JULIE MANGO

JULIE MANGO

JULIE MANGO

STORIES

N.D. WILLIAMS

PEEPAL TREE

This edition published in Great Britain in 2004
by Peepal Tree Press
17 King's Avenue
Leeds LS6 1QS
England

First published in the USA in 2000
by Xlibris Corporation

ISBN 1 900715 77 5

CONTENTS

For
Sandra
Jean-Ann F. R. and Linda K.

and for
Gordon Rohlehr
and all dem bassmen in the islands

She said to the driver: "Pas quittez moi a terre,"
which is, in her patois: "Don't leave me stranded,"
which is, in her history and that of her people:
"Don't leave me on earth."

– Derek Walcott
"The Light of the World"

you runnin' and you runnin'and you runnin' away
you runnin'and you runnin' and you runnin' away
you runnin' and you runnin' and you runnin' away
you runnin' and you runnin'

– Bob Marley
"Running Away"

JULIE MANGO: Or, Yu See Har Dere?

For months people on the island asking the same question: *what she see in he?* When rumor spread that the Doc declare his intention to marry her, is like they start playing the flip side of the same record: *what he see in she?*

If he and she were living in London or New York, in big cities where people mind their own business, nobody would be asking these questions. English people seeing them in a restaurant might raise an eyebrow or cough a dry cough. New Yorkers, from what I hear, too busy chasing the almighty dollar to care about a man and his mistress.

But islands are small places. Break wind in your bathroom and somebody passing by outside bound to look 'round and ask, *O gawd, who get shot?*

To step out your door, to walk these narrow streets, going downtown or to the market square, is to invite all kind of questions from the FBEye: *how you do, chile? who he think he is? what you drinking? ca ka fait, garcon, ca ka fait?*

And, *what he see in she?*

Seven years now I own this rum shop. The Doc's a regular paying customer. Came here from England ten years ago. This nurse-child he used to live with born and grow here. I have to tell you, I was curious at first when the two of them start living together like modern couple.

Curiosity killed the cat. Curiosity don't kill nobody here but sometimes it can suck you into gossip, scandal and intrigue. And on this island, particularly when you consider the state of politics and the woman situation, it have so much gossip, scandal and intrigue, conversation sometimes is like an open sewer running down the middle of the street.

Well, I don't care to walk that way, but a rum shop is a place where liquors flow and big mouths run loud like the rivers of Babylon. So sometimes you can't help overhearing things.

11

The Doc and I had a special arrangement. One night I was able to see down to the bottom of his soul. I could tell you now what he see in she; I could give you the real story, though please don't take it as gospel truth. After all, is a rum shop I have here, not an evangelist tent.

First, a few important facts.

The Doc is an outstanding man. I mean, he stands out from the rest, like a tamarind tree, *towering in stature*.

Other foreigners come here to work, stay two years, three years. Contract up, the money from the United Nations run out, they pack up suitcase and they *gone*! This fellow turn up one day from England; been working here for ten years now; learn to talk like islanders; make this place his home.

You look at him and you might think twice about letting him take out your appendix: face pudgy and blotched, hair straggly and thinning, eyes kind of bleary (because he like his Scotch). But when it come to childcare the man is a genius. *Towering in stature*.

Single-handedly, I would say, he was responsible for improving pre-natal care service on this island.

I mean, which doctor you know would stop on his way home from the hospital to check on this woman, check on that woman, give them advice on diet, ask them why they miss their monthly checkup? Which doctor?

Our own local boys returning from overseas as Doctors only thinking big money and building a fancy house; either that or sooner or later they running for political office. This fellow still in the same house the Government give him, up on the Morne; and people out of the goodness of their heart still bring him poultry, tomatoes, vegetables – everything from their farms. That's how much they respect the man!

As for the nurse-child, well, I don't know what to tell you. A badlucky child. Young, black and beautiful – but badlucky.

Her stepfather in jail still for killing her brother when she was a child. Beat the lil' boy unconscious because he used to pee his bed. Julie was taken from the mother and raised by nuns. Brought up like a nice young lady. Trained as a nurse. Till one day she get it in her head to enter the Carnival Queen contest.

Poor child, had to put up with a barracking from the crowd at the show. You know how some people attend the Queen show only to make life miserable for the contestants.

From what I hear, she should have won. But the judges thought she was too dark-skinned. At least, that was the word around town. Some people write angry letters to the newspapers about "color prejudice", and how beauty contests should be banned if the judges don't understand black beauty.

After that show she decide to reject islanders. Was like an amputation. Went about her business, keeping her head high, strong and proud and silent; turning down invitations from politicians, from young men in shiny cars; keeping herself to herself.

Fellows come into this shop, order round after round of beers, and talk nothing else but what they would do to the nurse-child if they get her in bed.

Now you could understand the consternation, the bacchanal, when she started living with the Doc. It turn a lot of women into vicious, cackling hens. A lot of young men pulling at their crotch vexed so, they ready to kill.

And *mauvais langue*, endless *mauvais langue*! How the doctor well in his forties; how he old enough to be her father; how she and he like the Moon and the Earth have nothing in common. And if she giving it to him, she's nothing but a slut. Gossip and scandal for days on the island!

But wait, you ent hear the intrigue!

Like I said before, the Doc and I had a special arrangement. You see, I like to close up shop at eleven. It's good for business. Rowdiness and drunken noise well past midnight could cause me no end of problems with the police and the neighbors. I have a reputation to upkeep!

So at eleven I close the doors. But shortly thereafter, the Doc would knock and ask to come in for *a nightcap.*

I liked the idea from the beginning: the hard working Doc stopping by my shop for a nightcap. Besides, the Doc was a gentleman of class. He'd order his Scotch – he's a Johnny Walker man! – and we'd talk man to man. No shouting and cussing; no susu and bobol. Civilized conversation. Man to man. Politics, bilharzia, the cricket Test match… *civilized*, know what I mean?

13

Well, suddenly he started coming on Wednesday nights. Only on Wednesday nights. In company with another white fellow, a young chap, who kept running his hands through his hair and writing in a notebook. They'd sit at a table and talk in low tones. The Doc would signal for another round – Johnny Walker for him, Heineken for the young man. I'd put it on his bill. He never fail to settle accounts at the end of the month.

At midnight he'd ask me to catch the BBC on my shortwave. They'd sit and listen to the news; the young chap would light up a cigarette; they talk some more, take another round.

Well, I curious like hell about what going on, but I don't want to ask the Doc since it's none of my business. At first I thought the fellow might have been his son from his marriage (his wife came out with him; spent about one year; went back to England saying she bored and she can't take the heat). Then one night I saw him squeezing the young man's hands and I said to myself, *O gawd, the Doc is one o' them!*

Then I start thinking maybe the young fellow – he had a knapsack and look like he always ready to catch a plane – this fellow might be some kind of Secret Service agent, flying into the island, conferring with the Doc, gathering information about political trends on the island.

Don't laugh! These were the post-Independence days. Politicians visiting Cuba and talking serious socialism!

To cut a long story short, what I'm about to tell you, *what in fact you're about to hear*, come straight from the Doc's mouth, his mind in a cloud of alcohol, his face shiny red with worry.

I remember it was weeks after a hurricane pass through here. It knock down a lot of trees, tear off roofs and cause enough confusion to last a fortnight. Left the economy in shambles.

The Doc came in on Wednesday night just when everything was getting back to normal. He looked tired; his jacket was rumpled, his tie was at half-mast.

Turned out he had just been to a christening for one of the babies he delivered. A lot of food and drinks and merriment; the Doc was a special guest. So he stop by to see if the hurricane blow away the shop. And for *a nightcap*!

– How is business, Sir Frank? he asked. He liked to call me *Sir* Frank.

14

– Couldn't be better, Doc. People have a lot to worry about these days, they dropping in here like flies. I ent see you in a long time, I said.

He gave a big sigh and shook his head. You'd think he just come from a funeral, not a christening. You'd think, too, that the hurricane break up his routine so much, he forget why he used to stop by my shop.

Well, we talked a little about this and that; 'bout the hurricane and how this time like it spare us grave loss of life; 'bout the banana industry in a serious state with all the trees flattened; how in times of crisis on this island people go out their way to help other people.

He poured a drink and shook his head like something else on his mind.

The Doc is a man who don't show his feelings. I mean, he would joke and laugh and tell you a funny story; and you could tell he's a sincere fellow in every way; but he kind of dry and tight when it come to his feelings, more like a green guava than a juicy mango.

Watching his face twitch you wouldn't think he was depressed. Not the Doc. More out of sorts, as he himself would say. *A bit under the weather lately*!

– Where's your friend? I asked, meaning the young fellow with the notebook.

He looked at me, and he said:

– *Friend*? I don't know what you mean? The only friend I have now is my work.

I watched that one go by. You don't swing your bat at every ball.

The Doc was silent for awhile, staring at his glass. He was looking real woebegone. In a situation like this you tell yourself, this fellow need real cheering up; the only good cheer I could offer was more Johnny Walker but I didn't want to push that just yet.

He took a deep breath and seemed for a moment to lift his head out of gloom. Then he said:

– Julie was my friend. The one friend I loved and trusted. Julie was my world.

– Julie? I asked.

15

– You know who I mean. The woman I was sleeping with, dammit! *My mistress*!

He really caught me there, leg before; took foolish seconds before I realized how mash up inside the Doc was over this woman.

Seeing as how the subject was kind of delicate, I wasn't sure how to proceed. And that is how the whole story come out, right there and then, with me and the empty chairs and the good Lord as witness, and Johnny Walker to the rescue when the Doc's voice tremble.

I give it to you now as I hear it, in the Doc's own words. He had a strange way of speaking, like a character in one of those old time radio dramas from overseas. If you listen carefully you can tell when he laughing at himself, and when he almost crying. Listen to the Doc:

"At 4.15, one damp Monday morning I slapped Julie. I remember the hour because the alarm clock usually goes off at 4.15, warning her she has thirty minutes to get dressed and catch the first bus. Julie works at a hospital at the southern end of the island.

"Our weekend terminates at 4.15 a.m. An ungodly hour for me to get out of bed, especially when you consider that Julie keeps springing up to check the clock in case there had been a power outage during the night. It's one of those digitals, illuminated red.

"Why I slapped her that morning, I can't explain. It was unpremeditated. I had never struck her before. I swore never to strike her again. I remember she gasped, touched her face with her fingers as if searching for a bruise or a swelling; then she marched off to the bathroom.

"I lit up a cigarette and waited.

"We'd have these frightening rows sometimes. She speaks rapidly, her dialect and English like switchblades, carving me up with passion.

"And what strange passion, what powerful emotions!

"They knocked you back; they slashed at you with jangling bracelets; they left you in shreds of astonishment and dismay.

"When she came out of the bathroom that morning she said nothing. Moved around the room, precisely, gathering things;

16

her mouth in a pout of anger; preparing to set out into the pre-dawn dark. Alone. Without my usual escort. Without a word.

"I couldn't let this happen. I followed her down the stairs.

– And just where do you think you're going? I asked.

– Open this door, please, she said, her anger still simmering.

"I toyed with the idea of *not* opening the door, but since everything so far had never happened before, I wasn't prepared at this stage to cope with more of the unforeseen on her part. I let her go.

"Damn movie actress behavior, I remember thinking, as I made my way back upstairs. I peered through the blinds of the bedroom window, not really believing Julie was out there, alone. The morning was so still, I could hear her footsteps on the graveled roadway. As she passed under a street lamp I could make out her straight shoulders, her free arm swinging.

"At this point I decided I'd had enough. She wanted to go, okay, she's gone. I got back into bed.

"Then I remembered the dogs: two fleshy Alsatians owned by an American couple down the road. They were fairly harmless overfed brutes, chained during the day, their bark worse than their bite. But at nights they were released.

"They prowled around, they romped, they sniffed at the grass and peed; sometimes they attacked late night strollers.

"Just last week a cane cutter, returning from the cinema and taking a shortcut through our street, was attacked. The next day a boisterous delegation of friends and relatives showed up en route to the hospital. They remonstrated; they removed bandages and pointed to the bite marks; they threatened legal action.

"The American couple, panicked by this show of grievance and rage, handed out dollar bills to everyone. They offered to take the victim to the hospital in their van.

"*The dogs*! What would they do to Julie if they attacked? Her soft, lovely arms. Her thighs, her solid ebony-smooth thighs!

"You see, God or some chromosomal accident had blessed that girl with the smoothest skin on earth. The price she had to pay for that blessing was that she couldn't pass it on. She could never bear children.

"The thought, now, of those dogs sinking their teeth like ice

17

picks into Julie's thighs, leaving deep wounds, leaving ugly scars, ruining for me the single source of pleasure on this island – the contemplation, the marvelous sensation of stroking Julie's buttocks, her smooth brown thighs – this is what propelled me down the stairs, to the car, swearing at the half-dead car battery, down the road, listening for screams or moans of agony. Determined to save those thighs!

"There was no sign of her, or the dogs. Actually I stopped near the American couple's house, wondering if perhaps she lay bleeding somewhere in the dark nearby while the dogs slept, satiated and content.

"No dogs, no Julie. And quite suddenly this rush to her imagined distress made me feel a little foolish.

"When eventually I drove up beside her – stiff-backed, her entire trajectory suggesting no forgiveness, no turning back – I was ready to repent, to throw cloaks over potholes in her way. I got out the car and walked beside her, appealing to her for forgiveness, trying to keep pace with her quick steps.

– Julie, this is ridiculous!

"She flashed a look of contempt and horror at the spectacle of me walking beside her in pajamas.

"I lost the headlights of the car around a bend in the road. The motor was left running. I remembered the handbrakes were not very reliable and I had a brief vision of the car rolling back and plunging over the hillside. I raced back to avert that calamity.

"When I caught up with her again there was a pothole I didn't see in time; my left wheel splashed her with water. She halted, examined her mudstained skirt and threw me one last murderous stare.

– Why don't you leave me alone, eh? she shouted, as if calling the entire island to witness.

"After that the best I could do was drive a discreet distance behind her, illumining the road ahead with my headlights.

"At the bus stop I parked on the other side of the road where I could keep an eye on her. Leaving her at this stage didn't seem right. I felt I had to demonstrate some loyalty, some concern for her safety. Secretly I was looking for the tiniest sign of forgiving and forgetting.

"Ah, those mornings – fresh as dew, invigorating! Long minutes before the light broke over the hills we'd sit in the car waiting for the bus, and Julie would listen to 'the sounds of silence' which she always took the trouble to identify – grasshoppers in the bush, church bells in the distance summoning people to mass. After a night with her I cherished those moments, those jewels of stillness before daybreak.

"The bus came laboring up the hill, its radio pounding the silence with reggae. Julie boarded, took a seat at the front and stared straight ahead.

"I buttoned up my pajamas and drove back home. I found the front door wide open, the light spilling out on the driveway like blood from a wound. I switched off the motor feeling sure there was someone inside.

"On the telephone you can hear Julie's voice firing down the wires. The lines are often bad. They don't permit even exchange. When I can hear her clearly, she can't hear me at her end. Sometimes it's the other way around. Sometimes she hangs up and dials again until she gets a line that allows her voice to come through.

"After that slapping incident I tried calling her. I prayed that the line would be good at her end so that she could hear me clearly. I wanted to tell her again how sorry I was, to swear never to hit her.

"Out of the blue, in the middle of the week, she called me. I shouted *Hello* over and over again to suggest my excitement and relief.

– I can barely hear you, she said
– I can hear you all right. How are you?
– You'll have to speak louder.
– Listen, about last weekend...
– Are they making preparations up there for the hurricane.
– Hurricane? I think I heard something about that. Listen, I...
– It's sixteen hours away. It's heading straight for us.

"All morning it had been unusually hot. As I looked outside – it was late in the afternoon – it did seem as if the wind had picked up and was becoming some kind of force. The coconut trees

19

looked restless. I supposed that meant some kind of storm was on the way.

– They say it's going to strike the island in the wee hours of the morning, Julie went on.

– *In the wee hours…* who said that?

– The hurricane *advisory*! We've been on hurricane watch for the past 48 hours. We're now on hurricane *alert*. It's moving at 85 miles. You know what that can do to us?

– Yes, that sounds serious. Listen, Julie, about last weekend, I'm terribly sorry…

– You'll have to come and get me.

– What did you say?

– You don't expect me to stay down here. The land is flat, the hurricane will sweep us like a broom. We're facing devastation! Will you come for me?

"Were my ears deceiving me? Did she say, *would I come and get her*? Of course, I'd come and get her. If indeed the hurricane was bearing down on us, there would be great danger, floods, dead animals everywhere, and a great mess for the survivors to clean up after. But for Julie and me, a silver lining, our moment of reconciliation, had come like a gift from the storm.

"I hung up. I had three hours of daylight. There was nothing to it but to go out and get her.

"There comes a point in every man's life when he hears the call to be hero; or simply to be brave. It might be a bugle call to action – the wondrous stuff one reads about of laconic men on horseback, or behind the wheels of machines; sometimes it's a quieter cry for help hidden in some mundane dilemma; the call is often fraught with risk one is never fully aware of until it's over. Whatever the situation, you must heed that call, you must respond.

"It wasn't until I'd got on the road that I realized how precipitous my action was. My alarm as I hurtled towards Julie deepened for I had not done that necessary checking of the vehicle. Was there enough gas in the tank, air in the tires, water in the coolant system?

"With every jolt and rattle I felt the real possibility of breakdown, of finding myself stranded in the middle of this hurricane night, trying to flag down cars racing for shelter.

"Fear and imagination can twist things out of proportion. Suddenly the sky was shrouding before my eyes; vexatious clouds seemed swollen with water, waiting for some signal to dump on us great fury. Coconut palms, banana leaves flapping like warning flags – the whole island was shaking in fear and anticipation.

"I heard the wind; I felt it lifting the car off the road; I accelerated telling myself firm speed would keep me rooted to the ground. The evening light was fading faster than I'd expected.

"When it started to rain I knew the Met office with its *advisories* had got it wrong. The downpour I ran into just ten miles from Julie's hospital was a savage. The windscreen wipers slashing at the water unnerved me. My headlights had little effect on the thickening rain. I slowed to a crawl. I knew for certain the hurricane was here.

"I kept thinking of Julie, waiting for me, glancing at her watch, her eyes on the hospital gates – not knowing what I was going through! I saw her face, I remembered her words on the telephone. Feeling a fresh surge of courage, I forged on, even as the storm waters now threatened to make instant rivers of the road.

"The road curved round a hill and for a moment the rains lifted. I looked down and caught a glimpse of the sea, boiling leaps of water that seem to reach for my heart.

"The car shuddered and hesitated; the tires spun on the wet surface. Panic like an icy claw gripped my insides and in an instant I knew I would fail. I knew I would never make it. And, worse, I was afraid I would die, swept off the road down the hillside into the foaming sea, or pinned under a coconut tree crashing through the roof of the car.

"The last remaining act for me was somehow to turn the car around and drive ruthlessly home. On any journey into the unknown you drive with greater faith, your grip on your destiny secure, on the way back, on the road home.

"The full force of the hurricane hit the island in the early hours of the morning, round about the time Julie and I had had our differences the week before.

"There was tape across the windows, on the sliding glass doors; and except for the flapping and banging of loose zinc sheets on the roof, the house was a wooden fortress.

"Outside the winds howled, trees rocked and swayed, the rains hammered. Somehow it wasn't as bad as had been forecast.

"I was thinking, as the morning light came up, and the force of the winds diminished giving way to hard rain, that, perhaps, with a little perseverance, I might have made it through to Julie. Judging from what I saw outside – the toppled trees, sheets of corrugated zinc – we had been spared *devastation*. Considerable damage, yes, but not devastation. Julie hadn't been *swept away*.

"I wondered what stories she had to tell about the storm at her end of the island; I pictured our next meeting, our feverish conversation, our laughter, happy together again.

"The hurricane had scrambled the lives of most everyone. What mattered now, surely, was the setting aside of past griev- ances and hurts. Our roofs must be restored. For each man, each woman this was a time of repair and healing. When the rains eased I would pick my way through the debris of fallen trees to the injured in hospital beds.

"I was just about to get to work, mopping the floor soaked from the leaking roof, when something else out there caught my eye: someone coming up the road, picking its way through fallen debris, in raincoat and rain hat, a mere outline of human courage or folly, head bowed against the rain, and, as the outline filled out into a body, looking incredibly, and then unmistakably, like Julie.

"I remember thinking that her feet must be wet, that despite the raincoat the poor girl must be soaked to the bone. I was waiting at the door as she trudged up.

"We must have stood there for ages looking at each other. People who live together like lovers don't really look at each other. I saw her face under the rain hat, soft and wet, as if she'd swum all the way from the south; and her eyes, sad and trusting, like a patient's after you've told them the bad news; and beads of water on her nose.

"I came close to tears at that moment, standing there looking at her, *really* looking at her. I felt like an old man, with an old man's longing to touch her face, make her eyes light up. Close to tears,

I tell you, which is as close as you ever come to loving someone.

"I reached out for the bag in her hand, a plastic bag full of mangoes. She always brought me mangoes from that side of the island. Said the best kind grew there.

– Where did you…? How did you…? My God, you're soaking wet, I stammered.

"If only I had said what I felt in my eyes!

"Julie brushed past me and marched up the stairs. Suddenly there I was, again, chasing after her. At the top of the stairs she paused to look around, at the furniture covered and pushed out of the way, at spread sheets of newspaper soaking up water on the floor.

– Water, water everywhere. Part of the roof went airborne during the night, I said.

"She was not amused. She was not in the least concerned. With water still dripping from her raincoat she swept into the bedroom, which, amazingly, had been spared drips from the leaking roof. I heard her rummaging about, heard the zipper of her bag open; it dawned on me slowly she was gathering her things. When I looked in through the door she was stuffing away the digital clock.

"Suddenly I wished she'd stop it, stop rooting around like a wet rodent amidst the chaos. I wanted to hold her, remove the leaves stuck on to her raincoat. I wanted to dry her face, make her comfortable in the driest room in the house.

– I was on my way to get you last night. Really, I was *halfway there*, I said.

"She stopped moving and waited, her head half-turned listening for what would come next; and in that pause I heard the storm moving farther away, I sensed the grey sky opening up tiny cracks for the sun. Half a chance, a promise of reprieve – and all that I had then were rain-soaked words, words of failure, words that to her ears sounded like thin lies. *Halfway there*!

"One night, one storm, one performance. One moment in your life, clean as a blade, comes to define you, or asks you to define yourself. All else, before and after, mean nothing, nothing at all.

– Julie… I'm so sorry…

"I had lost my claim to that name.

"She zipped up her bag and looked around one last time; then she sailed down the stairs through the door back out into the diminishing storm.

"I haven't seen her since."

The Doc! I tell you, with stethoscope or with words, no one can beat the Doc!

Right after that he was silent; he looked like a man who'd been horned and now didn't know which way to turn. I felt a little embarrassed and got up to get a fresh bottle of Johnny Walker.

But he'd had enough. With a flick of the wrist he downed the last shot. He stood up, tottering a little, as if he'd misplaced his legs; but he was all right. He fumbled in his pocket for his car keys then he straightened his tie. Before he left he slapped me on the shoulder and gave me a serious look. *Not a word of this to anyone, right, old chap?*

I knew what he meant. No badmouthing behind his back, no *mauvais langue!* At the end of the day a man must hold on to all he has left – his dignity.

So when the next piece of news break, about the nurse-child, Julie, I smile and play ignorant.

What they said at first was that she living in England. Staying with an Aunt. Working at a telephone company.

Next thing we hear, the girl traveling round the continent in company with a Lord Somebody or an Earl of Someplace. She send back pictures: the Lord and she posing in Trafalgar Square; Julie sitting beside the Lord; the Lord wearing a cape while pigeons *peck, pecking* round their feet; the Lord smoking a pipe and leaning on a walking stick in front of a fountain.

Then we hear she hook up with a photojournalist and she gone to some country in Africa. In the middle of a civil war. The fellow taking photos, while she nursing the sick and wounded. She promise to return to the island for a visit one day.

A picture is worth a thousand words. Those pictures the nurse-child send back home let loose more than a thousand words in this place. Susu for days: *who she think she is, what he see in she.*

You ask me what I see? I'll tell you what I see.

I see a face gazing out into the world, fearless and free. I see eyes

24

steady and sure. I see lips parted in a funny smile as if the nurse-child looking not at the camera, not at the photographer holding the camera. Her eyes soared over Trafalgar Square, cross the ocean, reach all the way to these island shores. There was message in those eyes, in the straight shoulders, in the smile. If you ask me, she was saying, *Don't worry 'bout me. I'm doing fine, thank you, just fine.*

TRINCULO WALKS THE DOG

First, let me say this: I did not return home with any foolish ideas about serving my country.

True, the Republic was where I was born, where I grew up, where I was eminently schooled. But England is where I completed my formal education, where I've expanded, joined the world. And where a perspective on life, like those first hairs on your chin, began to grow on me. It may not be fashionable or correct these days to admit something like this, but I shudder to think where I might be now if I'd taken another route.

But return home I did. At least for awhile.

My father wrote telling me there might be something for me, a position with the Government. They needed a French translator and I had done studies in French. It could lead to many interesting things, he said: trips to foreign countries, to the United Nations: accompanying various Ministers who needed an interpreter or translator. Now that we're an independent nation the Republic is expanding, he said. Trooping its colors. Marching in step with the world.

Then there was Pamela, this English girl I'd been seeing. I wanted to get away from Pamela for a while. I'd only been *seeing* her; we went places together – the cinema, the theatre, leisurely walks around London, and on good days an excursion into the countryside. Tickets to Wimbledon one summer (*Daddy* was an officer in the Black Watch and had connections). Mostly we stayed home – my place, her place – reading, watching the telly, tea and sparkling conversation.

This had been going on for two years until I began to suspect that Pamela wanted to become intimate. Sexually intimate. Astonishing as it may seem, during all the time we'd been together we had not been intimate. A kiss on the cheek, a goodnight embrace – that was as far as it went. It never occurred to me that

29

naked intimacy was something we would one day want from each other.

Now you may think what you like, but Pamela was very proper, very procedural and correct. I liked that about her. I liked how punctual she was, showing up at my door precisely at nine in the morning if that had been our arrangement; having the correct change for the bus, no fussing or haggling. A predictable human resource in a world of uncertainty is something you don't take lightly. It's something you value. At least for a while.

So when one afternoon – it was Remembrance Day, we were watching the usual somber stepping and wreath-laying on television – she hinted ever so delicately that perhaps our relationship had matured sufficiently to be moved from level #1, so to speak, to level #2, I remember crossing my leg and thinking: *what's gotten into her? has she gone off her rocker? and why now, on Remembrance Day?*

I wanted things to stay just the way they were.

Besides, I wasn't too sure about this sex business. To be honest I'm still not sure about this sex business. I know it's the fashion these days to be sexually savvy and all that, but I don't think I would have got where I am now – leaving Cambridge with a first, a Ph.D. – if I'd spent most of my time running my hands up women's skirts.

Nor was I sure I wanted to have sex with Pamela. I mean, once you start this *taking off your clothes* business, all ambition flies straight out your head. You know that drained feeling you get after you've done it? It's your *potential* reservoir being depleted. You pay a steep price somewhere down the line for that loss: the vital energy to build something, to *achieve* something. And before you know it, you're searching for your underwear and muddling your way through some squalid messy thing called a relationship. And then they're telling you maybe *we* ought to think of getting married. Good gracious!

Animum rege qui nisi paret imperat. His language might be considered dead but I think old Horace got it right. I mean, look around the world. Look across the road at your neighbors! See what I mean? Some sort of *imperium* is needed to keep encaged the animal inside us.

In any event I came home that summer for precisely these

30

reasons: see my Mum and Dad; drop by the old familiar places; talk to my father about this job with the Government. Allow the country take notice of what discipline and hard work – not rum and calypso – can do for any man from the Republic, once he sets his mind to the task like a nose to the grindstone.

It was 1973. The Government was giddy and champing at the bit with socialist theory, nationalist programs. Breaking out of the colonial mold. Embassies all across the globe. *Diplomatic ties with Cuba.* That sort of thing.

They need qualified educated people like you, my father had written to say.

Well, I wasn't sure. As I explained to Pamela the night before I left England, I was only twenty-two years old. At this point in my life was I ready to throw my life into the washtub of some grimy nationalism? I wasn't sure.

– *What do you mean you're not sure*, I remember her saying, passing me a cup of tea and beginning to work up a lather over something that really had nothing to do with her. But that's Pamela. She's the kind of girl who compels you to *look* at things.

That night she kept poking me with questions about my loyalties – about the need to belong somewhere, to be part of some great purpose like building a new nation. Back then, for anyone who liked waving placards, there were causes aplenty to demonstrate about. Student amusement themes, if you'd asked me. Like the boat race on the Thames. Made for evenings after of heady talk. A chance to change your hairstyle or your lifestyle.

Anyway, I knew what this was all about. Pamela was simply getting back at me for not taking her on, for ignoring her romantic overtures, if you can call it that.

She was not much to look at herself: thin narrow face, thin up-and-down body, though not bad calves. Made firm and appealing by long distance walking. A great walker, our Pamela. We took trains and walked all over England in raincoats and galoshes.

And she's blessed with a sharp mind; can cut like a laser to the essence of things; has a marvelous talent for organizing information which, as I told her once, would see her through postgrad school up into higher echelons of academia. A professor opening young minds to the mysteries of the world.

31

– What do you mean you're not sure, she went on, in that high-pitched manicured accent of hers. She was pulling her skirt over her knees and tucking her feet under her bottom.

– Well, for a start, I don't feel I belong to my country.

– How do you mean, you don't *feel* you belong? It's where you grew up. Surely you must feel *something*, you must have memories, you must want to go back and help.

That was quite a barrage. I sat staring at her little bird face, the beady eyes swollen behind thick lenses. And I remember thinking: no one will ever marry you for your good looks, dear girl. And I wondered: only a sentimental lost soul thinks of *going back* anywhere; and in any case, why was she getting so worked up over a tiny country she'd never seen?

I mean, it might have been *her* colonial possession once. It was *my* republic now: shores washed by the muddy waters of the Atlantic; a small place; a pocket-size republic making pompous noises in those days about its new independent path, its great national destiny. It wasn't India or Africa, continents with large resources and millions of able-bodied people wanting to be put to work.

I started to explain that although I was *born* there I hardly knew the place. I'd lived all my life in the city. Hardly went anywhere. The East Coast, the West Bank were places you passed quickly through, taking care not to run over some wandering cow, or some scampering boy grinning as he chased a stray pig. The Interior with all those Amerindians – I mean, I knew *about* them. I just didn't care to travel too far away from our house in the city. I wasn't the adventurous type in those days.

She couldn't understand that. She knew all about her world, her England. She had taken me around. The palace, her home in Yorkshire, the English countryside. She's a lucky girl, Pamela. Secure, rooted in her England. And a marvelous conversationalist too. I used to sit for hours listening to her go on about the Irish problem, the Labour Government. I like the way she tidied up evenings of chat by saying, *Ah, what a fine muddle we've made of this world*. I was fond of describing the Republic as a fine mess. Considering that we were a country of *mudlanders*, it seemed so correct to describe what our leaders were doing as so much *muddling*.

32

As I told you, Pamela was in many ways a nice girl to be with in a cold igloo country like England. I'm glad I met her. Glad, too, I got away from her.

Secondly, let me say this. My mum and dad held no illusions about the Republic where they'd lived all their lives and raised two sons.

My dad was a dentist. I won't describe him as "privileged" or "prosperous" or "middle-class" since those words have little meaning in the Republic; they're the epithets of choice among so many rabid nationalists back there, full of resentment, bad grammar and shit.

"Well-respected" would work nicely, I think, since his clients were mainly Government people, the families of resident foreigners: in short, people who wanted a dentist they could trust. In the Republic, torn and ravaged by racial passions even after its Independence, a dentist was like a Chinese umpire at a cricket match: someone whose ethnic background is perceived to harbor no bias, no residual resentment.

If I may say so myself, my father was an excellent dentist.

Now this doesn't mean he was completely neutral on the affairs of state. I think he played a shrewd game. I've learnt that from him: in volatile situations like our Republic, where people's emotions hang like raw meat on hooks in a butcher shop, where long knives of hatred can hardly wait for nightfall to open goblets of blood, one must be cunning, detached, extremely practical.

He had his opinions on the people who ran the country and the people who opposed the way it was run; but for the most part he kept them to himself. He shared his thoughts only with his two drinking mates: Mr. Agostini, who owned a funeral parlour, and Mr. Kissoondyal who owned a furniture store. He spent weekends of leisure with these two cronies on the balcony of the Chinese Benevolent Society where they were welcome guests.

I don't mean to suggest they talked only about molars or mortuaries or morris chairs. When they came to our house they spoke in low tones. They chuckled; they sipped tea or imported Scotch. What they all had in common was a businessman's interest in *the product*, in results.

33

My dad was obsessed with good results. When my brother and I brought home report cards, he glanced at the grades; he noticed we were among the top three in the class; he grunted and nodded with satisfaction. Good results pleased him. I think it bothered him that the country's leaders lacked his passion for getting the job done, for excellence and good results.

So why didn't he talk to them about excellence and good results? The Deputy Prime Minister came twice a year for a check up, or to have work done on his cavities. Why didn't my father speak up then?

I suppose when you're staring into the mouth of the country's leaders, or tugging away at stubborn plaque, the last subject you want to raise is the country's dilapidated condition, its failing public services, the general apathy, the racial bat and ball, street banditry and crime.

You must remember: these were the lean years after the Oil nations had raised their prices. The bottom had fallen out of our post-Independent buckets. The Republic had to import all its oil. The Government was saying, *It's the oil nations' fault things are getting worse. Ruined all our glorious five-year plans!* Belt-tightening and austerity were whips on the nation's backs.

When I came home that summer I discovered more disturbing undercurrents.

Our old house was just as I had left it: a sturdy two-storey wooden frame, a little weather-beaten; the front steps still creaked; my mother said they'd had to reinforce the door locks, and keep the bedroom windows closed at night; still it was our castle, our home.

At the dining table that first evening we ate in silence. As my mother ladled the soup, I told my father about my first at Cambridge; he nodded, pleased, the skin on his face tight and dry.

– Your brother is doing very well in Canada, my mother said. My brother was studying dentistry in Toronto.

– I don't think he's coming home this summer, she added.

My father sat with his chin propped under his fingers, brooding a little, waiting for the steaming soup to cool before taking the first spoonful.

As we ate my mother filled me in on the state of the country.

Things were getting a little difficult. Food prices were going up. Mrs. Pereira had moved to Canada.

My mother had her circle of friends, mainly Portuguese ladies and Catholics – the Fernandes, the Pereiras, the Rodrigues. Many of them had migrated to Canada soon after Independence, claiming they'd seen the writing on the wall. From the tone of her voice I got the feeling my mother wouldn't have minded moving to Canada; but that was not a decision for her to make.

When we'd finished dinner we sat thoughtful and silent, almost in a prayer mode. At some point my father usually scraped back his chair and left the table. It was a signal for us to gather the dishes, clear the table. This time he didn't move. He seemed more pensive than usual.

– The foreign exchange situation so terrible now, my mother said. Your father couldn't take his vacation this year in Canada. They only allowing you to take out fifty dollars. *Fifty dollars!*

I glanced at my father; he hadn't moved; sat there staring at the tablecloth, his face thinner, deeper creases in his forehead. Something was happening in the Republic, something rotten and deeply worrying, undermining the fabric of our family lives.

These trips to Canada on his vacation, I should explain, were intended to keep my father abreast with the latest technological advances in dentistry. He came back with equipment, magazines, improvements for the office. This is what impressed most people about my father: they could rely on him to provide the best, the most improved dental care. Knowing his passion for delivering the best service, I could understand why he might be depressed if obstacles were placed in his path.

But, you may be wondering, wasn't he after all a man of connections: those Ministers in the Government, those foreign diplomats? Surely he could have found a way around those travel restrictions: a phone call, a whisper in the ear of the Minster after his root canal surgery.

A universal practice, I know, making connections, asking small favors. Not my father's way. Not my way either. Compromise yourself to those bastards, give in an inch, *just one inch*, they imagine they've got you under their thumb forever. Then there's no telling what they may ask of you next.

35

Suddenly, still at the dinner table, my father spoke up, a short bitter complaint:

– You know that statue of Queen Elizabeth still lying in the grass outside the Law Courts? I have to pass it every day on my way to the office. *Every day*!

With that he touched his lips with the napkin, scraped back his chair, and left the table.

I sat there stunned. My mother shook her head and started clearing the table.

Stunned! Just when I was beginning to curse the Government for frustrating my father's simple wish to improve the quality of his professional service to the Republic, he makes this amazing statement about the statue of Elizabeth I lying in the grass. That, it seemed, was for him the most disturbing blot on his life.

This statue, let me explain, used to stand outside the city Law Courts. I suppose to some people it served as a symbol of the injustices of the colonial era. In the frenzied nationalism that followed our Independence, they were changing the names of streets, Government offices, villages: making them more identifiably local or national. The golf course, favored by expats and local businessmen, was taken over and turned into a national park. Before I left it was the favorite haunt of couples seeking sexual privacy; and rapists who preyed on these couples. Those once well tended greens were rapidly turning into jungle.

Some person or persons with the complete blessing of our leaders knocked or pulled down the statue of Elizabeth I. For centuries she'd stood in the malarial heat, erect, full breasted, frowning at colonials cycling by; then one day in a fit of anticolonial rage she was toppled; she was left to graze in the grass, her plump cheeks muddied, her stone eyes staring off.

People noticed, people gasped. A small crowd might have gathered and sniggered; a snapshot of the small crowd ogling or pointing at the statue might have appeared in the local newspapers. Life went on.

For my father, it was as if life had been summarily interrupted. It was the first insight I had into his interior life, or at least that part of it that was affected by events in the Republic.

Now, you shouldn't go jumping to conclusions that my father

36

was perhaps a colonial lackey, molded irreversibly by the colonial system, secretly regretting the passing of the old colonial order.

– But, Michael, why do you think he reacted that way? Pamela asked with furrowed brows when I mentioned this to her.

Pamela – let me slip this in – is also passionate about the peoples of England's former colonies. Might be something residual. She was born, she said, in New Delhi. *Daddy* and her mother lived there for awhile. The Foreign Service. Flapping khaki shorts, clenched pipe and cool lemonade. She even tried to get me to read *A Passage to India* which in her opinion was "a fabulously true" book. Now that I'm no longer in England it wouldn't surprise me if her next companion and friend turns out to be someone from India. I can see them now tucked in nicely, watching a rerun of that television series "Jewel in the Crown".

No, I've given the matter some thought. Dad might have been offended by the sloppy, primitive way in which the statue was removed; or the way no one cared once the job was done: just leaving her there.

Perhaps it goes deeper than that.

Once I heard Dad talking to Mr. Agostini about using the dead past to pay for the present. Mr. Agostini laughed, but my father pressed on with his point. No need to take revenge on old statues and old names. Put them in a museum some place; turn them into artifacts; filter away those useless emotions; make some money out of the past. The Americans on their Independence Day dressed up like British and held parades. It was all great national fun.

In any event, my first night home was not too restful. My father was far from happy with the state of the Republic. What else, I kept wondering all night, besides the fallen statue of Elizabeth I, lay festering in his closed heart?

This was the first sign of disturbing undercurrents in our lives. The second sign came two days later when I met an old classmate, Trinculo.

When Shakespeare wrote *The Tempest* he couldn't have known of course about the Republic. He couldn't have imagined that one day in one of the sugar-cultivating colonies far overseas an actor, or rather his cane-cutting ancestor, would be born, and that centuries later that man would step into the skin of one of his characters and give it eternal life.

Something like this happened one night when the curtain went up on our college production of *The Tempest*. Our Trinculo, born centuries after the play was written, stepped into his predestined role.

Actually all credit is due to the energy and ingenuity of Mr. Puddephat, who had come out from England on contract to teach us English. He was preparing students for O Level exams. Since we were to be tested on one of Shakespeare's texts he had this idea: why not get all examinees involved in a school production of the play?

In our O Level year the play was *Julius Caesar*. I was reluctant to get involved. I remember protesting mildly to Mr. Puddephat there were no Chinese people in Shakespeare's plays. He leaned right into my face, his orange moustache quivering, flecks of spittle hitting my cheeks.

– Nonsense, boy, utter nonsense! Of course there were Chinese people in his plays. There were Moors and Portuguese and Amerindians. Anyone with a love of the theatre in his blood could find himself in Shakespeare's plays.

No use my protesting I had not one drop of love for the theatre in my blood, that I was not a Moor, a Portuguese or an Amerindian. He gave me a part in the crowd scenes.

We came on stage trying hard not to smile, not to throw glances at relatives in the audience; and when Brutus made his famous speech about *Friends, Romans, Countrymen* we listened, then muttered *rhubarb, rhubarb!* Mr. Puddephat said that *rhubarb* spoken on stage – I had no idea then what the word meant – gave the audience the impression we were disgruntled and unhappy commoners.

Everyone who saw our college production of *The Tempest* agreed on one thing: even if they didn't understand the play, Trinculo was its star.

He upstaged all the actors. When he wasn't on stage our attention drifted. When he came on we cracked up laughing, often at the wrong time. He was so real, despite the costume, so recognizably real: wandering around frightened and drunk and seeing monsters, as if he'd stumbled out of a rum shop where he'd been drinking white rum.

What have we here? a man or fish? dead or alive? A fish? he smells like a fish; a very ancient and fishlike smell. And there was Trinculo holding his nose, recoiling in such horror, you'd think he was staring at a crocus bag of dead crabs.

Trouble was, once he'd stepped into the role Shakespeare had created, it was difficult for him to shed the skin entirely. The name stuck, as nicknames do at school, and so did part of the role: he became a character off stage, even after he'd been appointed Prefect; he was loud and clownlike, always ready with anecdote or joke; he was not an academic success – I don't think he had a disciplined mind – but he was popular.

He was good at soccer and athletics, and he was our House captain, which is how I came to know him well. He would turn up on the playing fields determined to coach reluctant House members like me into doing their bit on the track. He would declare, stop watch in hand, as I huffed toward the finishing line, *What have we here? A man or fish?* I have to admit I admired his outrageous manner; maybe because it was so much unlike my character. There were moments when I wished I had his nerve, his unselfconscious daring, the will now and then to occupy the center stage.

When I saw him again that summer he had changed. He had his hair knotted in that spiky Rastafarian way, and he was pedaling furiously and dangerously down the road; he saw me strolling, hands in pocket, looking I suppose like someone whose face had missed the daily massage of the sun; he thought he recognized me; he looked back, braked and shouted, *Michaelangelo... is that you? What's happening there, man?*

It was my third day back home. I was happy to be recognized in the streets. What followed was nothing short of extraordinary. It revealed to my astonished eye those dangerous undercurrents that ensnare us, that threatened to pull us all under.

– Hey, what's happening? I said, shaking his hand.

His skin was oily; he seemed somehow taller, leaner and he had that harried, tight-lipped look I'd noticed on the faces of many city dwellers, as if living in a country with no seasons was dangerous to their health. He wore a shirtjac, which was the national style, with two pens stuck in the front pocket; and, as was his habit ever since I can remember, he took out a large white handkerchief and got ready to mop sweat beads from his brow.

We took a good look at each other, smiling, pumping each other's hands, trying to determine what the last three years had done to us.

– You been in England, right? Studying? he asked.

–Yes… I'm back home for a spell… so what's been happening? I asked again.

He tilted his head back and said:

– *Ah, I have been in such a pickle since I saw you last, that I fear will never out of my bones.*

He spoke those words in such a theatrical manner, I suspect they were lines from *The Tempest.* So I laughed, acknowledging his trademark, his agility at jumping in and out of character with little prompting.

It was midmorning; the heat was rising in that rapid earnest way I had almost forgotten; wet patches were beginning to show on my shirt under the armpits, which made me think straight away of retreating from the streets, to the showers, some Yardley's talcum powder, a fan. We started walking, Trinculo wheeling the cycle.

He was on his way to work, late though the hour was. He worked at the Ministry of Youth and Culture. What did he do? He cleared his throat and told me he was a cultural officer. He was involved in organizing and planning cultural events. I nodded appreciatively. Being an officer and belonging to an office in the city could give anyone a vague sense of importance. He went on to detail what his Ministry was *trying to accomplish.* We walked in no great hurry. Occasionally he waved to someone driving by in a car, wearing a shirtjac, presumably on his way to his office.

Once he'd exhausted this national side of life he turned to mine.

– So what were you studying in England? he asked, making the word *studying* sound somehow like something bothersome but necessary, like pissing. I told him French.

– *French*…? Man, we need Spanish-trained people, not French.

40

The Government thinking of phasing out French from the high schools. Contacts with places like Venezuela, Cuba, is more in the national interest...

I wanted to raise the idea my dad had mentioned, about the need for French translators, but his tone had abruptly altered. Cheerfully informative at the beginning, it was now abrasive and judgmental. I felt as if I had made some terrible mistake in electing, first of all, to study in England; and then pursuing something as irrelevant to the Republic as French.

– Remember John Rasgullen...? our House captain when we were in Form 3...? He's back... Got a 1st in Economics... They have in the Planning Ministry... I hear he's now a member of the PM's kitchen cabinet.

He said all that in what sounded like the accent he used in the Ministry of Culture. Or the Ministry of Recruitment. I got the impression he was ready to recruit me on the spot and secure a place for me alongside Rasgullen in the PM's kitchen cabinet if only I hinted my interest. I pulled up as if suddenly remembering I had an appointment. He must have sensed my unwillingness to defer to him and, slipping once more into himself, Trinculo, House captain, he said:

– Listen, where you heading? Why we don't stop and have a beer?

– But... aren't you on your way to work?

– That's all right. They won't miss me for several hours.

I had had enough of his official presence that morning. I was gently but steadily perspiring under my shirt. I suddenly remembered I was on my way to my dad's office.

– Well, listen. How about meeting me after work?

He gave me the name of a popular restaurant. I wasn't too excited about eating in public. He suggested a quieter place, called *The Rendezvous*; we could sit and have a few drinks and talk about the old school days. I wasn't sure I wanted to do that but I agreed to meet him there at 4.30 that afternoon.

Pamela had introduced me to English pubs. A drink and a chat in the local pub seemed reasonable. Besides there was not much else to do that day.

41

He was late for our meeting at The Rendezvous. It wasn't the kind of place you could go in, order a drink, sit on a stool and wait for a friend to arrive. It was *down a yard*, as they say. Someone had enterprisingly converted the space under a house into a drinking spot. I could hear jukebox music pounding from inside its darkened interior. *Bang-a-lang, a-bang-a-lang*. Not the sort of place I cared to patronize under any circumstance.

But after three years abroad you feel somehow inviolable when you walk city streets again. You make their acquaintance as if for the first time, cloaked in your foreignness. You make comparisons, too, and sometimes you wish you had the power in the snap of a finger to bring a little order and civility to the routines of street life. Whip them into shape one way or another.

Just when I thought I'd had enough of standing around on the pavement, I started walking away and stepped right on tiny loaves of dog shit. I have to tell you, worse things could have happened: a bus out of control leaping the pavement could have mowed me down. But nothing was more devastating to my person than this.

I spent minutes wiping and wiping my patent leathers on the grass verge. You don't ever get all the stuff off your shoes. It was at this point, still trying to remove the last trace and smell of dogshit in the grass, that Trinculo showed up. I felt blind hatred for him, for the Republic he seemed to serve so proudly, for a Ministry that gave money to cultural officers instead of dogcatchers.

–*Michaelangelo*… what's happening there? he shouted. The look on his face suggested he understood what had just happened here.

I half-expected him to apologize for his lateness, offer some explanation; but this, after all, wasn't England.

He had company, two friends of his, co-workers; they wore shirtjacs and professorial goatees, which I came to associate with intellectual pretensions or simply *style*. We trooped down the yard, wheeling cycles, parking, then locking, the cycles; then into the place which had a bar and bar stools, a pretty Indian girl with overlarge breasts, a skirt too short and chafing thighs; and in the middle of the room a billiards table.

We sat around a table. The Indian girl came from behind the bar and began to wipe the wet rings left by the bottles of recent patrons. She smiled and tried to ignore crude remarks from Trinculo's friends.

They were loud jokey fellows, with thin bony faces, their thin bodies ravaged, you felt, by drinking sessions and bad eating habits. One of them had a cigarette tucked between ear and skull, and a toothpick in his mouth – for me always a sign of mental laziness and degeneracy.

For a while I sat looking around, not yet formally introduced, feeling distinctly like an outsider, traces of dogshit still on my shoes.

Just when I thought things were going to continue this way forever – jokes, laughter, cigarette smoke expelled with style, the head thrown back – his two friends decided to play a round of billiards. At this point they were introduced to me as Comrade "Snapper" Bobb and Comrade Wieve. At this point Trinculo and I settled in for more confidential exchanges.

– So what's happening, Michaelangelo? he asked again.

– Not much.

I was a little wary of where our conversation would wander this time.

– By the way, you ever come across Puddephat in England?

– *Come across*? England might be an island, but it's still a big place, I said. You don't *come across* people just like that.

– *Pain in the boodocks! You're a pain in the boodocks, boy*! he said. It was a first class imitation of Mr. Puddephat and I couldn't hold back a smile.

– When he left he told the fellows to look him up if they ever came to England, he said.

– Did he leave an address? Did he tell you where he lived?

– Yorkshire, some place, he said. Then he added, with a deep intake of breath, his chest swelling, Actually, it was his wife who gave me his address.

There was a pause, as in the theatre, where you're asked to watch the impact of one actor's words on the face of another. I don't usually show my feelings but this time my face was caught in naked wonderment.

Trinculo turned to order another round of beers. I balked. I'd been sipping cautiously from the mouth of the bottle, not caring

43

to pour it into a glass of ice cubes as was the local fashion. The Indian waitress came over with her tray and wiping rag; she got a hand around the waist and a whisper in her ear from Trinculo. Quite the lady's man, too, our Trinculo, even if you didn't care for his choice of ladies.

I wanted him to get back to Puddephat's wife.

– Yes, man. Gave me her address… and last Christmas I got a card. It said, *Merry Christmas, Trinculo… don't forget to walk the dog!*

– Walk the dog? Do you go walking dogs…?

Now he really had me shamelessly intrigued.

– *Aha…* and let me tell you a little secret. Puddephat might know a lot about theatre, but when it come to his wife there are some things he will go to his grave and never know.

Silence. The billiard balls went *poc, poc*; Comrade Bobb chalked his stick, knitted his brow and puffed on his cigarette, studying all angles. The *bang-a-lang* jukebox was playing something slow and syrupy, and Comrade Wieve sang along in a drawling lascivious manner.

Trinculo scraped back his chair, and said:

– Hold on! Got to unload these mules.

He got up and wandered away to wherever the bathroom was, leaving me twisting in the wind, so to speak, hanging from a tree limb filled with mystery and disbelieving leaves.

Let me explain something here: when I was a student at the college, teachers were like professional ball players: they were real only when you saw them on the playing field. They had no private lives, at least none that we knew about. We never thought of them as ordinary human beings who paid taxes, quarreled with their wives, shopped at the supermarket. They were men with special knowledge, men of habits and obsessions: men to be feared, sometimes tested, more often viewed with awe and resentment.

Our French teacher, Mr. D'Abreu, spent one whole week trying to get every boy in the class to pronounce the French word *l'horloge* correctly. Over and over, day after day, student after student choking and gargling tried to say it his way. He kept pointing to his throat and urging us to start *down there* – "L'horloge! L'horloge! It's guttural, guttural!" He was not amused when some

44

fellows made sounds like frogs in the gutter and the class went wild. That was Mr. D'Abreu's obsession: correct pronunciation of the French language even if it killed us trying.

Mr. Puddephat was the Englishman who put on these Shakespeare plays every year. We knew he was married. His wife helped the cast with makeup before the show and cold cream after the show. She made these incredibly neat cheese sandwiches. We knew they had no children because they lived in one of the houses on the college compound and we saw no tousle-head Puddephats running about in white socks and shoes. She was younger than Mr. Puddephat, about ten years younger, and quite attractive, though she always had a wilted look, like a flower that wasn't getting enough water.

When school was dismissed we left the college and its teachers and went home to more consuming realities.

Imagine, therefore, the turmoil in my head when Trinculo dropped his comment about Mr. Puddephat's wife. Snakes of prurience aroused and hissing wanted to hear more; at the same time they dismissed Trinculo's sly remark as preposterous. After all, what could he possibly know about Mr. Puddephat's private life?

He was taking his sweet time in the toilet. I grew restless.

At the door a stray dog, its belly swollen with pups, poked its nose in and stared; sensing no objection it ventured forward, sniffing its way among the chairs. The pretty Indian girl came rushing out with a broom shouting, *Shoo! Shoo!*

She came to our table, looking to clear away empty bottles, her short skirt revealing awful chafing fat thighs. She said to me, smiling, her eyes friendly, *You not from here, right? Is where you from?*

I was flabbergasted. Did I really look *not from here*? Was it the clothes I wore? Had she heard my university accent? And why did she smile at me like that?

Right at that moment the jukebox starting up on a fresh calypso swamped us; and here at last was Trinculo jigging and jigging to the music, his hands and head moving earnestly as if dancing was one of his minor, not often displayed talents, something he could hardly restrain when for instance he heard this particular tune.

He wanted to order another round. I started to protest.

– What's happening, Michaelangelo, you shy or something? Drink up, man. This ent England. They don't serve tea here. Drink up.

I swallowed my protest and made an effort to finish the first bottle. The Indian girl was already bearing down on our table with a tray of new drinks.

I wanted to get back to Mr. Puddephat.

– So you taking dogs for a walk these days, I said.

– *Aha! What have we here? What monstrous curiosity!* You can't wait to hear about Puddephat and his wife.

I laughed because it was true, and because whenever he slips into his Shakespearean mode I see that side of him that was always the clown. I should tell you: off stage Trinculo was a *raconteur par excellence*. He would hold us spellbound after classes with tales of life among the *hoi polloi*: tales of betrayal, sexual conquest, assault: gory and brawling tales that left me, I confess, shaking my head in mock horror and disbelief.

This time, knowing his audience was captive and cynical, he told his tale with an actor's accomplishment: pausing, speaking in hoarse urgent whisper, sometimes lifting his voice over the brassy noise of the jukebox. And as amazing as it turned out, his tale was credible and sound. Trinculo knew the Puddephats better than the Puddephats knew each other.

– You see, one night after the show, we got to thinking: *wait!* how come this young woman married to Puddephat? And they don't have no children?

Schoolboy questions. Idle college talk. But Trinculo had the curiosity of a bloodhound and he went sniffing for clues.

On the final night of *The Tempest*, the last curtain drawn, cheers and congratulations all around, everyone tired, going home, Trinculo and his friend Mombassa – *You remember Mombassa?* I did: he liked to close our Latin class with his Satchmo Armstrong imitations: *second spasm, second spasm!* – they decided to sneak back into the college compound and camp under the Puddephats' bedroom window. The Puddephats slept with the windows open and Trinculo was hoping to hear sounds of sexual passion: Mrs. Puddephat offering her body in adoring tribute to yet another successful cultural production by her husband.

46

They heard mutterings; they heard silence; they heard crickets and their own hearts pounding. When the bedroom lights went out they strained their ears but they heard nothing else.

– Then the next thing we hear was the front door *slam*! Footsteps coming down the front steps. Lo, and behold, Mrs. Puddephat! Wearing the same clothes, going out in the middle of the night – mark you, was near midnight! – to walk the dog! *Walking the dog*! Now you tell me!

– But, hold on! Maybe the man was tired that night. Besides, English people love dogs. They like taking the dog for a walk.

– If you ask me, they know more 'bout walking the dog than *dogging*!

In any event Trinculo and Mombassa decided to trail her.

Keeping what they considered an inconspicuous distance, they followed her block after block. With every step, as they passed under every streetlamp, they feared Mrs. Puddephat might turn and notice she was being followed by two young men wheeling cycles (Trinculo's cycle had a flat tire, so they would have been compelled to walk anyway).

They followed her until they came to Main Street with its tree-lined pathway for strollers. There she sat on one of the benches, slipped the leash off the dog, and looked around her dreamily.

– Now you tell me! What Mrs. Puddephat doing in Main Street at that hour of the night...*with a dog*?

I had to admit that was a difficult situation, fraught with risk. Main Street ran parallel to Water Street, which was near the sea. For a young woman like Mrs. Puddephat it was perhaps too near the sea, too close to a chance encounter with those denizens of the night: seamen and prostitutes, thieves and drunks. No, I couldn't imagine why Mrs. Puddephat would want to walk her dog there.

– What sort of dog was it? I asked.

– What sort of dog? *What sort of dog*? His eyes were bulging; his palms slapped the table in amazement.

– Bulldog? Alsatian? Dachshund... what sort of dog? I persisted. The question might have been unfair. In the Republic there are only dogs and stray dogs.

He laughed and emptied his glass, poured more beer on his ice cubes; then he said:

47

– I'll tell you what sort of dog... A bitch. A bitch in heat... in monstrous heat... a most poor credulous monster heat!

– All right, all right. I get the point.

– You couldn't *get* the point, 'cause I haven't *made* the point yet. Drink up!

It seemed that at this stage there were several points. To begin with Mombassa was getting bored and restless. He hadn't seen anything to warrant his hanging around the streets that late at night. Besides *his* bicycle was working fine; *he* didn't have to walk home with a flat tire. He grumbled and scratched his crotch; finally he said he'd had enough and he took off.

Finding himself alone, feeling vaguely disappointed, Trinculo was about to abandon his role as Mrs. Puddephat's midnight watcher when suddenly he saw the dogs. A pack of wild dogs.

– They must have been roaming the wharves. Pothounds. Mongrels. Six, seven, eight of them, out of nowhere, running like a posse. Must have been the scent. Dogs could pick up that scent for miles and come running. A bitch in heat is a siren call to every canine off a leash.

They came running because Mrs. Puddephat's dog was sniffing and wandering, lifting its foot to pee on a lamp post, then sniffing and wandering; while Mrs. Puddephat sat rigid, the rolled-up leash held tight as hate in her hand, her eyes staring blankly into space, oblivious to danger, indifferent to the night.

– What you think happen next? Trinculo asked. I ignored his smug manner, and waited.

– What happened was... both natural and unreal. The mongrels surrounded the Puddephat bitch. They sniffed and followed her wherever she turned. They came down the street toward me! It's something you hear most nights when you sleeping, but, boy, *this* was *monstrous*.

He was beginning to get on my nerves with his intensity, his Shakespearean words. But to tell the truth what happened was indeed natural and unreal.

The dogs closed in, he said, the biggest one taking first turn, struggling to get in position behind the Puddephat dog then silently, fixatedly humping away; while the other dogs snarled and bit each other, as if trying to decide whose turn was next. And

48

it continued like this for a while, he said, the snarling and quarreling for places in the queue; and the Puddephat dog let them have their way, though sometimes she snapped back if she was displeased with a performance, and ran off; but they pursued her, cutting her off, jostling for positions in the queue, mounting her again in the same quiet obsessed way.

– And all this time Mrs. Puddephat just sitting there, stiff and sad, staring into space, her hands in her laps. Eventually she got up, and start walking home, calling to her dog, *Come here… come here, Miranda… that's enough, now!*

He did that imitation of Mrs. Puddephat so perfectly it uncapped all the tension bottled inside me. I was shaking with delight and involuntarily reaching for my beer. Trinculo roared and slapped his thigh. It drew the billiard players back to our table.

The Indian waitress, her brassiered breast bulging ominously, came up to clear bottles; she looked at me, and remarked: "This man here really surprise me, drinking beer and enjoying heself." It sounded like some kind of enticement, as if I'd been singled out for special reward. One of the billiard players whispered in my ear, *Oi, oi, watch yourself! This giurl have she eye on you!* For the rest of the afternoon I ignored her.

But there was more, much more – mystery and revelation. After all, why would Mrs. Puddephat send Christmas cards to Trinculo? And was he now a walker of dogs?

When the billiard players sensed they might be happier chalking their billiard cues instead of sitting around our table, they moved away. And this is where Trinculo made his darkest, most disturbing disclosures. They remain wedged in my memory, the way important events or certain melodies sometimes get stuck there too, causing a little pain now and then, a stormy head, a roiling sleepless night now and then.

Trinculo had not done very well at those all-important overseas A Level exams. I think he passed one subject, which was not good enough to get you anywhere. I don't think he was altogether disappointed.

When I saw him just before I'd left for England, he was his usual ebullient self. He gave me the impression – talking fast, sporting American style sneakers and tube socks – that he'd cast away forever his school uniform as well as his education. He suggested there were other things to fall back on: his indigenous energy, that irrepressible humour, his memory of winning performances.

Yet even as he wished me good luck and told me to keep in touch, I sensed that day a bitterness in his heart.

Now that I was back home it might have been his intention to prove to me that his precipitous energy had got him somewhere in life: that there were roads you could travel right here in the Republic, roads to personal fulfillment which bypassed institutions of learning in England or America. There was something *here*, he seemed to be saying, that you couldn't find *out there*.

Framed in that perspective you might begin to understand what happened when just by chance he met Mrs. Puddephat again, one moonlit night, sitting with her dog in Main Street.

– I swear to you on my father's grave: I just happened to be passing down Main Street. Had a few drinks that night. Was on my way home. She was sitting in the *same* seat, *same* position, sitting like a statue, and the dog lying at her feet.

I shook my head, cynically rejecting this set of circumstances. A third round of beers, apart from encouraging loud talk, might have sneaked in some capacity for easy distortion. I sat back determined to be sceptical; he leaned forward, his fingers quivering.

– I stop. I wheel the cycle back to where she was sitting. The dog look at me like he want to attack. I said, *Goodnight, Mrs. Puddephat.* She look at me like I was the devil.

Like he was the devil! Mrs. Puddephat was probably more irritated than frightened by his intrusion.

In any event she apparently didn't recognize him right away, and the dog was growling, getting ready to charge.

In an instant he did something that flashed his identity like a badge before her eyes, dispelling all her fears. He fell into his Trinculo role from *The Tempest,* reeling off a few lines:

– *Were I in England now, as once I was, and had but this fish painted, not a holiday fool there but would give a piece of silver.*

Mrs. Puddephat smiled, bright as a full moon, and patted the dog in restraint.

– *Alas the Storm is come again*! she answered. She knew for sure now who he was.

– Trinculo! Good heavens, what are you doing here?

– I was going to ask you the same thing: what *you* doing here?

Mrs. Puddephat laughed. A strange, happy laugh. And Trinculo, who was no expert on women's laughter, felt a gust of power inside his body that made him fearless and strong. Dog-taming fearless, wild-man strong.

She told him she'd come out because she had a sudden urge to drink water coconuts. He told her there weren't any vendors around there. He told her she really ought not to be hanging about these streets at night; he offered generously to escort her home.

– So we start walking. I wheeling the bike. The dog running ahead and sniffing the grass. And she walking beside me *close, close*, touching my arms, my legs, walking *close, close* – and talking up a storm.

Mr. Puddephat had renewed his contract; he was staying on for two more years. She was returning to England. No, no there was nothing terribly wrong with living in the Republic. Of course, there were problems. But then every developing nation had its problems. No, she was returning home because she felt the time had come to move on.

On and on like this she talked. It reminded me a bit of Pamela. When *she* got ready, usually on similar long walks, she could talk herself to the end of the earth. Only, to hear Trinculo tell it, a storm must have been gathering inside Mrs. Puddephat. He could hear it, he said, in her nervous laughter; he could feel it like electrical sparks when her body touched his.

– She would stop walking and come close up to me to say something, staring up into my face, he said.

– English people tend to keep a little discreet distance in conversation, I said.

– Well, not this Englishwoman, believe you me! I could feel turbulence in the air. Like when the clouds begin to pass over the full moon.

Turbulence in the air! Clouds passing over the moon! With his face shiny from the strain of memory, the beers were evidently spreading vapors over his mind.

They entered the gates of the school compound, the moon high and bright in the sky, so that the old school building, all shuttered and empty, look like some huge ghost ship moored forever to the earth.

– She stop talking the moment we came through the gate. Her head was lowered like she deep in thought. I thought of Mr. Puddephat. I didn't want him to see me. I getting ready to say *Goodnight* at the gate, but then I said to myself, *Wait a minute! This ent the Queen's property! This is our Government property*. Just before we get to their house, the dog was already up the front steps. She stop; she turn; she look me straight in the face. And she said, *Thou shoulds't have been Caliban*! I tell you, Michaelangelo, it was as if she'd reached out and grabbed me by the balls.

In the next instant Trinculo's mouth fell gently on Mrs. Puddephat's lips like the start of rain.

It was, he said, a fantastical kiss. It was a kiss Shakespeare might have written for him on the stage. An incredible kiss, their mouths finally touching after centuries of travel and circumstance.

– Then she took my hand and we started walking away from the house toward the playing field and it was weird, 'cause I'd never been out there before at that time of night and I let go the bike and put my arms around her waist, she had a tiny waist, and, boy, I tell you, her whole body *shudder* and she squeeze me and squeeze me, and the moon lit up the cricket pitch so bright, I was sure the whole world could see us.

Mrs. Puddephat looked up in his face and said, *Misery acquaints a man with strange bed fellows*… and a woman!

Hiatus. The jukebox, a hammer of brass battering my senses.

– Then what you think happen next? Trinculo asked.

I looked at my watch and muttered my dismay at what time it was. I glanced at the doorway, at the bicycles leaning one on top the other.

– What you think happen next? he asked again, shouting.

I knew and I didn't know what happened next.

Trinculo was grinning, a wicked schoolboy grin. With his right hand balled up in a fist, he was punching the open palm of his left hand: sure and smooth like a greased piston: *Smack*… *smack*…

52

smack. The old schoolboy way of re-enacting sexual conquest. Only now, that gleam in his eyes hinted at something else, a kind of revenge.

I found myself recoiling. I wanted to hear no more. No cheap boast of how unforgettably sweet it was.

The billiard players who had had enough of billiards came over, and straightaway knew what we were talking about; they made the noise of simple men who'd been cheated of some manly joke:

– What the rass you two *auntie-men* going on with? one of them said.

The other leaned toward me, and speaking loud enough for Trinculo to hear, said:

– Don't let him fool you. Is only white meat he eating. Local girls not good enough for him. Strictly white meat.

Trinculo drained his glass and called to the Indian waitress as if he didn't mind what lesser mortals said about him since in any case they were not in his league.

I wanted to get up and leave. I was sick of this bottom-house bar, sick of its weak fluorescents, sick of the crass vulgarity – *only white meat he eating* – the humping dog tricks it encouraged in men like Trinculo. I didn't come all the way back from studying in England to be part of this.

I smiled weakly and asked the friendly billiard player which way to the back room. He erupted in rude laughter, pointing his billiard cue at me. *All right*, I sighed, *where de piss house?* He pointed to a curtain near the bar.

I got up and started walking towards the bead curtain, dreading that journey, dreading even more what I would find back there.

I flew back to England, of course. What else could I do, given my potential, but pursue a Doctorate? I made the mistake of telling all this to Pamela. She was reclining on a fat embroidered cushion, her *I missed you* face lapping up every word, her *I like you* eyes riveted on my lips. There I was spilling my guts out, all the time wondering what was different about her. Finally noticing: she had done something to her hair, cut it short so that more of the nape of her neck showed; she had apparently done something to her body too; she seemed somehow sturdier, and her breasts had a new unsupported lift. It was all so distracting; I couldn't quite say what I wanted to say about the folly of going back home.

And her reaction? A most peculiar thing: she fell back laughing and clapping her hands like a girl guide, quite delirious.

I had expected some sensitivity to my dilemma, certainly not wild laughter. And then:

– Oh, Mikey, Mikey…

– What's so funny? I asked.

– Oh, Mikey…

– Stop calling me, *Mikey*. What do you take me for, a child?

– I'm sorry, I didn't mean to be rude.

– I don't know why I bothered telling you all this. After all it's really none of your business.

– It's just that… well, you're a grey person, so to speak. I mean, that's why you're *here*, not *there*. You cleave to all that dull damp greyness outside. You don't want the light, the wonderful energizing light back in the Republic.

– What are you going on about? I said. No one builds a life, or a country for that matter, on *wonderful energizing light*.

It was so unusual for Pamela to miss the point.

– I mean, you're here, and you're so smug about what England has done for you, while your country's fairly pleading for hardworking men and women, pioneers and frontiersmen, willing to sweat out the tough times.

She wasn't listening to me. All this time wasted, pouring out my guts, and she hadn't understood a word!

Then she said:

– *Michaelangelo*, what it boils down to is this. You're not much of anything really. Hard in your chest, soft in your trousers. That's what you are. Whereas, your Trinculo…

So that was it! *Your Trinculo. Puddephat's Trinculo.* And that unused and undecorated night companion inside my trousers! I must tell you, right at moment I was disappointed in Pamela. Very disappointed. I felt angry and betrayed.

I said to her, putting down the teacup and saucer, and reaching for my jacket:

– What it really boils down to is that you're not much of

54

anything yourself. Why don't you get yourself a little doggie? Take it for walks. Feed it those clever dog biscuits you call conversation. You don't need me around here.

And that in one swift showering thunderclap was the end of that.

One other thing I should mention. The reason I felt moved to share all this with you is this: just the other day I came across an article in newspapers sent by one of my mother's friends to her here in Montreal. It announced that a delegation was about to leave the Republic for Canada to seek economic assistance. There was a photo of the travel party about to enplane at the airport. And, yes, you guessed it: there among the officials smiling and waving to the reading public was the face of Trinculo.

A member of the delegation. Moving up in the world, the little twin-horned *pioneering* bag carrier. Getting ready to perform some begging bowl act for his country. Well, a new Republic gets what it deserves, and performers like Trinculo no doubt have something to offer, like the *smack... smack... smack* of sweet lashings; that neck-gripping ride on the backs of its people.

Our family got out when things were beginning to crumble around them. Mum had wanted to leave long before. It took my dad a while longer to see the light. I prefer not to go into details. Suffice it to say we're doing very well here, our family is.

My brother, the dentist, is married to a Canadian woman. He has a thriving practice up in Calgary. Dad's retired now, though he did work for a while here in Montreal. I don't think he has any regrets about moving up here. As for me, I'm a college professor. Doing what I must to keep body and mind together. Dad is quite pleased with the way things have turned out for all of us. I couldn't be more content. As a family, we've joined the world, so to speak. And all's well in our world. I walk these Canadian streets, an achieved man, a free man. No fear of stepping on tiny loaves of dogshit here.

YOUR SLIP IS SHOWING, COMRADE!

On their way to the airport that humid afternoon it hadn't occurred to Julienne that she was leaving the Republic the way most people left it, wrenching themselves from its pincerlike grip of low wages and unending misery; leaving relatives behind like bits and pieces of wailing flesh trapped in the pincers. She was content simply to be moving: toward the airport, where a change of transport would set her in blissful drifting motion again; to an island, and the next stage of blissful drifting motion, during which she would fall asleep and wake up to wonder where she was now – what day, what year – then back to sleep: moving on toward some splendid distant goal.

Leaving hadn't crossed her mind until Romesh who'd been chattering to her about his own plans to emigrate to Canada, *and maybe they would see each other in Toronto one day,* suddenly fell silent, puzzled by her stiff brooding manner. Then he said sharply, irritably:

– So you leaving us.

Which sounded so foolish and sentimental, Julienne sucked her teeth. At least he hadn't said, so you're leaving *me*, which would have been really foolish and sentimental.

Romesh laughed as if being ignored was nothing to get upset about. Then he said, still baffled by her silence:

– So you leaving the Republic. You are an *émigré*!

– Don't be stupid. Émigrés are poor European people fleeing communism.

– Then, you're a *migrant*.

– Migrants are third world people fleeing poverty and job-lessness.

– But this is a poor third world Socialist Republic, and you leaving. So what are you then?

At this point, wearied by the exchange, unimpressed by what struck her as an attempt by Romesh to be funny-clever, she tried to change the subject. She reminded him that they'd been driving for ten minutes with the car windows rolled up. The air-conditioning was supposed to be working. She was hot. Evidently it wasn't working.

– Give it time, comrade. The system takes time to warm up! Like when you making love, Romesh said.

She let that answer go. Romesh was in a flippant mood; he was also in a bit of pain and confusion, not knowing where he stood with her, whether he'd see her again; not knowing who she really was; driving her to the airport, anyway, because she had asked him to, his hands on the wheel light and cavalier, as if he were flying a kite.

She looked at his hands, then at his handsome face, and she smiled because she really liked him and probably would miss him. She put her arms on his shoulders and played with his long hair – it was styled like the hippies in America – and she rubbed his neck affectionately. But her body felt damp with perspiration from the stuffy car.

She was wearing a bright summery dress that showed off her legs in a way Romesh had never seen before. He'd always considered her a "free spirit", by which he meant someone who wore American blue jeans, with a strange mannish voice, and a brooding passion for sex. He was seeing her for the first time now as a bright young woman with pretty legs; and she was leaving. Was he in some foolish sentimental way falling for her?

– And, please, if you writing me letters, don't address me as *Comrade*, she said.

– Alright, how about *My Darling*?

Again she let that go. Conversation on the way to the airport must be as painful for people leaving the Republic as for those left behind. The feelings you struggle with as you stare through the window at people going about their drab business, unaware of your good fortune!

Julienne wanted, suddenly, passionately, to be alone up in the sky, jet-propelling far away, the drone of the engines dulling her senses.

60

On the plane she settled in placing her travel bag under the seat. She looked at the assortment of documents in her hands, the cards, the papers, her passport. She looked again at the photo in her passport; the camera had caught her scowling. The photographer speaking as if his job, linked to prospects of overseas travel, was of great national importance had told her the passport office didn't like photos of smiling comrades.

She put the passport away and took out a writing pad, a farewell gift from Romesh; and because passengers were still boarding the aircraft, and she was buckled into her seat with nothing to do except stare out the window, she started scribbling answers to questions that nobody in a uniform would ask.

I am my mother's child. Her pride and joy. My love and hate, she wrote.

She liked to think she had nothing in common with her mother. Nothing at all. She was delivered into this world, into this century, and on this obscure piece of earth, by some quirky hand of fate, which had inflamed her mother's heart with powerful illusions. The illusion, for instance, that she was in love with the Minister of Finance and Foreign affairs: a divorced man: graying handsomely at the temples: a big wheel in the Party.

At moments when Julienne hated her she told herself: my mother was probably attracted by his status in the Party; or his mixed race background; or the fact that he studied in England.

Or maybe it was his power to make life comfortable or miserable depending on your response to his wishes. And since her mother's loyalty to the Party was as fierce as lust, she must have succumbed one night in a confusion of loyalty, fear and desire, to the Minister's casual request for sex.

In the Republic if you were young and pretty and excited about politics, one thing led to another. Then another. And then to birth or death.

In the early months of her pregnancy her mother tried to be evasive about her swollen state; but rumor and gossip reminded the nation of her dalliance with the Minister. She decided one day to put a bold face on it, a defiant untouchable face. *Let the people gossip about their leaders. We're the Royal Family of the Republic*, her mother declared jokingly one evening to a working committee of women, party comrades and friends who had gathered in her living room to discuss preparations for the next congress.

Her mother arranged for her to be chauffeured to school. Her mother insisted Julienne sit beside her sometimes on the dais at party functions. She was pressed into helping on social evenings at their home. This was all the result of her mother growing into a new radical person of the 70s: the liberated single woman raising her daughter alone, the working woman setting an example to the fickle masses of duty and responsibility.

As she grew older, Julienne was left more alone to ponder her own liberation. She hungered for close friendship. She searched for ways to secure the closeness of friends.

Most people she grew up with at school regarded her with a mixture of envy and contempt. They were as friendly as classroom friendships go, but she was still after all the offspring of a powerful Minister. She may not have taken his name, but she wore his features (the set of the eyes, the texture of his hair) like birthmarks of his enduring presence. This led to some confusion and uncertainty among her admirers.

Young men, fearing the Minister's displeasure, weren't sure how to approach her. Young ladies, secure in their own families, viewed Julienne with condescension.

Slowly she drifted away from the dailiness of friends. Secretly she longed for intimacy. Bored, left often to *her own devices*, as her mother liked to say, Julienne devised.

Daughters, beware of the dogs. Your mother's pets. Pacing, snarling, baring their smiles. Like Cerberus. Behind the gates of your precious virginity, she wrote.

The first young man she tried to seduce was Corbin, their driver. She imagined it would be simple. He was trained to follow instructions. He was a voluble courteous fellow, a private in the Defense Force. He was also a soccer player; he played for the national soccer team. The party had arranged the chauffeur job for him as a gesture of support to young sportsmen.

Julienne liked his lithe springy movements on the balls of his feet; she liked his bowlegs, the neat fit of his shirt around his torso, and his constantly dry appearance. He wasn't bony faced and oily skinned like so many young men she saw pedaling cycles around town in shirtjacs. Besides, she was amused and touched by his clumsy efforts to be courteous as he opened the car door, avoiding her eyes.

One afternoon she asked him in on the pretext of helping her with shopping bags from the market. Once inside she got him to sit in the living room. He looked uneasy. She offered him a beer thinking that might loosen his restraints. She changed into shorts and sat hugging her knees, revealing her thighs. When finally he understood her deep wish he started stuttering and looked plainly terrified.

He got up to go, smiling sheepishly and claiming he had club practice that afternoon; and as he backed away toward the door his shoes left prints on the polished floor. The terror on his face deepened, as if those footprints were irrefutable evidence he had trespassed and gone beyond the call of his duties. He fled.

Julienne was left embarrassed and angry; embarrassed and chastened: she had stooped to the level of her mother's driver. How terrible her desire, how pitiful her efforts! She locked herself in her room and indulged in thirty minutes of self-pity.

She cursed the Republic, which at that time was negotiating loans with the IMF; she cursed her mother's stupid loyalty to the party; she cursed her father and the circumstances of lust that brought her into this world. She wondered if she was doomed to spend the rest of her life unwanted and unloved.

One evening, unexpectedly, with nary a hint of premeditation, that quirky hand of fate threw the dice and snapped its fingers again.

Her mother was in the bedroom trying on African wraps. There was to be a reception at the Prime Minister's residence for a visiting dignitary from one of Africa's republics, ideologically entangled and economically mired like theirs.

– How do I look? she asked. I don't know how they manage to *walk* in these things. I feel like a Japanese in a kimono.

She was turning this way and that, her hand smoothing her bottom; and she waited for Julienne's approval. Actually she knew more about African women in wraps than about Japanese women in kimonos. She was advisor to the Party on cultural

63

affairs; the first lady in the Republic to have met and spoken with Miriam Makeba; the first admirer of her music long before it became fashionable to own her records.

– So how do I look?

Julienne looked. In the gasp of hesitation before she responded she realized the great lengths her mother had gone to maintain a youthful attractive figure. And since her mind was prone to certainties these days, she now felt sure her mother's nights of surrender to the Minister must have been the only nights of pleasure she had allowed her body. Her mother had pledged her soul to something beyond pleasure, beyond the party and the Republic, to something obscure and fearful.

– Did you breast feed me when I was a baby? Julienne asked casually.

– What kind of question is that?

– Never mind.

– How do I look? Tell me.

– You look… convincing… If a helicopter dropped you right now in a Lagos marketplace you would vanish without a trace.

Her mother laughed, very pleased with that response: still turning, still looking down at the hem.

– They'd probably declare me *persona non grata*. Backside not big enough. Are you coming?

Julienne had decided she wasn't coming. She muttered something about a migraine. Then abruptly she changed her mind; she *was* coming. She was thinking: it might be possible after all to meet someone interesting, one of the Africans perhaps, charming and resplendent in flowing robes, speaking in an educated accent, and after a few drinks whispering lasciviously in her ear.

Then she balked. Her mother was insisting they dress as twins in African wrap. She ignored her mother's wish. She chose a leopard print dress with a slit at the side. Since it was getting late and Corbin was already outside with the car, they finished dressing in stony silence.

– And by the way, you weren't breast-fed.

Corbin was stiff and formal, as if the occasion at the PM's residence called for a special effort at correct deportment. Once in the car Julienne's mother encouraged him to talk. Informal chats, with Corbin glancing occasionally in the rear view mirror, gave her that sense of unity with the workers in the Republic. She'd boast to party comrades that she had her fingers on the pulse of the people. She was invited often to the PM's residence for dinner and conversation. He picked her brains, she said, about the mood of the people, their willingness to make sacrifices in the struggle.

Corbin was asked about the performance of the national squad in the last World Cup elimination match.

– We didn't score a goal. What happened?

– Bad luck. We had plenty scoring chances, *plennnty scoring chances*, but the fellows slip up.

Julienne, who had been indifferent and silent so far, said:

– Typical. Just typical! Give them a wide-open goal and all the chances in the world, they still wouldn't score.

Corbin laughed like a good sport. Julienne wasn't sure he'd grasped her point. His knotty head was so dimwitted he'd miss even the crudest irony.

When the car turned into the Prime Minister's residence, the tires making that reassuring sound on the gravelly driveway, Julienne declared her migraine had returned. She wanted to go back home. At this point, near the gleam of parked cars, lights on the lawns, the sound of a band entertaining the guests, her mother was in no mood to argue. She could see the Africans, tall and statesmanlike in robes, mingling with the locals in their imported dashikis. Her blood raced, the glow of first greetings shone on her face. Not a moment to waste. If Julienne didn't feel drawn to the occasion, so be it.

Driving back, feeling ridiculously dressed up, Julienne was sullen. Corbin was no longer loud or voluble. He drove with dutiful care.

Suddenly he turned off the main road onto a rough dirt track that led into one of the villages. Taken by surprise, a little fearful, Julienne said in a calm voice:

– Where you taking me?

– I have a sweet spot. A place with plenty scoring chances, he laughed.

So he had caught on. So his footballer's little knotty head had caught her meaning.

65

She said nothing. The car bounced its way deeper into the dark; there were no lampposts; the sweep of the car lights illumined a canal running parallel to the road; then a hump where the old train lines ran the other way, over which they bounced; then they plunged forward again, along a straight path deeper into the dark, the headlights revealing coconut trees and peasant huts on one side, bush on the other; driving on and on as if Corbin was forcing her to ask once again in naked fright, *Where are you taking me?*

She breathed not a word. She sat erect in the back seat biting her lips, her racing heart refusing to disclose its fear.

Finally Corbin stopped; he turned the car around with some difficulty and grinding gears; then he backed it into what looked like a field of sugar cane stalks. He switched off the ignition and the lights and they were swallowed into pitch darkness.

He turned to her and said:

– This is it, my sweet spot.

His voice was loud again, full of strange assurance, as if he were trying to erase from her mind the retreating apologetic person that was last seen fleeing down the stairs of her house. She couldn't read his face in the dark; she sensed something slightly deferential in his manner, suggesting that despite his newfound courage he was awaiting her consent. At least he wouldn't harm her, she thought; he wouldn't *do* anything stupid to her.

She looked outside. There was nothing but surrounding walls of sugar cane stalk. In the heavens a litter of indifferent stars. This was *not* how she had imagined it would be; not in her wildest fantasies.

She said to him in a little strangled voice:

– *Here?*

He glanced outside, then he said animatedly:

– The seats go back. I can fix it… By the way, my first name is Felix.

The car was one of six offered as a gift to the Republic from the government and people of North Korea. The Ministers who had their own roomier cars anyway had assigned them to several Ministries; they were deemed too small for private use.

Corbin groped for something below that let the seats go back.

66

By this time he'd sensed her acquiescence; he clambered over until he was beside her then boldly fumbled with the belt on his pants. Just as he loomed over her, running her hands slowly up her thighs, she felt a rush of excitement, and, partly to calm her nerves, she said to him, sternly:

– Don't get me pregnant.

This brought Corbin up short. He turned and was fumbling again for his pants. She slipped out of her panties and waited.

Her mind drifted away to the Prime Minister's lawns, mere miles away. She could see her mother moving comfortably now in the wrap, holding her glass tightly, sharing humor and light-hearted speculations with members of the African delegation about Third World problems, the need for fiscal discipline, sacrifice and more sacrifice. And asking about her good friend Miriam Makeba.

A whimsical shift of mood like a snap of a finger, and she might have been *there*, in the glow of the lights strung around the lawns; rather than here in this bushy backdam dark, with Corbin, who was making rather loud sounds now with his rubbery thing.

A new feeling rose inside her, stronger than her first desire; an inchoate feeling which, despite Corbin's business-like determination not to slip up on this, his big scoring chance, was springing not from below her waist but from the pounding delirium in her young heart.

My mother will not forgive those who trespass on her kindred and her kind, she wrote.

Whenever she looked back on that night with Corbin in the Korean car it was with complete satisfaction and joy at the risk she had taken, the courage she had shown. The way things unfolded made her first attempt to seduce him seem so foolishly desperate and unromantic. No longer would she trust herself to arrange these things. They would happen just like that, without premeditation or design.

For days she lazed around the house living off the memory of that night. She had gripped his fleshy buttocks with her fingers. She was sure she'd left marks on his skin, for in the dark when she felt that first rupturing pain all she could think of was grabbing hold of something. She'd closed her eyes; she'd bit her lips and uttered barely a whimper. She smelled the cologne coming from his shoulders and his neck and she gripped his buttocks and marveled at his fierce concentration.

He'd said not a word, breathing a little raggedly, measuring her satisfaction in the dark. And when she gave no indication she'd had enough, he came into her a second time, still quiet, business-like and oddly deferential.

A night like that could not be repeated. She couldn't dream of asking him to take her back into the cane fields one more time. So she waited for chance to throw them together, hearing the car drive away racing in first gear after bringing her mother home.

These were the hot dreamy days of August '74. Popular American songs about rebellion, soulful love and casual sex flooded the airwaves. Everyone in the city was talking about *Last Tango in Paris*, which opened that week at the Plaza cinema. Julienne bought a ticket and sat tight-lipped and unblinking for the first ten minutes.

She'd graduated from high school and, following her mother's wishes, was getting ready without great fuss to start undergraduate study in September at a university overseas. These were days, therefore, of lassitude, of wild fantasy and a tremulous readiness whenever next happen-stance beckoned.

Her mother came charging up the stairs one afternoon, slipping in her haste, swearing blasphemously, then stomping on up. Curled in a chair Julienne saw her drop her bag and office folders, watched her as she approached pointing a trembling finger:

– You…you…common slut!

Julienne winced at the words, uncomprehending. Her mother snatched the thick paperback novel from her hands and hit her across the face, hit her on the head, on her hands raised in startled defense. Over and over, the blows emphasizing her words:

– You *think*…I brought you up…to be nothing but a *slut*…? a common *slut*? After *all*…I've done for *you*…in this house…you *behaving*…like…a…common…slut!

And she might have gone on hitting had not the telephone rung, pulling her away; for as enraged as she felt, her mother could not bear to hear the telephone ringing again and again.

68

Julienne quickly escaped to the bathroom in whimpering confusion.

She examined her face for swellings and bruises. She suspected her mother's wrath had something to do with her night off the main road in the Korean car with Corbin. She'd found out about it only today. What fury must have possessed her all the way home! Betrayed by her own flesh and blood!

Her mother's voice on the telephone reached her just before she hung up:

– As for him, don't worry. Somebody going to fix his behind. Shoot him in the knees like the IRA people in Ireland. That should fix him.

When she heard this Julienne was horrified. Corbin, her knotty-head football lover, to be shot in the knees; to be punished for so silly a transgression! It was not beyond the power of her father, the Minister, to arrange these things. He liked doing things to troublemakers that set an example to the nation.

What could she do to prevent this cruel fate?

The matter didn't end there. The very next day her mother, speaking in a modulated tone, in contrast to the near hysteria the day before, announced there would be changes in Julienne's future. Bare months before she enplaned for University, it was now considered unwise to send her off in so naive and vulnerable a state. She'd had no experience of *the real world*; she'd been too sheltered, too coddled all her life. What she needed was *experience in the world of work*.

They found her a job in her father's Ministry. Simple clerical duties. At the bottom of the ladder. And no more Korean car privileges. Public transport was cheap and reliable.

Julienne received all this in pouting silence. She considered it below her dignity to protest, to argue for her rights, her independence. Besides something of that beaten, haggard weariness hanging over the Republic, touching everyone's private lives, made protest futile.

In any event she sensed her mother waiting for precisely that: a shrill display of defiance, tantrums, tears: just that opportunity to lay down some crude reminders about *whose house this is*, and other hints at constituency and control everyone had come to identify with the Party. For the woman out there laying down new laws was no longer her mother. She was the Minister's consort. And like the Minister, she knew how to impose her will on vagrant souls.

In her room, behind a locked door, she curled up and stared for long hours at the walls. At times a shudder of helplessness overwhelmed her. She buried her face in the pillow to muffle her crying. She turned over and stared for long hours at the ceiling.

The next day and the day after she confined herself to her room. She ate very little. She did not answer the phone fearing it might be her mother, wanting to normalize things; not apologizing, just carrying on as if nothing had really changed.

The time had come, she thought, to strike out on her own. That much she knew. But where? And how? Could she ever escape the clutches of her mother? Her father, the Minister? The Party? Was there some place in the world away from this dry city where she could plant the tender shoots of her life and bloom like a rare flower?

In the Republic of desperate dreaming, happiness is a pig wagging its tail in the mud, she wrote.

At the airport Julienne was hot and irritable. She saw the crowds at the terminal building, friends and family outnumbering passengers, and her discomfort grew.

Romesh honked his horn, drawing stares, and inched the car forward to the curb. He'd told her to be prepared: there might be a flight delay, flight over-booking, flight cancellation; for these were the bedrock days of socialism when everyone schemed to flee the Republic as from an advancing swarm of locusts. But he swore he would get her on the plane. He knew people, he said; he had connections.

He had no idea of the power and connections behind Julienne's name since she'd never really told him who she was. When he drove up to her gate she was waiting at the door. He looked around curiously. She urged him to load the bags quickly and get going.

It wasn't as terrible as Romesh had anticipated. She got her bags tagged, received her boarding pass and she was waiting for

Romesh to park the car. Not in the parking lot. He'd chosen a spot some distance along the roadway close to the fence near the perimeter of the landing field. That way Julienne would have no problem spotting the little red car and waving at his solitary figure from the plane.

He was taking his sweet time getting back to her. She stepped outside for a final idle walk around. She heard footsteps behind her. She turned and was surprised to see Col. Puneshwar, Chief of the new Security Branch.

– How *are* you? What are you doing out here? he asked, loud and friendly.

– I'm fine, she said.

He fell in step with her, his boots crunching the gravel in military stride. He wore his army uniform, his dark glasses, and he was carrying a swagger stick, which he wiggled behind his back like a happy puppy's tail.

Julienne had met him before just once. He made her extremely nervous now. It seemed he enjoyed making people nervous, perhaps because people were not yet familiar with the workings of the new Security Branch. People were not even familiar with his name and his role. He'd recently returned from a training course in London and was described in one local newspaper as the Republic's most eligible bachelor. His favorite author was Erle Stanley Gardener.

– So you're traveling, he said.

Julienne wasn't sure if he was posing a question, but she said, yes, she was traveling.

– Off to university, I hear. Well, that's a very good move. The Republic needs all the young bright minds it can get. Especially when they belong to lovely young women like you.

Clumsy with compliments. Julienne gave him a weak smile, wishing he would run out of things to say and drift away. But he stuck to her side, wagging his puppy tail stick, stiff and smug, walking beside her because one didn't often get a chance to walk beside lovely young women. She began to sense danger in this man, still new to his job.

– I wish I were traveling myself. You know how it is, once you get the travel bug, that sort of thing…

71

He'd slipped into a British accent, topping off his sentence with *that sort of thing*. He liked doing that, dropping borrowed phrases, slipping in and out of accents. It reminded people he had traveled; he was a man of several worlds of which London was one.

Julienne looked around, ignoring him for a moment, as if she really had to say a last farewell to someone else.

– Anyway, have a wonderful trip, he said.

– Thank you.

She walked away in search of Romesh. She heard him call after her:

– Oh, don't forget this. Your passport. You must have left it somewhere.

She walked back, took the passport from him, weak-kneed all of a sudden and trembling. She thought she'd put her passport away safely with the other travel papers. How the hell did it get into his hands? And where on earth was Romesh, who had gone off simply to park his car?

They were asking her to board the aircraft. She wanted to say farewell to Romesh, a quick embrace, and a promise to keep in touch. He was nowhere around. She hurried inside pushing her way through knots of non-travelers who stood around tight-lipped and useless. He said he'd park his car in a conspicuous spot. If she could see him she'd wave to him.

In the Republic of desperate dreams, frequent shortages and power cuts, a young woman follows the fires in her darkened heart. Or shrivels like a seedless prune. Unready for the world. Unfit for love, she wrote.

She had met Col. Puneshwar once before and it left her with distinct feelings of loathing.

She had come home one evening after another dull day in *the world of work* – sealing envelopes, ignoring crass whispers around her, reading a novel – to voices in the living room. No problem. She would quietly slip by into the kitchen for a glass of water. Then to her room. Silence. Icy resolve in her heart. Sleep.

Her mother's voice calling to her – its tone demanding she show her face, not just *answer* from the kitchen – made her bristle. She walked wearily into the living room. She stared at her mother's face as if she hadn't seen it for days.

72

– Have you met Boysie? He's our new Chief of Security. Comrade, this is my daughter, Julienne.

Col. Puneshwar smiled and nodded.

Awkward silence – through which like a window she saw him the way he wished to be seen. Clean-shaven, thin moustache. A narrow good-looking face. His legs crossed, an air of aloofness, which he didn't wear with natural ease, so that he seemed haughty and stupid. An unlit cigarette between fingers. Crisp well-cut army uniform with no sweat marks under the armpit. A man who was most himself on public occasions. A man who could be frightening, she sensed, in small rooms, in solitary places. Fixing other people's behinds.

Awkward silence.

– Julienne is working at the Ministry of Education. Getting to know the system, her mother said.

Abruptly Julienne said she was tired and retreated to her room. Hating her mother for putting her through this: introducing her to someone she instantly disliked because as she walked away the first words he spoke to her – *Your slip is showing, Comrade!* – were like a pat on her bottom from a man who couldn't keep his eyes to himself.

To her room, with its fluffy pillows and color posters on the walls; where she couldn't completely shut out their laughter and conversation; where it suddenly occurred to her that this introduction might have been cleverly arranged by her mother to divert her passion from knotty-head footballers. She was being asked to take note of a more suitable prospect when next she contemplated romance.

It was at this juncture quite fortuitously that Romesh came into her life. She would have opened herself to anyone who dared at that point to tap on her shell of sadness and resentment. Romesh showed up and revealed precisely that daring.

Most afternoons as the working class cycled home or rushed to the market square for buses and taxis, Julienne walked home. She strolled along the sidewalks, a solitary lovely young woman; and she drew curious stares and whistles and remarks from young men on cycles. She enjoyed every bit of attention though she rarely smiled back or looked at anyone.

73

She was now a creature of impulse. A glance at a cinema hoarding, a double feature that looked interesting, and she would plunge into the flickering darkness for four hours. A bus would take her for a ride to the sea wall where she gazed at the horizon and followed solitary men in fishing boats heading out in rough seas. She discovered the ferry, which crossed a muddy river; it seemed somehow exciting to be on water for a change, sailing away from her city of sad duty;   crossing to the other side, buying another ticket and returning, as if she had traveled for miles and miles into the hinterland.

Romesh came up to her one afternoon on the ferry. Later he would explain he had noticed her often leaning on the rail, always near the stern, looking down at the boiling water, or watching with great interest the docking procedure. He was a city worker. The ferry took him home.

One afternoon drawing on all the courage of his curious young manhood, he came up beside her, cleared his throat and said:

– I know exactly what you're thinking.

She turned her head, saw a foolish grinning face, a quivering lip. She looked away, pretending to be bored and unimpressed. Since he didn't feel shunned and, in fact, had stood his ground, she said, her face still averted.

– Okay, what am I thinking?

– You're thinking: my life is a slice of cheese, he said.

She glanced at him, puzzled, not getting it.

– *Golden Grove Cheddar cheese*? he said.

She got it. She lowered her head and she laughed. She tried at first not to let him see her face, not to let him know how mired in boredom and misery her body, her whole life, had become – until his intrusion, this *knock, knock* on her forbidding shell. And he was right. Her life was a slice of cheese.

Golden Grove Cheddar was a local brand of cheese which had recently appeared on supermarket shelves. People were encouraged to support it. It would save the Republic foreign exchange on imported brands. When people protested that the cheese tasted fair, but the smell was offensive, the Minister of Health went on radio to explain its important properties. He ended his speech with an exhortation to listeners: *Hold your nose and eat our national cheese!*

74

She took a deep breath for no apparent reason, then she said:
– I hate the city.
– Me too! I only work over there. I live on this side of the river.
– I hate socialism
– This boat is run by socialists. See how rusty and broken down everything is? You smell the piss from the toilets…? Those fellows… in grimy sailor clothes… socialism got them that way.

Drawn by the light humor in his voice, rather than his words, Julienne looked at him: a slender Indian, several years older that she was, with a moustache and unruly shoulder-length hair. A slim relaxed body; and of course his clever remark about the cheese. He lived on the other side of the river.

When the boat docked he stopped someone, borrowed a bicycle, and invited her chivalrously to tour his village. She accepted.

He pedaled away along a rutted country road, sometimes splashing through muddy puddles of water; past dingy shops and unpainted dwellings and wandering animals. His village. It seemed somewhat drab but it had a strange charm, unlike the white city over there with its capital pretensions, its weeds and cracked pavements, peeling paint and clogged canals, its terrible neglect.

They arranged to meet more often at the ferry at the end of a working day. They stood side by side gazing sullenly as the ferry glided away from the city. The city was the seat of arrogance and mismanagement, where people waited in long lines and the dry heat bred thievery and resentment. On the other side of the river she went for strolls and bike rides. She found release and enchantment.

Romesh was attentive to every shift in her mood. If she fell silent he tried to cheer her up with amiable chatter, usually anecdotes about city life, the black market in goods and foreign currency, the bizarre strategies city folk came up with to survive another day.

She listened; sometimes she laughed; sometimes she asked him to stop talking.

One evening they were passing a deserted churchyard she had seen from the road. She wanted to go inside. It was an old English church that must have thrived in the old plantation days. Peering inside you could see rotting pews, broken stained windows and the board where they placed the hymn numbers. Stray goats roamed and left droppings everywhere; the bush had taken over and the grass covered a few gravestones.

At the rear of the church Julienne was overcome by the sweep of its neglect, the powerful quiet that seemed to hang over its abandoned state. She told Romesh she wanted to make love. *Right there. Right at that moment.*

Caught off guard Romesh looked around, not sure if she was joking. She lay on the grass and closed her eyes until he realized she was serious. She had unzipped her jeans. He could see the elastic of her underwear. Wasting no more time he slipped quickly beside her and unfastened his belt.

Wordless, tears welling up in her eyes, she held on to him, her arms around his neck long after he was done, until Romesh began to wonder about his exposed bottom, and gently, firmly, pried her arms loose.

– This is where real life is, she said, almost in a whisper.

Romesh looked around the churchyard, a little perplexed.

– What do you mean? he asked, checking his watch.

– On this side of the river. Do you know the city lies several feet below sea level? It's a tomb... for all the self-centered...corrupt...stupid people who want to run every moment of your life.

Romesh laughed a little nervously. He was still tidying himself, wondering whether his lovemaking was all right. This sudden outburst about the city as a tomb and its ruthless people sounded fine, like good poetry, but it was weird coming right after their quick coupling minutes ago.

– Listen, we have to hurry, or you'll miss the next boat.

She was staring up at the sky, not worried in the least about missing the boat; she was a little disappointed in him; he seemed to lack imagination; he'd been frantic in his lovemaking, as if he thought rapid skinny-flanked movement was expected of a man; but he kissed her when he was through, softly, on her cheeks and on her neck. She liked that. And in other ways he seemed not afraid to take risks, to say what was on his mind.

She told him her name; she said he didn't need to know much

76

more about her; it would spoil the romance of their meetings; they could pretend they were the lovers in *Last Tango*. He thought about that for a while, laughed, then said he agreed. He took her back to the ferry and waved to her as to a lovely woman in a poem. At least that was how she felt as she waved goodbye to him.

In the Republic of bitter farewells, as you wait for the aircraft to lift off, you feel again the mournful flame of love. It flares for as long as it takes to light a cigarette, she wrote.

Brandishing her independence, Julienne had told her mother she would find her own way to the airport. Her mother was puzzled, but agreed; she had an important meeting to attend at the Ministry; they hugged and kissed; her mother checked her watch and said she had to dash.

Romesh made the whole business of leaving a little frightening by recounting recent airport incidents: travelers had been turned back in the departure lounge, pleading and tearful; some had been snatched off the plane because their papers were not in order. He advised her to secure her seat quickly and not relinquish it under any circumstances.

– If they ask you to give up your seat so that a honeymoon couple could sit together, tell them no, you not moving! If they tell you they overbook the flight, and they ask you to come off and catch a later flight, tell them *later my backside*!

It all sounded so ridiculous. Where did he think they were – in the Soviet Union?

She'd boarded the plane with no difficulty. No one had approached her, not even someone vaguely resembling a honeymoon couple. A little girl in a lacy pink dress had taken the seat next to her. Her Indian parents on the other side of the aisle kept passing instructions to her; she looked frail and sad in her seat.

Now after interminable minutes buckled in and waiting, she felt the first stirrings of anxiety. The plane, it seemed, was ready for take off, but something was holding them back. It sat frozen and heavy, its engines patiently whining. The FASTEN SEAT BELT sign was on. The stewardesses walked briskly up and down the aisle, glancing left, right; they looked exhausted and worked with a tight-lipped urgency; the captain had said something about a slight delay, but that was a long time ago, and the delay now seemed anything but slight.

Julienne lifted her head warily and looked around. Her ears pricked up for some clue as to what was holding them back.

A young man appeared, struggling with his hand luggage, his long hair and slim body resembling Romesh's. Ragged cheers from the back of the plane, and some banter.

– Man, is you holding up the plane all this time?

– What happen? You wife won't let you go?

The young man smiled sheepishly, walking sideways, searching for his seat number.

– I just talk to the captain, he said. I ask he to do me a favor. Fly over the Prime Minister's residence so I could go the toilet and drop a load.

The remark sounded risky and premature but it caused some softening of tension, a fresh conversational buzz, someone unbuckling and changing seats, a muffled cough; then the silence returned; the waiting, the foolish fear that some development outside might delay the takeoff.

Romesh had said that most travelers these days had no intention of returning to the Republic, despite what the Embassy had stamped on their visas. So many lies told to get this far; so much money passed to officials; so much currency or gold jewelry hidden away despite restrictions and penalties. The plane felt heavier now with its luggage of fearful secrets, the swelling fear of discovery.

An airport official appeared with a stewardess at the front of the plane; they conferred over the passenger list; he walked down the aisle counting heads, scrutinizing faces; another conference over the passenger list; more waiting; a sour pain like acid in her stomach.

Comrade, there is a little problem with your papers. Would you come with us, please?

A man in a blue suit two rows behind her got up and followed the official to the front of the plane. Raised voices, swearing. The man returned, his brow shiny with perspiration. He shouted to a frightened audience, *I have an American passport. You can keep your blasted passport. I know my rights. I'm not leaving this plane.*

Julienne lowered her head and tightened the buckle of her seat belt.

Under no circumstances, you hear? Romesh had said.

She started drawing lines on the pad in a criss-cross pattern, scratching, scratching until there was a wiremesh of lines on the page: a screen behind which her resolve to get away hardened: then she was on her way, already moving.

Racing down the runway so that, looking out, she could see Romesh and the little red car. His back was against the perimeter fence, and there were two men in army uniform talking to him. She wanted to wave but it was no use; he seemed locked in fierce conversation with the men standing on either side of him. His arms were spread wide like the wings of a plane, and his fingers seemed to be gripping the fence.

In any event Julienne was already airborne despite the fresh stirring at the front of the plane, the stewardess conferring in heated whispers with another official; her spirit gaining altitude, secure behind her mesh of crisscross lines, refusing to look up, even though she heard someone clear his throat, and then the words – *Excuse me, Comrade*! – like a pat on the bottom from a man who couldn't keep his eyes to himself.

LIGHT
OF THE WORLD

I

What could you say about the sea if you're an islander?

It's always there, around and beyond us: churning and receiving; washing up all the dead stuff of the world: sunken histories, green bottles with messages of lost ambitions, the loves we abort and throw away. On Sunday afternoons our islanders come down to the beach; they show off bathing costumes and muscles; they gleam and splash about like carefree porpoises; then, salty-skinned, with sand in their hair, they turn their backs on it and go home.

What could you say about old ladies if you're an islander? They're always among us, in straw hats and headkerchiefs, beneath and beyond us like ancestral graves. On Sunday mornings our old ladies go to church. They startle you in their starched church clothes many decades behind the times. If you stop to say, "Hello Aunt B.," they lift their bowed heads; trembling fingers of memory reach for your face; they squint at you, then smile, for they'd seen you coming long before you had arrived; and they ask about your mother.

These days, of course, I know better.

Old ladies are somebody's mother and somebody's grandmother. They're not waiting to die. They are dreaming souls, lighthouses to so many ships, ancient and new, adrift in the world.

As for the sea, it's the last resting-place for the useless and the used; for skeletons and bones that rattle only what is real; a place for sunken vessels stripped of vanity riggings. You could step off our island and cross over seas, the way you cross borders from France into Spain, or Canada into the USA.

And you could call me caretaker of the sea.

Before, I used to be a journalist. *A journalist*, you ask, raising eyebrows. These islands have journalists? These islands have all breeds of men and women, let me tell you.

83

I was fooled once by the magical possibilities of that word. Plucked from high school out of the stampeding path of scholarship winners and exampassers, I was told I had a knack for storytelling; I could develop into a correspondent, reporting back to the island. This was how Mr. Pinks, my father's friend, explained it to my father:

The boy could write (True. I wasn't much good at math and science). The boy could be my apprentice (Mr. Pinks was editor of the island newspaper). Start there, move up gradually, just like me (Mr. Pinks liked to brag he never went to college). Until – who knows? – maybe people at the American Embassy might spot his talent (and send me up North on a training course).

I was fooled by all that; became an apprentice; wrote articles and stories. Year after year after year.

Now I understand how young men like me feel anywhere in the world: in Dublin or Soweto or Port au Prince; up against walls of no hope, your parents threatening to dash you away because once *you* were *their* only hope; tempted to join groups of scowling anarchic youth lounging at street corners in every city; then one day something extends itself: a hand reaching through the sky, pointing at you; you feel uplifted; separated from the rest; spared and chosen and uplifted, as each of us in times of hunger and the wolf, in cities of downcast eyes, wish with all our hearts to be noticed, to be redeemed.

Fooled by all that, as I was saying. I don't mean to sound bitter. For a while with one foot on the career ladder, it did appear as if I had been saved.

I became a "rookie reporter"; it was exciting to be part of an office team. I sported my press pass and breezed through the door at functions, festivals and sports events. I learned to type and I used to think my writing in some way shaped the policy of a Government Ministry, and that the Prime Minister was secretly indebted to me.

So what happen?

Blame it in part on the delusions of gullible youth, the glow of self-importance, the feeling that success would last forever.

Right now I can point to only one source of my demise: Mr. Massareep Pinks, Editor (Maz to his cronies and friends, Mr.

84

Pinks to his underlings) who often took this *rookie's* reports and turned them into pontificating editorials; whose style was laced with apologies to Churchill and Shakespeare and Wordsworth and Bertrand Russell; whose body in its coffin when he dies should be cushioned by the books of these dead authors.

I see his fat, smug face, and hatred wells up in me. I see his pinstriped trousers held up with braces, his eyes large and round like those Martian creatures in comic books, his face speckled with warts; and on the nape of his neck those boils, disgusting shaving boils, big as sores. I see all that and a desire to kill consumes me.

Islanders have a foolish respect for men like Mr. Pinks who write and speak like Mr. Barkis in Charles Dickens' *Nicholas Nickleby*. This man of words sat on my dreams all these years. Suddenly one morning I began to wonder: what will become of my life, pinned and squashed under this old fart?

Call it a romantic hunger for freedom. I became caretaker of the sea. And strange as this may sound it was Mr. Pinks who pointed the way.

Puzzled? You sense a story behind all this? I'm coming to it. I was waiting for a wave, for a rhythm on which to ride to its beginning. Caretakers are, if nothing else, men of patience.

All right, catch this wave:

On the morning of my twenty fifth birthday I woke up thinking that twenty five was an ordinary number, like twenty six, twenty seven; not deserving of notice or celebration. I switched on the transistor and heard steelband music and then the calypso chorus: *"We go beat them/lick them/destroy them."* The cricket test was on, West Indies vs. Australia. For the next six days our island would be the center of the world.

I wasn't a sports fanatic, but this was my birthday; and with a press pass I could be *there*, in the stands, watching boundaries and sixes and shots like miracles. I put on a special shirt and had my sun hat all ready.

Imagine my shock when I got to the office and found an assignment from Mr. Pinks marked *Urgent*. He needed a human-interest story for the weekend edition. The deadline was six o'clock that evening. I had to travel miles outside the city to August Town to interview an old lady, reputedly the oldest lady in the island. Possibly the oldest lady in the world, Mr. Pinks added.

"Why me? If this story so important why he didn't go himself and interview this old lady?" I exploded.

There were one or two fellows in the office hammering away on typewriters, with their sun hats and their flask of ice cubes, and sunglasses perched on their heads. They were going to the test match; they were determined not to miss the first ball; they sniggered and ignored me and pounded away on their stories.

You know those moments when you're alone with desolation as bright as a stab wound, and you wish you could grab a shiny cutlass and make some people slump to their knees begging for mercy? You know those moments?

I stepped outside feeling like a small boy in the office sent out on an errand by the boss.

I searched the sky for rain clouds that might burst over the island, forcing the umpires to abandon play for the day. I dreamed of reporting the sudden death of Mr. Pinks – from cardiac arrest, his sins catching up with him at last. I went in search of a van to take me to August Town.

You could feel the island's center of gravity shift towards the cricket ground as from every quarter, on bikes and on foot, people streamed to that place where two captains were about to toss a coin. You could sense in the air all the electricity of world communications, as transmitters crackled beaming commentary back to Australia, England, India, all over the globe.

The driver of the minivan was a skinny Indian man with wavy hair, quick darting eyes and overwashed clothes. A fidgety man with little time for sleep or meals. Probably the only man at that moment on our island who couldn't care less who won the toss, or which side batting.

He had to be an illegal resident; a runaway from another island, scratching out a new life here.

Normally I might have felt inspired to do a piece on people without work permits on our island. It would have pleased Mr. Pinks and his political masters (we all know he had Scotch and soda cronies in the present Government). But I was in a vexed and vengeful mood.

I understood this driver's indifference to events that had nothing to do with his livelihood. Soon we were moving away from all the cricket frenzy. We were brooding, silent men nursing hatreds or dreams. It is at moments like these that destinies are chosen.

We got to August Town so quickly, it occurred to me I might be able to do the interview and get back to the cricket ground to see most of the day's play. I might not get a good seat, but if the West Indies were batting good seat or bad seat made no difference.

First, I had to find the old lady. Ma Memu.

We have these houses on our island, outside the town centers: boxy structures, leftovers from the plantation days. Miniature weather-beaten wood things. You can't imagine a whole family living in them. A giant bird could swoop down, plant its giant claws on a roof and fly away with one of them easy, easy.

It was to these boxy houses that I was directed by people who smiled when I asked for the old lady. "You mean, Ma Memu?" Mr. Pinks had forgotten to give me her name. *Just ask for the old lady in August Town*, he'd said. "It just down the road there," they said.

I walked for five, ten, fifteen minutes, past bushy vacant lots, the ruins of an old sugar mill – and still couldn't find this place. I began to curse country people with their poor sense of distance.

I almost walked past it, telling myself this couldn't be it: a boxy house, alright, festooned with vines and flowers; no TV antennae; a gate, a fence, a concrete strip from the roadway to the front door; and a flower garden. I looked back down the road: nothing but dry grass and a bony stray cow. This had to be the old lady's place.

The front gate opened easily; I half-expected a yapping dog to rush me. The front door was open. Wary, I shouted, "Hello. Anybody there?"

Silence. No dog. No old lady. "Hello… Ma Memu?"

Someone answered: "At the back. Is that you Waverider?"

I stepped nervously round the side of the house, bowed my head under the low branches of a cherry tree, cleared my throat

87

and prepared to introduce myself in a manner befitting a newspaper reporter from the city.

"Oh…it's you… I thought you was my son Waverider come to wish me happy birthday," the old lady said.

She thought I was her son! Well, as my eyes clapped on her face, I thought this old lady sitting under the breadfruit tree was my grandmother! The spitting image of my grandmother! Whom I had seen only once on her sick and dying bed!

I remember they had to lift me up to look down her face. I must have been five or six years old and she was lying on this four-poster bed, large and blanketed and breathing in a frightening nostrilly way. Everyone around the bed her that day whispered and seemed drenched in sadness. It was my first visit to a house of death.

This old lady, this Ma Memu, was *the spitting image*, I tell you. That was the first shock. The second shock hit me like a ricochet.

I was expecting the oldest woman on the island to be someone shriveled, bony, confined to a rocking chair; wearing a headkerchief; giving off an odor of folk medication; hard of hearing, her jaw working up and down; her voice raspy and complaining.

This old lady was a heavyset presence fanning herself under a breadfruit tree (despite the leafy shade and the breeze sweeping up from the ocean below) with slow thoughtful motion of her wrist. Her face was a shiny black moon; she had hair copious as butterflies, and bosoms that looked large and unused.

I waited to be summoned closer.

Her backyard was swept clean; a few chickens had scooped a bowl of repose for themselves in the ground; there were banana plantings and sugar cane stalks and short papaw trees. Everything seemed lush and friendly with green life, so much so I began to wonder what force of nature kept it flourishing this way.

You see, the island was going through a dry spell; there were water restrictions in the town centers; yet somehow the front garden here seemed in full bloom, as if it had rained just yesterday and every day before that.

My eye fell on seven calabashes laid out on her backsteps, their insides turned up to the sun. I had always marveled at the smooth clean insides of a calabash; they made such perfect dippers of water; I used to keep my collection of seashells in a calabash.

"So he sent you to see me?" the old lady said out of the blue.

"Who?"

"You know who. That man of newspaper words. Couldn't come himself. He must be getting old and lazy these days."

She laughed in a way that startled me. Not an old lady's raspy laugh. A young woman's coquettish laugh, her bosom heaving a little with a young woman's contempt for pretentious young men.

"Last time I saw him was twenty five years ago. Came to *interview* me, he say. Century-maker, he call me. Said he was going to make me famous. Said it was a miracle how I live so long. I told him he should have been there the day I was born. Every birth is a miracle. And every day after that is a celebration of that miracle. As for making me famous…fame is a cologne for the mean flea-bitten dogs of the world."

"Twenty five years ago? Mr. Pinks came here twenty five years ago?" I could barely contain myself. "You know, today I am twenty five years old," I said.

"*Mon Dieu!*" she laughed again, shaking her head.

Discombobulated was a word Mr. Pinks was fond of using. It made him sound educated. I considered it ridiculous, a word filled with wind and too many syllables, like a shoe several sizes larger than the foot it was meant to cover. But I have to tell you: discombobulated was the exact fit for the state of my mind.

"He asked me fool questions… like if I born here, if I remember my parents…"

I made a note not to ask her any *fool questions*, though to tell the truth her accent was strange. And add to that her lapses into French, I was thinking: she must be from Martinique. There was voodoo in her eyes, her ample body, her chicken-cluttered yard. No, not Martinique. She had to be from Haiti.

"Kept asking me what were the secrets to my long life. What foods? what faith? what habits? You know what I told him?"

"What?"

"I said to him: Mr. Pinks, I have no time for fool questions… I am going to tell you a bedtime story."

89

"A bedtime story?"

"That's what I said: a bedtime story."

I cleared my throat and said, "Well, listen… I didn't come all this way to listen to bedtime stories."

Suddenly she lowered her head and for a moment it seemed she had abruptly fallen asleep. I got the strange feeling, however, that under those heavy eyelids she was watching me, that she was offering me a blind chance to slip away.

What happened instead was that my legs became weak, as if tired of holding up my body: body holding up the weight of my spirit: spirit and body manacled like prisoners in Ma Memu's backyard: legs complaining, unwilling to assist me in flight.

So I lowered myself on my haunches and I waited.

My body felt even heavier squatting on my haunches. I thought of moving, sitting on her backsteps, but I was seized by a cramp and locked in that squatting position, muscles tense and aching; I would have been forced to crawl on all fours like a dog if I tried to move.

The sun was sprinkling through the leaves of the breadfruit tree. I became aware of the odor from the soursop tree as if the fruit was ready to be picked. In fact there was the odor of ripeness everywhere unlike what you might expect from an old lady's backyard, given the fowl pen, the chickens and the rooster. Ripeness, not the odor of things rotting; no fruit lay squashed and decaying anywhere.

I looked up at the old lady – still fanning herself, head still lowered, chest moving in a faint breathing rhythm. I stared at her – *God help me, the spitting image of my grandmother!* – and I wondered: she's supposed to be 125 years old, where were the years? They were nowhere on her face, unless the wrinkles and creases of age lay on her insides. What I saw outside was an unblemished surface, like the insides of the calabash.

And this way she had of speaking, in sliding tones like notes on a musical scale – now a child, now a girl, adolescent, woman! You could hear the passage of a hundred and twenty five years in her voice, in the silences that punctuated her words during which you smelled odours of the world around you.

"Who is your son?" I asked.

"You are my son," she said, smiling.

"No…I mean, Waverider… the fellow you were expecting?"

"Oh, he will come. He brings me a birthday present every year."

"Where does he live?"

"By the sea."

At this point, tired of stooping like a tribesman in a forest, and puzzled by her answers, I tried to heave myself up on my feet. Suddenly it was easy. Whatever was holding my thighs in a vise had released them. I jumped up in surprise; I told myself it was time to make a retreat; not too hasty, not too obvious.

"Listen, I have to go soon," I said.

"No… stay and wait for Waverider… he should be here any minute… he could tell you many stories."

Since I still had an article to write I began to take note of the yard, a few more details about her person. I would have to invent more back in the office. Still, I was puzzled: considering the importance of this assignment why hadn't Mr. Pinks sent a photographer with me?

"I told Mr. Pinks a story about Waverider and he didn't believe me," she said.

"What did you tell him?"

"I told him that once, long long ago, back in the colonial days, when pirate ships use to sail these Caribbean waters, islanders used to hang lanterns in coconut trees. Waverider's father would do that. He'd hang the lanterns in the trees and lure the pirate ships onto reefs. The ships would sink to the bottom of the sea with chests of gold in their bellies…"

She caught me staring at her and once again she laughed. This time I laughed too; I had never before heard so preposterous a tale.

"That is where Waverider gets his gifts. Sometimes they float up from the bottom of the sea and wash ashore. All kinds of precious ornaments… I told Mr. Pinks I could make him a wealthy man if he listened to me. He wouldn't believe a word I said."

The lime tree was giving off a scent that swirled around my head and drifted away with the wind. My mind was in turmoil. My legs were light and springy and ready to rush away, but now I couldn't tear myself away.

91

I had heard stories from time to time about discoveries on our beach of old coins and medallions. I remember our history teacher, Mr. Gravesande, had jokingly given the class an assignment: we were to walk the beaches at the eastern tip of the island and search for lost treasure: for *doubloons and guineas*. Someone did find a few gold coins and took them to the bank. An article in the newspapers about the rare value of the coins and the possibility of sunken treasure off our shores threw our island into a frenzy.

For weeks after people actually combed the beaches with flashlights during the night; tourists, too, all hoping to become instant millionaires.

A part of me views such stories as fodder for stupid, gullible folk from rundown neglected villages – Choiseul, Bathgate, Pompey. The behavior it encourages is often shameful. Another part of me, hearing this tale again as if from its source, was hanging in limbo: wanting to dismiss it as a joke by a crazy old lady; at the same time, half-expecting her to reach into her bosom and offer proof, a shiny necklace, for instance; or pull from the folds of her dress a tarnished gold coin, large and round, with strange inscriptions.

Instead, a soft voice, croaky, like my grandmother's on her sick bed, said, "Come over here. Come and give the old lady a birthday kiss?"

Now, I'm not the kissing kind; I didn't come all this way to kiss an old lady. But when someone summons you in your grandmother's voice, you tremble and pout; you lower your head like a schoolboy; you shuffle forward, praying for release from the next few seconds of agony.

I moved toward her, prepared to peck her on the cheek; I had to look into her face, that shiny black moon. I leaned forward awkwardly. There were a few pimples where crinkled eyebags should have been.

Then a voice that was distinctly that of a young woman said, "You so shy. Come closer." Broad arms reached out and pulled me into the waiting folds of her lap. "So shy. Close your eyes and kiss me."

I could feel the warmth of that massive flesh (there was

nothing, no bodices, no old-fashioned slips under her clothes). I could hear inside her body the sound of her enormous breathing, like a furnace burning up the air she inhaled. I let myself be wrapped and enfolded, then squeezed gently and long in those fleshy arms.

I raised my head, placed my cheeks against hers, and was surprised at how soft they felt, how tender and yielding like baby fat. In the next instant with my eyes firmly closed, her lips had found mine.

It was this kiss that woke me up. Her lips were those of a young girl in the first flutter of passion, giving herself nervously, heart racing. Her hands found my hands and directed them under her arm sleeves to her breasts. There the flesh was smooth and firm; there the nipples were hard, wanting to be pinched; there I thought this had gone far enough.

I opened my eyes; I found her eyes wide open; they'd been open all along. I felt awkward and frightened and I pulled away. It snapped the spell. Her chin fell down on her chest and for a moment I was afraid she would topple over to the ground. Instead she started rocking gently back and forth, humming and chanting strange words.

I backed away. She made no effort to stop me. My hair got entangled in the branches of the cherry tree. I thought I saw a smile tugging at the corners of her mouth, but by then I was in full flight, determined to let nothing get in the way of my escape.

Only once before had I fled from someone's grasp and ambivalent intentions. A police officer, a friend of my father, promoted to Sergeant and a desk job, had playfully arrested me. He'd surprised a group of schoolboys raiding the mango tree in the yard at the back of the police station. It was a daring raid. The tree because of its location was considered off limits, its fruit left to rot in the yard. We thought all the police were out on duty. The Sergeant surprised us.

In the scramble to get away, each man for himself, I tripped and fell and was paralyzed by the Sergeant's voice ordering me to stop. He dragged me inside by the neck and showed me a cell. He threatened to lock me up forever, and pretended to push me in the cell. Crying and pleading to be spared, I was eventually released with a warning.

That warning and that incident, I think, has scarred me for life. I have a foolish fear of our island policemen in helmet and khaki. Each time I am approached for any reason by one of them fear rises inside me like acid.

Fleeing that old lady's arms, her yard with its poultry and abundant trees, I felt an older fear: of badly lit villages, shabby dwellings, crumbling bridges and mud-cratered roads; of people trapped there with their children and goats and bony stray cattle; an older fear of spending the rest of my life in so desolate a place.

I hurried toward the main road. I twisted my ankle but didn't stop to inspect it. I wanted to get back to the town, to my office, familiar streets, my house.

To my surprise and relief the same skinny Indian driver who had brought me here was parked off the main road, his engine idling. He was waiting for travelers.

I jumped in and told him to drive. He scanned the road for more passengers. My ankle began to pain and I became irritable. I told him I was a newspaperman. I told him the Government was about to announce a crackdown on illegal residents working on the island. I told him to drive if he knew what was good for him. He flashed me a look of fear and contempt, then slowly, still looking around for fares, he put the minivan in motion.

Back in the office I wrote a story about the old lady; I told our readers about lanterns hung in trees and Spanish galleons blown off course by hurricane winds and gold bullion lying at the bottom of the sea in moss covered hulls just off our shores. I told them there were fortunes to be made by anyone with patience roaming the beaches. I wrote all this and hobbled home.

People who go to Test matches expecting miracles would believe you if you tell them that fortunes like chocolate cookies were made in heaven then dropped from the sky through a chute. People who watch and wait for one glorious shot, that stroke of wondrous magic, to last a lifetime, could be led by the nose through portholes into the paradise. They'll find nothing, but never mind, the shot of a lifetime always beckons. And the paradise, we know, is always elsewhere.

94

In the following days I never felt such pain and discomfort. My foot was bandaged; my movements were excruciatingly slow. Imagine my horror at what I had become: a young man hobbling around town; people staring, people asking, *what happened?* then looking disappointed when they find out it was only a sprained ankle.

I decided to ask for sick leave.

Sick leave? Mr. Pinks was incensed.

One of his favorite complaints about islanders was their failure to adapt. A little rain falls, what do islanders do? They walk through the rain getting soaked, or stand for hours under shop awnings as if they'd never heard of raincoats and umbrellas and galoshes.

Sick leave? For a sprained ankle? *Get a walking stick*, he railed at me.

Let me tell you: at that moment I felt like bashing his breadfruit of a baldhead with a cricket stump.

The old lady's story set fire to the island. It was the talk, in between cheering and barracking the players, all around the cricket ground for the rest of the series. I stayed in the office nursing my ankle and waiting for telephone calls.

A professor from our island university called asking for more information; he said he was doing research in "African Retentions". Another professor, an anthropologist visiting from California, wanted names and addresses and was willing to cover all expenses if I led him to the source of "this fabulous tale". People started scouring the beaches; even well-off islanders drove up in their cars at night, carrying flashlights.

For a while nothing much happened; the excitement began to die down; then somebody made a discovery of six gold coins – "I turn around, I see these shiny things lying there, under a rock, just like that!" – and the whole gold-hunting madness started again.

Tourist people who you would expect to know better were now shamelessly walking the beaches with toy spades, towels around their waist, ignoring the surf, eyes cast down. The Tourist Board called to ask if the paper was going to do a follow-up on the old lady article. They spoke to Mr. Pinks. Mr. Pinks decided a follow-up would be good for tourism.

This is where we came to the crossroads, the parting of the ways.

Because of his prior involvement in this story (and some undisclosed anxiety over its subject) Mr. Pinks insisted I see the old lady one more time, sprained ankle or no sprained ankle.

I refused.

He reminded me that the people at the U.S. Embassy were still following my development with keen interest. I sucked my teeth and pouted.

He accused me of laziness, lack of ambition.

I told him he was acting like "a pussy".

For long steaming seconds we stood in the office, glowering at each other like gladiators in a Roman arena. He said he was "appalled" at my language; he told me I was about to walk alone into my future.

Islanders reach a point in their cramped lives where the longing to take wing, to stretch their limbs, overpowers good sense. In fact, good sense is what keeps some of us trudging along, always yielding and dreaming, year upon year. In calling Mr. Pinks "a pussy" (I'd borrowed the word from a disgruntled character in an American movie) I was revving up engines. I was looking at empty blue sky and I was saying: *enough is enough. Time to take off.*

I remember how I felt walking out of the office that day: loose-limbed, untouchable, not seeing anyone, brushing past desks, not caring, heading for the last doorway to freedom.

II

Sunshine and beaches, palm trees and lovely blue water are good for vacations, but you can't live well on our island unless you have money. You might get by on the goodness of neighbors, or raiding fruit trees in season. At some point I knew I had to get out and start all over again looking for work.

Pride forbade me from crawling on my knees back to Mr. Pinks. Shame made me falter the moment I stepped out into the streets to face the sniggers and looks from a public whose daily existence I once influenced with my columns.

Was it the hand of destiny reaching out the sky that led me to the east end of the island where I now live as caretaker of the sea? I could say that. I have to be honest. I came here – to this side of the island where weeks before people were tramping the shore-line in search of gold coins – because I was a desperate man; so desperate, I was willing to believe the story I had written. I came here hoping for a small miracle: scuffing the sand with my toes I might find enough of that sunken treasure to last the rest of a life removed from this island.

I remember that day like your first day in a new job or a new country: clear blue skies, the tide out, the beach littered with stones, shells, sea residue, the horizon empty and compelling: a day to fill your heart with wild hope and sweet despair. I stood for a while staring out to sea, wondering how many young men had stood here centuries back looking out for the riggings of ships bringing supplies, newspapers, more slaves, chests of gold.

I started walking, my head cast down, not really searching for anything. A plane had taken off and now caught my eye as its nose pointed to destinations up and faraway. I felt a chill ripple through my body, and this cold thought: *you're going to live and die here, marooned forever on this island.*

Vexed by that thought, wishing I could tear myself apart and scatter the pieces into the sea, I fell on the sand, dug a hole and brooded for awhile.

I thought of Ma Memu. I blamed her for everything. Crafty spinner of tales! Fat old voodoo woman from Haiti!

The odor of marijuana tickled my nostrils. I paid no attention to it at first until it circled my head, strong and distinct, as if a stream of smoke had been directed at my back from somewhere among the leaning palm trees. I was not alone on this beach.

A man was sitting in a chair under a beach umbrella, his legs crossed, a straw hat shading his eyes. There was a freshly painted boat next to him. He must have been watching me. I tried to ignore him but the marijuana seemed a deliberate intrusion. I decided to confront him.

The chair looked borrowed or stolen from someone's fancy

living room. The boat might have been waiting for those idle tourists, bored with hotel service, eager for something different. (They'd rent the boat, sit in the middle of the ocean, draw on a little marijuana till they were stoned.) It all seemed to fit this character under his red, white and blue beach umbrella.

"You look like a man with no family. No job. No home. No nothing," he said, his voice clear and ringing.

"And you look like a lazy beach bum," I shot back.

He laughed as if the remark had missed by a mile.

"So what's happening, young man? What you searching for in this life?" he said.

Lord, help me! This was no ordinary beach bum! This was a mouth-running old geezer, his chest raggedy with grey hairs, the flesh slack on his rib cage: bony legs crossed, rubber slippers dangling on knarled feet: with not much time left in this world, though that voice was as clear as church bells; and eager to engage this young man in some foolish test of knowledge. You learn to stay away from some oldtimers on our island, cross-legged on the beach or under shop awnings; watching and waiting; and always warning the youth about the ways of this world.

"I have something here that could take all your worries away," he said. The thin, paper-rolled cigarette stuck out through long fingers.

"No thank you, I don't smoke weed!"

He laughed again. He watched me from under his straw hat, drawing on his cigarette.

"I don't have any worries," I said, trying to be casual.

"Then why you standing out there staring at sky in the water? I'll tell you why. There's a hole in your life. A big gaping hole. Something missing in your life." Silence. "You're a man with no home, no future, a very unhappy man. No place left to turn but to the sea!"

"Excuse me, I don't have time for foolishness," I said.

"Exactly. You young, you have all the time in the world, but no time for foolishness! You're a serious fellow…you have the sloping shoulders of philosopher…no skylarking for a man like you…which is why I can give you what you searching for."

Some oldtimers need to be humored.

"So what you have to offer…drugs… women?" I asked.

"*Cho*! Listen… I have something here more precious than that. Worth more than a treasure chest of gold."

Behind me I heard the sea racing up, firing cannons of emancipation in the air. And hissing at me: *Back away from this old fool; his life is finished; go back to town, start looking for a job.*

I heard the old man say, "I can give you diamonds of living memory to fill that void. Stuff that myths are made of. Yes, I can tell you stories dredged up from the bottom of that raging sea in all of us."

Suddenly it hit me: this was Waverider, Ma Memu's son.

"Sun getting hot," he said. "Come into the shade, man. I have something I've been longing to give to a fellow like you with all the time in the world."

I don't mean to make this any more mysterious than it really was.

I'm now caretaker of the sea. If you chance to visit our island, drive down to the eastern tip. You'll find me there in an easy chair, under an umbrella (the sun wash out the colors; I might have to get a new one) and the boat (which could use a fresh coat of paint soon as I get around to it). And I will tell you, if you're willing to listen, the story of Waverider. I will show you the diamonds of living memory he passed on to me.

For now what happened was this: he got up, removed his hat and he said to me with a schoolboy's bravura grin, his teeth sparkling white, "Watch this! Watch me closely now!"

He jogged out toward the sea, bowlegged, the upper half of his body tall and lean, the faded football shorts staying up by a miracle on his tiny waist. His gait first caught my eye. He wasn't trying to impress me with *how youthful he still was*. It was a smooth gait, without huff and puff and stiffness.

He trotted up the beach, limbering up like an early morning riser performing some meaningless ritual before taking a quick dip. I stared because his body, out of its chair now and in fluid motion, seemed neither old nor young. Or put it this way: his legs and arms looked as if they had been oiled with some concocted mixture, the hairs, say, of an aging lion and an agile monkey.

If he was trying to tell me something, it was this: he was his mother's child; his navel cord had been snipped from its tie to the womb of the old Haitian woman. Of course, he had no way of knowing I had seen her.

I watched him intently, half-expecting him to pull up, tear an old muscle, then come limping back to the chair, panting and wincing.

Suddenly he stopped and faced the ocean; he stood there for long seconds, staring out, his body erect and poised, waiting for some signal. Naturally I followed his gaze. There was nothing out there; no aircraft cutting across the sky, no speedboat slapping and skimming the waves. *What the hell was he staring at?*

Then he waded into the water and started swimming.

You saw only the motion of his arms and head; he didn't back-kick the water as I'd been taught to do. He was swimming like a sea creature, up over the ocean swells, gliding forward and on and on. At times I lost sight of him; then I'd see a splash of water, like a marker in the waves, telling me how far he'd reached. I found myself shading my eyes, squinting in an effort to locate him.

At some point he ceased being a swimmer, a man who had left his clothes and keys on the beach; he became instead mysteriously self-propelled. Every time it seemed I'd finally lost him, there would be a disturbance in the water, like the flash of a fin, urging me to pay close attention.

A rumbling in my stomach reminded me I hadn't eaten in a long time. I felt foolish all of a sudden, just standing there looking out to sea. I started walking away throwing sideways glances at the waves. *Where the hell was he now?* Suppose he'd gotten into trouble and was drowning out there! It became hard to simply walk away.

Then out of nowhere a gull flew over my head, low, almost clipping me with its wings. There was a loud flapping in my ears and a violent screeching as other gulls swooped by; then they all flew back out to sea where Waverider, now a man in the grip of some stupefying folly, was still swimming with all his heart.

I followed the gulls' trajectory until they began to make ecstatic circles over the water. I saw Waverider; his body seemed to leap into the air like a porpoise; I saw his hands waving, his teeth gleaming in a broad sun-capped smile. It happened quickly: one

100

split second he was out of the water, waist high, waving like a man frantic to attract someone's attention. Next moment he was gone: diving or sinking, it was hard to tell.

At that moment I knew what it was I wanted to do with my life: to disappear from far away from this island; to slip into the water like Waverider, roll on my back, wait for some serpentine current to take me out to a spot where the sea was calm, where the waves would enfold me in gentle forgiving swells.

Next thing I knew I was crying. Tears of amazement. For no apparent reason. I looked around, ashamed of the tears, and thankful no one was watching. I wiped my eyes in my shirtsleeves.

I decided I'd wait for Waverider. I wanted to see him wade out of the water, lurching in the shallows; his head garlanded with seaweed, his body shiny with sea brine. Just the sight of him, I thought, would fill me with a new confidence. I'd be released from this strange feeling of hopelessness.

I settled back in his beach chair. It smelled of salt and marijuana. Never before had my heart felt so wound-up, my eyes locked on the horizon.

Noon passed. The ocean breakers hissed and foamed as if sharing some private joke.

Waverider. A man of the islands. Who was this old man?

I imagined him *fathoms deep* strolling the ocean floor, schools of fish gamboling around his head as he stepped over a rusted anchor, or opened a half-buried chest, letting pearls and jewels pour through his fingers like sand. I played with those images, and waited for him to come back.

On the floor of my stomach hunger pains like a million worms started crawling. My head felt light and dizzy. The heat shimmering off the scorched sand encircled me. I raised a weak hand to swat at insects buzzing around my ears. Now, strangely, if I tried to get up and walk, I knew I wouldn't get very far; I would stumble and fall; I might lose consciousness! It seemed my only salvation was the return of the swimmer at sea; he'd laugh and offer me once more "diamonds of living memory". Only he could restore the energy to live.

I looked at his boat, at the umbrella above my head. Does a man swim away and leave all his property behind? My eyes fell on two objects on the sand near the chair. A lobster pot and a shiny cigarette lighter. I peered into the lobster pot; there were six or seven rolled up cigarettes, thin stems, one half-smoked.

Vagabond weed. The kind of smokes you would expect someone to indulge in on an empty beach. The kind of smokes made into a sacred need by our island Rastafarians. Touted for its curative powers – glaucoma, asthma. Illegal substance. The refuge of the poor and befuddled.

I could almost hear Waverider's voice urging me: *Light up, man, make yourself at home, I soon come.*

A desperate man grasps at any straw. I lit up the weed; I inhaled; I closed my eyes and felt the parting of the waters inside my stomach. I inhaled again and again deeply, filling my lungs, my heart. The tension and fear inside me evaporated. I was all set to move, when I saw Waverider coming toward me.

He was standing at the front end of a boat out at sea, like a lookout man on a man-o-war, while behind him six men worked at the oars, leaning and heaving, leaning and heaving. He was struggling to keep his balance for the choppy waves threatened to hurl him overboard. He seemed to be searching the curve of the beach. Suddenly he pointed to the spot where I sat and he must have said something to the men for the muscles on their shoulders rippled and shone as they put their backs into it, finding new inspiration.

It was magnificent, this view: Waverider coming toward me, his shape shifting in rhythm with the rise and fall of the waves: splashing through the shallows, the men in the boat exhausted, slumped over their oars.

Then he was standing over me, shielding me like a fatherly cloud from the angry glare of the sun. There was a mischievous boyish smile on his face; the smile concealed his secrets; it had been with him through all the manifestations of his life.

III

I used to think once that only handsome boys and girls grew up to be successful men and women on our island. Whatever they

102

achieved came to them easily; they were twice blest. But the ugly child had to struggle. With luck he might manage to build for himself a small career; he became a civil servant, a disgruntled police sergeant, a stevedore. He never worked in a bank or in an airline office or in city offices. For him, only the sweat and unfairness of life.

The boy standing over me had handsome features. As he stepped back I noticed his calabash haircut, his dry skin blackened from overexposure to the sun. Straightaway I thought: this is a stray boy, fathered out of wedlock, his mother poor and pretty and barely past puberty. He had inherited her good looks. He should have been in school.

"What you looking at? What you doing here?" I shouted.

"None of your business."

"Hey, watch your mouth! I know you cutting school."

"My mother send me here."

"Liar! Your mother send you to school!"

"You don't know my mother! You don't know me! If you so ambitious, what you doing here? Like you cutting and running from something yourself."

Cocky little stray boy! Scuffing the sand with his toes. Roaming the beach with a stick searching for crab holes. Answering back with the ease of ragamuffins these days.

"And I have plenty pride. My mother gave me pride to last a lifetime," he said.

"So what you doing with yourself to make her proud, eh? Tell me."

He fell to the sand and lowered his head as if he'd been wounded by that opening skirmish of words. I sat back and looked him over again.

He was about fifteen, long-limbed, sway-backed, scrapes on his shins; teachers must have found him wild, undisciplined; schoolmates must have teased him every day about his tar black skin. But those eyes! Burning fierce like hot coals in those white sockets! And those well-set cheekbones! How to explain his vagrancy by the sea?

Easier to understand was my desire to berate any youngster who stepped out of line. On our island it used to be that small boys

103

were pounced on and punished for the slightest misdemeanor. They were expected to know their place. This boy wandering on the beach, evidently friendless, wearing his handsome face like a good luck charm, was most certainly out of place: poking his stick in the sand and hoping for sympathy and affection.

I heard him say in a whimpering voice, "In school they use to tease me all the time. I was always fighting. The teachers don't care. They too busy planning to cut and run."

The stick in his hand was still poking at the sand. My eyes were closed but I heard clearly the sadness in his voice.

"School is the only bridge from the island to the world," I said.

"That's what everybody say."

"At exam time, crossing is a mad stampede. You might come through trampled and bruised. But once you pass, the world is your oyster."

"My mother used to tell me that."

"Tell you what?"

"The world is your oyster."

"Well, you should listen to your mother."

"Oysters are happy at the bottom of the sea."

My body was still weak; Waverider was still somewhere out there; I pulled on the vagabond weed again and closed my eyes.

"My mother say there are other ways into the world. You don't have to run through no gauntlet, get whipped for nothing by teachers always asking you: *what you going to do with your life*?"

"But every boy your age has some dream, some ambition."

"When I told them what I wanted to be, they laughed," he said.

"What was that?"

Long silence. I opened my eyes wondering if he was still there. He stabbed me with look straight to the heart and said:

"A fisherman."

I sank back in the chair, my mouth shut tight, my eyes suddenly moist.

Oh, the howls of disbelief that must have echoed round the classroom! The mocking laughter spilling out the windows, racing round the schoolyard. Oh, the stunned look on the poor boy's face – *What had he done? what had he said*? – the wish to scuttle away to the nearest hole.

"A fisherman," he repeated, poking my face for a response.

A fisherman: requiring few mental skills; a half naked man, hairy-chested, bowlegged; in one hand his scale, in the other his slippery catch from the night before; his tie-head haggling customers, his weather-beaten face; his fierce muscled upper body staggering across the road under the weight of an outboard motor; the smell of fish in his hair, on the pillows at night beside his woman.

What's wrong with all that on our island?

Well, for many, our island is still a place of no second chance. In the stampede across the bridge connecting the island to the world, you could stumble and fall under someone's spiked heels: a teacher's contempt for your cheekbones, a father's indifference to your tears, the cruelty of the schoolyard. Stumble, fall, then crawl away in shame, the remains of your life washed down to the sea with white rum.

In the sand the boy was drawing triangles. The stick in his hand dug deep and angry furrows, linking the three corners over and over like connections missing in his life. How do we save the remains of our lives?

When I opened my eyes I had the distinct feeling that not just hours but a complete day had passed. Same sky, the sea pounding and frothing up the shore-line again; the boat, the umbrella; my body weak, my spirit pleading for a return of its daily routines.

I reached once more for the butt ends of vagabond weed in the tin.

Then I saw the cruise ship, huge and magnificent in the sun, anchored in the water. I saw the boy standing in a pirogue bobbing in the water: the same stray boy I'd been talking to hours or minutes ago.

He was waving at passengers leaning on the rail of the deck. He seemed so tiny and frail and dangerously close to the stern of the ship, I had this bright fear: the propellers might start up at any minute and drag him under in a cauldron of red bubbles.

The faces on deck looked down with fascination at the black head below them in the water. As if responding to their stares, the boy stood poised for a moment then plunged into the water.

I dragged myself to my feet, took a few stumbling steps and fell to the sand. Some befuddling *thing* seemed to hang over this beach

105

like a mist. How else could I explain the strange behavior of people who talked, then waded into the water and before you could determine what was going on, they dived into the ocean? Never to appear again, for the pirogue remained bobbing near the side of the ship, and the people on deck craned over and pointed down at it, some smiling, and rushing over to the other side of the deck thinking the boy might have resurfaced there.

Where was the strength? Where was the will to get away from all this?

A superstitious side of me, which I'd never acknowledged till now, took over. It assured me I was here for a purpose. My body was under some spell; it had been weakened so that I could not run. I was held here against my will so I could hear and behold these apparitions: first Waverider, now the stray boy.

Someone else was bound to show up. I would ask him not to go into the water. I would plead with him to help me walk back to the road. In a state like this your defenses shut down. You're vulnerable to the vagaries of wind and sea. In a state like this life leaves you little choice: you pray to absent gods and reach for the vagabond weed.

The next stranger to approach was dressed like busboy or a waiter in a tourist hotel: neat white shirt, bowtie, hair well groomed, the folds of his black pants rolled up and wet at the edges – he'd evidently been walking too close to the water; he wore no shoes and carried a stick he might have picked up idly from the shore.

As he came closer I stared at him hard. I had the feeling I knew him from somewhere but I couldn't be sure. The face, the contours of the face: this fellow could have been Waverider in his younger days; could have been the older brother of the stray boy on the raft; or maybe just another hotel worker taking a break. But there were no tourist hotels at this end of the island!

He came right up to me, planted his feet in the sand and he said: "You still here?" *Still here!*

I gave him a startled, searching look.

"Who're you? What do you want?" I asked.

He looked around pretending to be puzzled by everything, the boat, the beach umbrella. He seemed amused by my proprietary manner.

"What do *I* want…? Nothing… I just taking a stroll on the beach… Anything wrong with that?"

"You looking for hotel work or something?"

"*Looking*…? I not *looking* for anything. I have a job. I was at the Colony Club for six years. Now I'm at Coral Reef."

There were no hotels at this end of the island. I was not going to be drawn into more delusion and rigmarole.

"What happened to the ship? There was a cruise ship, and a boy in a dugout," I said, trying to sit up.

The young man followed my gaze out to sea.

"You mean *Strayboy*! He comes down to the beach every day. I bet you he was born under a water sign. You know, that boy… if he were given a gambler's chance to climb the anchor ropes of the world, show people what he can do, he would have *developed*… he would have been world famous."

"Wait…wait…! You *know* this boy?"

"Of course, I know him…! Know him like my own flesh and blood. That boy could have been a marine biologist… or an Olympic swimming champion… given a chance. But then, that would have changed his life completely. You have to give up the island to join the world, and once you're out there, it's hard to find your way back."

What in heaven's name was he talking about? What did he *know*… a hotel waiter…whose livelihood depended on people coming here… where did he get this talk about joining the world?

We listened to the chafing sea. He heaved a sigh as if dispersing clouds and he said:

"Yes… when you step across this white shoreline, wanting so badly to join the world, you run the risk of getting choked and robbed in the first dark alley of progress."

Enough was enough. I had no more patience with this fellow. I wanted to draw his attention to my condition. I thought of asking if he could get me food, or perhaps a shot of rum. Was he carrying a flattie in his hip pocket? But right then to our left two people appeared, out for an evening stroll too: a tourist couple, the man smoking a pipe, one hand behind his back, balding, shoulders hunched in thought; the woman companionably beside him, enjoying the sea breeze in her wispy hair, looking at everything around her with friendly interest.

"English people!" the busboy said, "That fellow there remind me of a guest at the Colony Club, years back. Peter Cartwright was his name."

"What makes them come here?" I asked.

"Oh, they hear about us, same way we hear about them."

"Yeah, but why do they come to *this* island… on the fringes of the world?"

"Same reason islanders want to get away from here. To plant green stems in places where nobody knows you. To please no one but yourself. Nothing more complicated than that."

We watched the couple: the woman lagging a bit behind the man, who walked as evenly as the sand would let him, self-possessed, looking at everything around him with a studious air, as if disappointed there was not much more to this vacation spot than beach and vacant blue sky and locals with nothing to do.

"You know, when I see them here outside their cities and fog, under our bright skies, they're as ordinary as… cattle birds." The busboy said, as if he'd traveled and seen them in their cities!

"Look here, man," I was desperate now. "You have anything on you to eat? Coco bread… sugarcake? Anything?"

The fellow ignored me. He went right on: talking about the table manners of the English, those horseback-loving Americans and their women, the Germans always formal and brusque and "racial". He went right on: giving imitations of their accents and habits; saying he was "an encyclopedia of insights into the naked souls of these folks".

I heard him interrupt himself in mid-sentence, his voice trailing off. A pause, then, "Uh, oh!" I raised my head.

The wispy-haired woman was running, or making her way rather urgently in our direction, holding up the hem of her floral patterned dress and moving as fast as her frail limbs allowed.

I couldn't tell straightaway what the problem was but the busboy had taken off his shirt. He must have sensed trouble the moment he saw her coming; he was already on the move as the woman came up, flying past her, snatching her words like a lifebelt. "I think he's in trouble," she said, meaning her husband or companion whose head the rough waters were tossing back and forth as he made a futile effort at swimming.

She glanced quickly at me – she did look as plain and rumpled as any beachcombing tern – and said almost apologetically, "Peter's not a particularly strong swimmer," before running after the busboy in case there was something she could do.

I watched as the busboy plunged into the waves, which immediately reduced him to a puny swimmer, bobbing head and chopping arms. Somehow he made it to that other bobbing head, the Englishman, while the woman stood at the edge of the wet sand, the hem of her dress wet from water racing in and for awhile you couldn't tell what was happening out there – a drowning or rescue.

The busboy found a way to get back. He was helped by a huge cresting wave that seemed to lift and dump their bodies closer to the shore. Next thing I knew he was helping the Englishman through the shallows, stumbling and swaying, his wife or companion standing still like a marker of safety. They collapsed finally in a breathless heap near her feet.

Minutes went by. There were now four people on the beach in separate states of exhaustion, anxiety or near death. Then the woman was helping her companion to his feet and they started walking away, throwing glances over their shoulders at the busboy who lay stretched out on the sand.

The woman broke away and started running toward me. The Englishman called to her sharply. She turned back, shouted something over her shoulders I couldn't hear. They walked away. They'd had enough of the beach, enough of strange impulses to run or swim for your life; they were walking back to a well-lit room where one felt dry and safe.

I had to drag myself down to the edge of the water. The busboy's body lay there unmoving, all vital signs sucked out of it. The surf washed around its head. I tried pulling him by the arms away from the grabbing tide. I dug my heels in the sand and pulled him by the wrist, inch by inch. The body felt stiff and gave off a sharp odor of seaweed. The effort of pulling exhausted me quickly. I crawled over and with the last ounce of strength heaved it over on its back.

Shock of my life: the white goatee, the pouches under the eyes; it was the face of Waverider.

Discombobulated, staring in disbelief, wanting to get off my knees and run, knees frozen to the spot, eyes locked to that face in bewilderment and fear.

Then he moved. I felt his callused hands grab my wrist. His eyes opened and a sea-weary smile wrinkled his face. He said:

"So the life-giver come down to rescue the life-saver! Took the plunge without knowing why. This man is not without heart."

I fell back on the sand and stared up at the sky.

"Was an Englishman, alright!" he continued, in between gasps for breath. "Know what he told me when I got to him? *Bugger off, leave me alone, you black bastard*! I don't think he wanted to live…"

At this point I felt my grip on the sand and the light slipping. I was ready to surrender, to let everything – sky, beach, sea, screeching gulls, wandering souls, confounded heart – simply fade away. Say welcome to that blissful dark peace.

Just before I passed out an orange light played down on me from the sky. A family of gulls passed overhead, seven of them, unconcerned, heading out to sea.

Waverider's body gave a cold shiver that rippled through the sand. I heard him expel the longest sigh or breath of contentment, like a man who had savored life's bittersweet stuff, and was once again astonished at what he'd found.

That orange light playing down on me must have been the glow from the setting sun. The orange turns pink, then a flaming crimson, which drenches the whole island before the sun slips away.

I don't know what people see when they faint away but I saw the beach through the filter of these shifting hues and I thought that for brief moments I had escaped to some sort of paradise, leaving body, pain and hallucination behind.

I was back in Waverider's chair. It seemed I'd never left it.

I looked toward the spot where I'd last seen his body lying in the sand. There was a body there, or something that looked like a tree trunk, or maybe the wreckage of a boat: something solid and inert over which the waves spumed and washed.

I tried closing my eyes, determined to erase the scene; I'd keep them shut until I sensed some semblance of normalcy had been restored. The ocean had quieted; the water licked the shoreline in a friendly feline way; night was closing in.

When I opened my eyes and returned to the spot where I'd last seen Waverider I found an even stranger sight.

A woman was standing in the water, a fat woman, wearing a strange hat, a gentleman's hat she might have grabbed to *cover her head* as she hurried here. There was only one woman on our island that corpulent and heavy – Ma Memu. She appeared to be sprinkling flowers from a basket in her hand; pausing, to say a prayer or mutter an incantation, then throwing more flowers into the sea.

When she was through, she turned and walked heavily to the spot where Waverider's body lay, not flat on its back as I'd left it, but half-curled as in sleep. I saw her pull up the broad sleeves of her damp clothes, reach down and heave Waverider up on her shoulder. I thought she would stagger under the weight, but no, she adjusted the body a little on her shoulder as if it were her last and only possession, more precious to her now in death. Then she walked away.

I was bobbing on some sea of high fever, I was babbling in delirium. When eventually my body felt relief there was a full moon in the sky. The palm trees rustled behind me. I felt someone's arms lifting my shoulders, then resting my head on a soft cushion: a woman's bosom, a smell of herbs. A voice was urging me to drink; I opened my lips and drank; it tasted like hot soup; I wanted more; something was lighting lanterns inside me, making me warm and whole again.

She was sitting broad-bottomed on the sand, alternately feeding me the soup and cradling my head. I inhaled the herbal oils she must have rubbed on her body, feeling stronger with every passing moment, sitting up eventually and looking around like some shipwrecked sailor grateful to be alive. She looked down at my face with a strange happiness.

"How you feel now?"

111

"I feel alright."

"Thank you for saving my son," she said. *Saving her son?* "He said you gave him the kiss of life when every force of breath had been sucked out of him." *The kiss of life?* "I gave thanks to Erzuli. She has been in a generous mood all day on this beach"

"Who are these people…going out into the water…nearly drowning…? And what's this you gave me to drink?" I asked.

"Turtle soup."

"I didn't know we had turtles on this island."

"Many things you do not know about this island, this lump of rock you've lived on all your life… Turtle soup… seasoned with celery, thyme, saspirrilla, other boiled plants."

She spoke in the same slow deliberate manner, and she kept throwing her head back to inhale the salty air from the sea, her hair loose and wet under a gentleman's straw hat.

"You ever thought of swimming around the island?" she asked.

"Around the island…? I'm really not a strong swimmer. Besides, why would I want to do that?"

"Why would you want to climb mountains?"

"I don't know…These past days all I thought of doing is leaving this place… *disappearing*…without a trace," I said.

She shook her head, as if what I had just said was reason for disappointment in my character.

"Anywhere but here," I said, "Some of us have ambition, you know. Islands are small places. Out there life offers you a second chance."

"Give a man a second chance, he'll repeat the same mistakes," she said, rocking back and forth as from some unshakeable habit of cradling a child. "If you could swim around the island… of one man's whole life… trace every heartstep …you would discover… a place where you belong …there's nothing out there… nothing but cells of loneliness, streets of pain…tired old imperial nations with no place left to conquer…new independent nations shedding blood like bad memories …tribes of amnesiacs rushing for trains, trolleys and buses…zombies hooked up to picture tubes for life support. There's nothing out there for you, my son."

I squirmed in the sand, not sure what to make of all this. I stood

112

up. I was feeling my normal self again. It seemed a long time since I had done something as ordinary as walking. I wondered what I looked like: my unshaven face, my itchy scalp, dirty clothes.

"Alright…alright…! The world is full of mysteries," I said. "Right now, I'd like to go home."

She made no attempt to stop me; she sat there muttering and rocking and humming like my grandmother. I was ready once more to walk away – from Waverider, exhausted bodies on the beach, the tricks played on my mind by this sea. I waved goodbye and moved off, determined not to look back.

I had taken only ten steps when I heard a sound to my right, a distinct *splosh* in the water. It stopped me in my tracks. I thought that something – a meteor, a swordfish – had fallen from the sky, making a clean entry into the water. I could see nothing. The sound released inside me that feeling of being a stranger to myself, a fear of unreal happenings about to assault me again.

This time I heard a voice say – so close to my ear, it could have been someone standing behind me – *Some of us will stay at home. We are the light of the world.* The words, soft and distinct, sent ripples and tremors through me. Like a snagged fish, I surrendered. I turned.

Ma Memu was sitting up erect as a tree trunk, her face luminous as the moon; she was clapping her hands, singing, her body swaying – left, right, North, South – as if the last piece of a human puzzle was finally in place.

Recently I've been trying to bring back from the grave the face of my grandmother. She'd been dead many years and I had no clear memory of what she looked like. I had only a frightening image of her, as a hard wiry woman who smoked a pipe, walked barefoot and shot fear into my heart whenever she called my name.

The last time I saw her I was six going on seven. My mother took me on a bus that raced with thrilling recklessness through the villages. It should have been a simple visit to her village, with the promise of guava trees, the rusting hulk of an old Bedford truck, its steering wheel stiff. Instead I was told minutes before it was time to go home, that I would be left with my grandmother for a week. It was a week filled with terror and tears.

Bare minutes after my mother disappeared down the road my grandmother announced she was going to give me an enema; I had never been given an enema before; I didn't think I needed an enema. They had to hold me down, screaming and kicking, while someone stuck a tube up my anus. A terrifying time. I never forgave my mother for abandoning me that way in that village.

Now I find myself reaching behind that week of terror (my grandmother's voice shouting at me to be still; the pipe clamped in her mouth, her knarled hands) and groping for her face: not the wrinkled earth mask she took to her grave, the face that linked her to me and the people who came before us: the original face, you could say, from which my face and hers were only variants.

I've painted the boat blue and white. I haven't taken it out to sea yet.

People drop by: tourists, young couples mostly, on honeymoon or on vacation, with fresh white faces, asking questions in an innocent childlike way. The boat intrigues them; they push it into the water and paddle off, waving back at me.

Other people, not tourists, show up. They approach as if they'd known me all their life. When they discover I'm not much interested in idle conversation and have no cigarettes, they call me dirty names, urge me to get off my backside, get a job.

Months ago a film crew showed up: cameras, dark glasses, baseball caps, bright colored fabrics, surveying the landscape, pointing in every direction and shouting at each other. Americans. They acted like new owners of the island. The cameramen took still shots of everything around – coastline, incoming surf, tilting palm trees; they took shots of me (without my permission, the straw hat low on my forehead) lounging under the beach umbrella.

The following morning just before breaklight they showed up again to shoot the first scenes. It had to be shot just as the sun was coming up.

A man dressed in a dinner suit, tall and elegant, walks along the beach accompanied by a woman wearing a white dress and carrying her shoes in her hand. She seems a little inebriated, but it's the sea, the morning breeze, and the breaking light which intoxicate her. He strolls in a disinterested manner, careful not to

114

get his polished shoes wet. The camera follows them as they walk, as the man smokes and walks, as the woman, still strangely intoxicated, frolics and dances about.

The following morning they shot another scene. The woman, impulsive creature that she is, takes off her clothes and dashes into the water. She laughs and waves to the man inviting him to join her. He refuses. He is content to smoke, so vertical, aloof, one hand in his pocket, intently watching her.

They shot this scene many times. The director wasn't happy with the way she held her shoulders when she laughed and waved. He showed her how to do it. He wanted her to get it right.

Zombies hooked up to picture tubes for life support.

I think I understand what Ma Memu means. She's not just *using words*, as islanders say. What she knew about the world out there had a lot to do with the images her son Waverider brought back after a journey overseas. Yes, Waverider was one of those islanders who crossed the seas on ships bound for the shores of England in the 1950s.

Fists of clenched handkerchiefs waving from the deck. Ships bound for cold grey harbors. Astonishment. Fear white as bone. Bedsitters. Shillings of heat.

Waverider in several amazing situations: as a male nurse in a London Hospital; selling tickets in the underground railway; in a nightclub as a drummer in a band. Jumping here, there; coming up for air; trying this, that. In a small room of bearded men, reading the Bible and speaking of Ethiopia. At a bus stop smiling at white faces, which stare back at him, their cheeks hollowed out by the cold, their thin lips sewn tight. Knocking on doors that won't open once they saw his dark face. Smiling as he walked away for he could see right through to their skeletons.

Always smiling, was Waverider, in those cold hard cities, as if he knew something was waiting to reel him back here.

Dream and fear rose inside him like a tide: *why was he here – in this choky sardine room called a bedsitter? Why call this cold place home?*

Two weeks ago a party of tourists appeared from nowhere: chatting to each other, ready to picnic on the beach. Baskets,

115

umbrellas, a dog, sunglasses, suntan lotion, large beach blankets: all the paraphernalia visitors feel obliged to bring along to sit for a while on strange shores.

Minutes went by. The ritual of spreading blankets. Baring limbs. Suntan lotion.

Then a shout went up. *Someone's in trouble.* The picnic group assembled at the water's edge, clutching each other; some shading eyes and pointing out to sea; no one quite sure what was happening; no one quite sure what to do.

There was a man out there holding on to a raft; another on the beach who'd managed to swim to safety, exhausted, happy to be alive, pointing back out to sea, insisting there was someone in trouble out there.

The picnic group huddles, horrified. They've had no practice in saving lives; someone comes running with a rope; wades into the water; a big wave hurls him back.

"You've got to catch the wave," I shout at them.

They draw back as I come up, surprised, a little mistrustful – *"Where did he come from?" "He was over there sitting under that beach umbrella, I saw him."* – and in their eyes the terror of losing their own lives one day by drowning. Their thin lips plead silently for deliverance from this beach.

I took the rope and rode out with a receding wave. I got to the raft. A man was holding on for dear life. The rope wasn't going to do us much good. You've got to wait for a really big wave bearing down, only instead of thinking you'll be buried under churning heavy waters, you try to catch it, by the mane, you might say, and ride it bareback to the shore.

This is how we made it back. A big wave brought us on its camel's back straight to the feet of the picnic group.

Someone call an ambulance, is he alright, is he going to live, he's breathing, he's going to be okay, stand back, let me take a look at him, Josh, you haven't even started med. school, what do you know? Mark said there are sharks out there, that's absurd, take it easy, take it easy, he's going to be alright, Brad, your hands, how can you think of sex at a moment like this?

Say fellow, that was pretty good swimming, we want to thank you for what you did, he was outstanding, wasn't he outstanding? listen, why don't you join us, we're at the Colony Club, we'd like you to meet everyone there, I mean, this was outstanding work, you're a hero, say, what's your name?

Back in my chair hours after everyone had cleared off, I thought of the moment I stared into the face of the man clinging to the raft, saw the surprise, the absolute terror, the pleading for help as the next big wave bore down. Thinking how all life leads up to one single moment that blinds you with light or snuffs you out; the rest, so much tedium, the heart-aching hope that the future will come to save you.

Here I am, stripped finally of all desire; feeling no more those heart-pistons of ambition, that urge to cross overseas, following old footprints; wanting no shiny trophy on a shelf, no tiger head on a living room floor.

Life has come down to this: a place in the world where someone knocks and asks to borrow sugar, or *What time is it?* or *Please take my life, I am weary.* A readiness to act – free from envy, hatred, fear. Always marveling at what the bilious tides throw up at your feet or take away.

For me that place is here near Waverider's boat. Ma Memu explained there is no need to travel the world, or kill someone to get there. Sometimes I ask myself: *why this island, why not Rome? And why this time, not 1893?*

She still grows those flowers in her front garden, which she cuts and throws into the sea. She still brings me turtle soup – and ochros, cassava, dumplings, plantains.

Once as a hurricane approached and I sat entranced by the winds, the scowling grey skies, Ma Memu showed up. She sat beside me for a while, silent, holding her hair with one hand and shaking her head in wonder at the raging sea. It boiled and heaved as if a lost city buried in sepulchres of clean sand had broken loose and was surging to the surface.

Then quietly she said, "Time to go home." There was a van waiting to take us from the seashore. The thin Indian driver at the wheel. He smiled as patient and mannerly as a limousine chauffeur. Was he too under her spell? We were battened down in her house, the rooms lit with old hurricane lamps, and there we waited out the storm. She made us paint our faces with colored clay and she danced about holding a white rooster like a lover to her breasts.

We could hear the winds outside, the world howling in turmoil, roofs and trees ripped from their holdings, swirling through the sky; but Ma Memu's house was a rock embedded in the earth.

I suspect she wants to adopt me, make me an apprentice of her voodoo ways. For now I am content to sit under this umbrella – I don't care too much for the sun – caretaker of the sea.

She says there is a price we pay for choosing this place. We can't pretend forever that the world out there will leave us alone. When she said that the color of her face darkened to brooding coal beneath those shiny layers of purple and blue. She means those modern day pirates and buccaneers, no longer searching for gold or coffee beans. Wanting instead a place to bury receptacles of deadly waste; a place where they believe life hardly matters.

She made it sound like something I might wish to be armed and ready for, a fishnet I should struggle, twisting and flipping, to escape from. I know that given a shout, a whisper, a song, she would rush to my side. She would free me, hug me to her bosom; she'd never let me go.

MONKEY WRENCHING
SNAPS

1

Hunter Michel Valcin. Child of his island's Independence. Citizen of the world.

Given the reforms in education, the ceremonies and euphoria on Independence Day, he might have formed some lasting attachment to the island, to that necklace of beaches and sugar cane fields that stretched across turquoise waters from Cuba to Trinidad. But all those years growing up had been a preparation of sorts for his departure.

His father, once a highly respected Magistrate, had lived and worked on the island all his life. On his retirement he left for England to live out the rest of his days. That final move was for him the ultimate reward, the planting of his flag of personal achievement. What came before, starting with his good colonial education, was simply preparation, the packing of his psychic bags over the years.

Hunter had to admit that like his father he had looked upon the island as a springboard to various distant futures.

Had he won the island scholarship (he'd lost it to the son of a local businessman) he might have vaulted overseas to Oxford, England; he might have acquired a British accent instead of this hybrid falsetto that now escaped his lips.

He had to settle instead for three years at the University in the islands before vaulting finally to doctoral studies in Buffalo, New York.

2

"I've been trying to place your accent. It's so intriguing," someone said to him one day (Fall '83) – this at a college in upstate New York where he taught French to freshmen, and where he was beginning to think he had at last found a new permanent home.

They were in an elevator going down, Faculty members three, and this fellow whom he barely knew except for the occasional passing exchange of nods and pleasantries, punctured his composure with that casual remark.

Why was this fellow trying to *place* his accent? What accent was he talking about – his island accent? He'd thought that accent had been varnished away after years in North American classrooms.

His alarm deepened like pain for he took himself rather seriously, and was never sure how to respond in situations like this. Was the comment an attempt to pry open his character? Was it little more than a gesture to crack the silence, to introduce some small talk among colleagues riding a slow elevator?

"So you've been trying to place my accent?" Hunter said, a little abrasively.

He was looking up at the floor indicators and shifting his body in a way that suddenly struck him as typical of islanders back home, uneasy in the presence of foreigners. When it seemed the conversation would lose momentum and founder, Professor Ros Miscuri, the third Faculty member in the elevator, came to its rescue.

"If you think his accent intriguing, wait till you hear his name," she said. This was followed by formal introductions.

Anxious to answer the firm American handshake with a matching grip of his own, he never caught the fellow's first name. He also missed some reference by Professor Miscuri to the French Revolution, but he laughed along with collegial good humor.

"We've had merely a nodding acquaintance before this," the fellow, a Professor Cubbidge, said.

"Yes, we pass each other every day like merchant ships in the night," Hunter said, recovering his balance, and chuckling to clear the air of misunderstanding.

Outside, just before they separated into the prematurely dark night, Prof. Miscuri identified Hunter's island as a place once ruled by the French and then by the British.

"Actually I was there as recently as last summer?" she revealed.

"Oh, really?" Hunter said, eyes wide open, hands in his pockets.

"It's a lovely little island. Lush vegetation, lovely banana fields and winding roads, *lovely winding roads* going up into the hills…"

Professor Miscuri went on with considerable passion, swiveling her head evenly from Hunter to the Cubbidge fellow to Hunter, and although he stood there with a fixed smile of interest on his face, Hunter felt pain and discomfort in his bowels and chest.

He didn't care to be regaled with descriptions of quaint little houses and the charming island folk she'd met. He didn't really want all of that brought up again; yet here was Professor Miscuri, her pointy nose reddened from blowing into tissue, scuffing and scratching with a puppy dog's interest in what lay beneath Hunter's pedagogical surface; and laying bare like so much fossil and with obvious delight bits and pieces of his island history and geography.

To add to his discomfort he sensed the Cubbidge fellow staring at him with an oily mixture of suspicion and disbelief; a little envious, perhaps, of Professor Miscuri's travel insights, but clearly astonished to discover that a fellow colleague with an earned Doctorate had origins on an island of lovely banana fields.

A chill wind had begun to encircle them. It was drizzling. Unlike his colleagues who seemed oblivious to the weather, Hunter found it difficult to ignore the raindrops pattering on his bare head.

"So how are you guys going to spend your long weekend?" Hunter asked, not meaning to, but putting a stop to Professor Miscuri's effusions. She looked away, displeased at being cut off. Hunter, sensing he'd committed some breach of etiquette, bit his lip.

"Well, I'll tell you," the Cubbidge fellow said, leaning into Hunter's face, "*this* guy has in *this* briefcase scripts with the potential to ruin what few pleasures he might have arranged this weekend. And so I will bid you all *adieu*."

Hunter walked quickly to his car, his mouth tight, his glasses speckled with raindrops.

"These Americans are stupid people… stupid people!" he muttered to himself, fumbling with the ignition keys.

The journey home, a twenty-minute drive from the campus, was somewhat perilous this time. The conversation he'd just had kept replaying in his head. There was a blotch or smear on his windshield just out of range of the wipers. On close inspection it turned out to be bird droppings. It tormented him, this Rorschach blotch of bird excrement on his windshield. He almost rear-ended a car on the highway, so frantic was his distraction.

On the roadway, a mile or so from home, he got the feeling he was being followed. At the next Stop sign he idled for awhile and the car behind him with its stone-faced occupants simply waited. It looked like a local police cruiser. What did they want? Had he infringed some traffic code as he came off the highway?

When he pulled into his driveway the car stopped. He paid them no attention. He grabbed his briefcase and searched his pockets for his house keys. A voice from the police cruiser shouted, "Hey…you! What're you doing here?" And Hunter felt in his stomach a tearing sensation as if a bayonet had ripped open a seam of pain from his chest right down to his bowels.

His first act soon after the police car left was to squirt Windex glass cleaner on his windshield, then wipe it off with furious circular motions of his hands.

Home, since he had landed on these shores, was the uncertainty, the lacerating encounters on the streets; the sanctuary of his well-lit rooms, placid routines, carefully arranged furniture; his books, his computer with its heavenly blue screen, his bachelor's austerity.

Home was once the presence of his father, his magisterial silence, his muted pleasure at learning that his boy was making progress at school.

Home was his fear of displeasing his father whose ghostly presence he felt whenever, as was the case that evening, his spirit shuddered and the memory dust raised in delightful puffs by Professor Miscuri settled back into a grainy patina on the prairie of his heart.

Sunday afternoon with Hunter. He'd had lunch, washed the dishes and ironed his shirts.

He'd settled in an armchair with the Sunday papers when a picture of one of NASA's spacecrafts flashed across his television screen. It caught his interest. There was a shot of the spacecraft being ferried out to the launching site, moving slowly, inch by inch across the open tarmac, taking half an hour to travel half a mile or something like that.

With an intake of breath he realized he had found it: the metaphor on which to hang his life.

Those early years on the islands were a preparation for the big launch overseas. All his teachers were like the many technicians working at the NASA space centre, fixing this, checking that, while he sat in his space capsule on the launch pad awaiting the final count, the billowing cloud at the base, then lift off.

He played with the metaphor for a long while. It left him very unhappy.

The NASA people kept in touch with their astronauts; they sent them up and brought them back to earth. Far from contemplating any return to his island, to his piece of earth, Hunter felt at times as if he were spinning weightlessly around the planet, void of purpose, with no connection to mission control anywhere.

At this point, the pain of that reverie threatening to paralyze him in his chair and stop his heart, Hunter reached for the Sunday newspapers.

5

He bought the Sunday New York *Times* from a candy store. The owner of the store was a balding portly unsmiling white man who always turned away and looked busy whenever Hunter walked in; never spoke to him, never looked him in the eye, his hands feverishly shifting stock.

His mind on his mission, Hunter was careful not to appear to be loitering. He deposited exact change on the counter; he nodded to the owner's chubby bespectacled daughter, who always smiled and urged him to have a good day, and hurried out to his car.

Reading the London *Times* (which arrived in the middle of the week by a British aircraft laden with tourists) was one of his father's rituals, on the verandah, a crinkled sea below in the distance, while from an old record player in the living room an Italian tenor, or the Irish John McCormick, sang scratchy favorites.

Reading the New York *Times* was the one solitary pleasure Hunter looked forward to on weekends. No waiting here for aircraft to bring news of the world to his doorstep. In fact, this was his moment of exploration, a blast off into orbit around the world.

And the world out there as reported in that leisurely, sometimes amused style of the *Times*, seemed forever in turmoil, its populations boiling in huge iron pots of folly, misery and discontent.

Pass over the continent of Africa, look down, and there, again, glimpses of human misery: the tribes at each other with spears and machine guns, undoing their colonial past; starving women and children on dusty treks to beggardom and death. Pass over Asia, with its monsoons and religious wars, its rice-fields of skulls, its bloated cattle floating in watery graves. Nearer home, over Latin America, where the earth perpetually groaned, forced over and over to swallow more bodies, more blood, the cannon fodder of peak-capped generals and dictators.

Other places – where transfer of power was more orderly, its citizens absorbed in fashions, sports or fiscal planning – he gave little more than a cursory reading.

What fascinated Hunter, what caught his planetary eye, was the playing out of human conflict on so catastrophic a scale. Secure in his capsule, free of any obligation to report to anyone, he thought he was watching that evolutionary flux – slower in some places, more advanced in others – that had always characterized human life from the days of the dinosaurs.

He considered lucky to be here in far upstate New York. He had struggled with single-minded purpose, fighting off all manner of distraction, to be here! It had meant sacrifices; he'd tried to

126

bury all traces of *back there*. This hereness with its access to everything, he would not exchange – never mind how empty and frightening it felt sometimes – for any other place in the world.

6

Someone rang his doorbell one Saturday morning (Spring '84). Hunter was slow getting out of bed, reaching for his bathrobe, and slipping on his wristwatch. The doorbell rang again. He wasn't expecting anyone; he felt somehow rebuked for keeping whoever it was waiting.

He opened the door into the smiling face of the fellow in the apartment above, whose footsteps (and those of his female companion) he recognized going up the stairs late at night, but whom he'd never really met. The man held an envelope like an olive branch before Hunter's eyes.

"The postman left yours in mine," the fellow said.

Hunter thanked him, cleared his throat, and the man was gone.

The doorbell, a neighbor's kindness, in themselves benign, small happenings. Yet after he had shut the door Hunter was thrown in disarray.

He'd been caught off guard. The man's smile quickly disarmed him; his canyon deep voice stripped him of defenses; the swift glancing way the man had made contact, before going about his business left Hunter with little more than a fading impression: a receding hairline, a thick moustache, the shades of an aviator and that blinding smile.

These Americans! They shoot at you first, then they gallop away!

Why couldn't the fellow just slip the letter under his door, and remain the unseen tenant upstairs? And what if anything lurked behind this act of kindness?

7

An airmail envelope. He thought the letter might have come from his mother. It hadn't. Stamps from England were tiny and

127

functional. On this envelope there were four, not too carefully aligned, with all the colors and pictures of a new nation advertising itself. An island nation. How had anyone back there get hold of his address?

The letter was from Christopher Yardbrough, a lecturer at the island university. He reminded Hunter of their freshman years; he mentioned the names of other university professors "still here"; he was writing, he explained finally, to request from Hunter a letter of recommendation.

Hunter sat staring at the wall, at his thin hairy exposed legs, at the envelope, which like a stone weighty with omen had come crashing through his morning.

Yardbrough tracking him down, contacting him after all these years – transmitting a message to his circling spacecraft! Yardbrough wanting a letter of recommendation (never before had Hunter been asked to recommend anyone). Yardbrough indicating that he was making plans to complete his Doctorate in the U.S. In short, coming up here; entering Hunter's sphere of orbit; greeting Hunter one day with island jokes and accents and memories; spending time in Hunter's apartment, altering his routines. It disrupted his entire day.

Hunter liked to think of every day as clean and unblemished, like a windswept beach awaiting his measured footprints. That morning wherever he went he saw other prints on the sand; he felt the shadowy presence of Yardbrough.

By mid-afternoon he gave up trying to drown his thoughts in busy chores. He sat in his living room, the television set flickering; he stared; he read the letter again and again; he scratched the hairs on his thighs.

What if he simply ignored Yardbrough? Pretended he'd never received his letter?

8

Mens sana in corpore sano.

Inspiring words of an old Latin teacher, a friend of his father. Words that had guided him all these years through the snares and bushfires of sexual need. In fact, those words had been his salvation after a particularly frightening day back on the island when his school (on instructions from the Ministry of Education) had spent its morning hours lecturing students and passing out pamphlets on venereal disease.

Those words had shielded him from the brazen behavior of a girl from his high school days, Daphne Licksamber, who, he was convinced, envied and resented his father's position, and never missed an opportunity to taunt Hunter: *Hi, there, chimpanzee face. What a way your arms long! Want a banana?*

Daphne Licksamber was loud and coarse and common, but to this day he still could not erase from his mind her tantalizing breasts, the dark mysteries her thighs revealed when she sat in a careless unladylike way.

Mens sana. Hunter believed resolutely in a sound mind, in pure reason, imposing its will over the unruly passions of the body. Even now when he caught himself staring after a woman's bottom, sordid images flooded his mind: the sounds of dogs roaming island streets at night, sniffing the anus of a bitch in heat; the grotesque sight of two sadfaced dogs, locked together after copulation, whimpering and tugging to get loose; the cruel laughter of schoolboys throwing stones at the dogs. The cruel taunts of Daphne Licksamber.

9

One evening, while he was a student at the island university, Hunter found himself trapped and cornered like an animal, his *mens sana* unable to rescue him from total humiliation.

It was his first night in the student dormitory, and he was told that as part of his freshman initiation he should prepare for a visit from a black virgin, The Goddess of Poo. It sounded outrageous and stupid. *The Goddess of Poo!*

Just as he was settling down to his first letter home – expressing doubts about his decision to live in a Hall of residence "among cretins" – there was a knock on his door. A messenger in red robe, a freshman who stammered and held a towel wrapped between his legs like a dhoti, shoved a packet of condoms in his hands and instructed him to turn off his lights: The Goddess of Poo was on her way.

The second knock on the door he ignored; the third knock sounded like the knuckles of a shy hand rather than a fist. He sighed irritably and opened the door.

He saw a young girl's smiling face; he opened the door wider, saw the smile dissolve into a knowing giggle; he sensed her right leg moving forward so he gave way. She slipped quickly past him. Befuddled, his heart suddenly pounding faster, he shut the door.

The Goddess of Poo. She stood a little shamefaced, still giggling, not sure if she was expected to make the next move; a slip of a girl, skinny arms, in a plain dress, one shoulder bare from a loose brassiere strap, wearing sneakers. A mere schoolgirl. In fact, Hunter thought she couldn't be older than those girls he went to school with on his island, who giggled at him behind his back, friends of Daphne Licksamber.

In swift seconds she sensed his fear and confusion, his still uninitiated manhood; and as if she'd been in this situation before, she turned her back to him and began removing her clothes. Before he could say *Stop*, Hunter was staring at her bare back and buttocks. And to his horror he felt the stirring in his pants of little Willie.

Little Willie was what his mother used to take to the bathroom when he was a boy, shaking and instructing him to pee. Little Willie was the son of Big Willie whom he had once glimpsed lying large, serpentlike and frightening between his father's legs as his father slept. Until ways had been found to tame him, little Willie had caused Hunter all kinds of embarrassment by coming to attention at the most awkward moments of his sleeping and waking life.

What happened next happened fast. The girl turned to face him; there was an odor of Lifebuoy soap coming off her body; Hunter's eyes fell instantly on her poo; there was a fourth knock on the door, followed by hammering; little Willie fell limp and mercifully still.

Hunter was startled, then relieved; then alarmed at the thought of a third visitor, who would now find him alone with a girl in a state of undress.

130

Without a word the girl reached for her clothes. Hunter hesitated, sneaking one more glance at her bare buttocks, giving her time to be decent. And that was how Hunter came face to face for the first time with Christopher Yardbrough.

He was tall, slender, bearded, and bedraggled; he stood at the door slightly apologetic but furious, for apparently he'd found out what was about to happen, and like some morals officer on duty he'd chosen to intervene to stop any further indignities.

He spoke firmly but gently to the girl, telling her to go home and never return. He gave Hunter a searching look and told him he'd be back.

Hunter waited; he felt he'd been rescued from certain humiliation of the flesh; he wanted to thank his savior.

Two hours later Yardbrough returned; they talked. Deep into the night they talked of the idiotic indulgences of students privileged to be at the island University; of the exploitation that poor girl had been spared (for which she had nevertheless been paid). And Yardbrough displayed his wide knowledge of many forms of exploitation.

The island Government was a ruthless exploiter of the broad masses of the people. His own father, he confessed in a voice shrill with anguish, had engaged in shameless exploitation of his servant girl's body after his wife died. His father had tried to initiate him into manhood by urging the servant girl to seduce him.

Yardbrough spoke as if his life-mission on earth was to rescue or protect defenseless bodies from all forms of cruel exploitation.

Hunter was touched by Yardbrough's restless intensity, the instinctive way he seemed to trust Hunter with his confidences. Hunter knew only the painful silence and secrets of his own heart. He'd always disdained that island way of joking cruelly about other people's frailties. He'd always longed for a mate, someone to whom he could bare his soul with no fear of betrayal.

He was touched, too, by Yardbrough's revelations about his father. Paying his servant girl to seduce his own son! That detail was the final bond in their friendship. Hunter couldn't help wondering how radically his life might have been altered had his father, Judge Valcin, thought of such a scheme to accommodate his son's deepest longing.

131

10

Hunter preparing to go to bed. He loved his American bathroom with its globe bulbs, the mirrors, the tiles. He'd strip, then he'd examine his teeth. He loved using dental floss. Then the shower; slapping powder or lotion on his body. In the bedroom his pajamas laid out. Back to the bathroom for an examination of his face: deciding, for instance, to put off shaving until the following day.

But now the memory of Yardbrough floated by, leaving him with a distinct sense of a wasted day. He stood at attention looking at himself, pleased with himself, unhappy with the still unresolved problem of Yardbrough. He felt more than a little tense. Angry.

He slipped his pajamas off his waist and looked at little Willie. He closed his eyes and summoned before him the body of Daphne Licksamber, still giggling and smirking after all those years. He felt the pain of desire harden in his loins until he was as firm as a tamarind rod.

He ordered Daphne Licksamber to get on her hands and knees. Her face looked puzzled; it turned to wide-eyed fear; she pleaded with him not to; she told him she was very sorry. His hand gripped the tamarind rod. He bent over her, ignoring her screams: *Serve you right, Daphne Licksamber, serve you right!*

11

Yardbrough, the student activist, always on the run, distributing fliers. Yardbrough, the Assistant Lecturer, raising the consciousness of his students, drilling and grading his troops for the defense of the island's body politic. Yardbrough, his rescuer and friend, his buddy and mate.

What after all was so difficult about writing a recommendation for someone to whom he felt indebted?

Yardbrough had also invited him to revisit the island; offered him a place to stay. There were weekend flights from New York city advertised in the *Sunday Times*. He could take advantage of early bookings and bargain fares. What was so objectionable about that? And wasn't Yardbrough's letter that signal from mission control to his orbiting capsule? Would it not guide him back to earth, bring him home?

A four-day trip – what really was the problem there? A short retreat. He could return here recharged, a solid man, having jettisoned in flight that vulnerable lonely feeling that was his wooden cross in America.

12

The flight to the island was late taking off. Hunter had to join a long line of islanders shuffling forward to the ticket counter, with bulging suitcases, boxes, barrels with hand-written names and addresses everywhere. *Who in God's heaven were these people?*

They made scenes and attracted stares. They sucked their teeth and grumbled about airport inefficiency and racial prejudice. To be viewed as one of these people, their bags crammed with cheap sidewalk purchases, their destination an island of lush vegetation and lovely bananas, was more than his dignity could take. Biting his lip, Hunter shuffled forward and tried to hide his chagrin behind his scholarly glasses and a book.

He was seated next to someone who reeked of liquor; an islander, for sure, whose farewell party must have ended mere hours before his departure time, the car racing recklessly to the airport. The man placed a handkerchief over his face and slept throughout the flight. Hunter threw glances of disgust at his unwashed presence, and stared through the window at fluffy white clouds.

At the island airport the immigration clerk viewed with suspicion his passport, his accent and the contents of his immigration card. The impertinence of the man, with his shiny ballpoint, and his clean-shaven good looks! What criteria, what tests did they use to select these people?

He emerged finally from all this telling himself how wonderful it was to breathe the open air, to live one's life free of the multiple abrasions, the petty incarcerations that was life on any island.

The fierce heat assaulted him, mugged him as if he were a tourist. He felt sticky and self-conscious, in his jacket with the leather patch at the elbow: ignoring the predatory scrutiny of taxi-drivers and other idlers; hoping the bag at his feet wouldn't suddenly vanish; wondering where the hell Yardbrough was.

He heard his name being paged; he found the airline counter and was delivered into the arms of a Rastafarian who seemed at first to be simply standing about with a deranged smile on his face.

"You the bredda from Stateside?" the man spoke up suddenly. "My name is Bikesman. Brother Chris couldn't make it. Him ask I man to pick you up. Him give I description of the bredda but me couldn't remember everything him say."

The man laughed; Hunter looked stern and unforgiving; the man continued:

"Is *long time* I man searching for this bredda looking at all the passengers coming through the door till I man decide to *page* cause me have your name written down right here."

Hunter frowned as if, no matter what the explanation, he was far from pleased with this arrangement.

The Rastafarian walked ahead of him, his head slightly cocked, with that dip at the knee that made him look jaunty and sure of faith. Suddenly he couldn't remember where he'd parked his car; he tried to make great humor of this, scratching his beard and looking around like a man who had misplaced his glasses. Hunter seized this moment to study him.

He saw a wiry fellow in a tricolored Tam, wearing the dark glasses of a movie star and the beard of a New York Hasidim. A real Rastafarian? A student dressed up as Rastafarian? Either way he sounded like one of Yardbrough's cadres, a runner of important errands.

On the road, finally, at the wheel of Yardbrough's car – a noisy downtrodden Volkswagen, its backseat littered with pink leaflets, a newspaper, a few textbooks, a few empty soda cans – Bikesman felt compelled to display his erudition.

"Is *long time now*," he began, settling back, his elbow sticking out the window: "Long time I man study this island/world situation… the futility of politics, or the politics of futility – *See't?* – either way you deal the cards, is sufferation for the righteous… Now, I & I reach one conclusion: the only true salvation from and for the *hege/money – See't?* – of oppressor nations is for I & I to recover that original ground of the spirit… Selassie I, the true vine!"

Hunter was flabbergasted. He couldn't think of anything to say. Just off an aircraft, a survivor of Customs and Immigration impertinence, here he was being sermonized by a fellow named Bikesman about *man's search for that original ground of the spirit*. And, next, being asked about his *position* on this issue.

Hunter bit his lip and kept his silence; occasionally he managed a weak smile; he squirmed, shifting his long legs in the Volkswagen front seat; unaccustomed to someone else at the wheel he clutched his travel documents and looked straight ahead; and although he didn't mean to be rude, his silence must have struck the Rastafarian as indifference, if not aloofness.

The fellow suddenly turned off the main road; the Volkswagen hesitated, then began to labor up a narrow hilly road; running water coming down one side, weatherbeaten houses, a cement mixer with no sign of the cement mixers at work. A depressing place. An all too familiar place.

The Rastafarian stopped the car; he shouted, *Soon Come*; he disappeared. Hunter felt a sharp sense of abandonment.

People who seemed to have lived there all their lives walked by; they looked inside the car, and smiled at Hunter as if they knew him from somewhere; a few skinny boys jumped on the bonnet of the car. Hunter was tempted to shout at them, to wave them away. He felt fatigued and displaced.

Out of nowhere, the voice of his old Latin teacher started speaking to him words he'd often quoted to Hunter's father during sunset conversations on their verandah: *Odi profanum vulgus et arceo*…

Hunter had come to believe there was profound correctness in those words. His father, the Judge, and the Latin teacher had spent their entire lives summing up human failure (in the courtroom) or trying to nourish human potential (in the classroom). They were men of learning; they ought to know about the

135

unchanging condition of *the vulgus* through the centuries and across seas.

Favete linguis! Shaking his head gravely the Latin teacher would roll those words off his tongue, as if their mere pronouncement was all any reasonable man needed to insulate himself properly from *the vulgus* of this world.

When the Rastafarian returned – there was the odor of marijuana on his breath – he found Hunter much more relaxed; he had removed his jacket; he seemed congenial, apparently chastened and ready to respond to further flights of erudition.

14

Christopher Yardbrough the student activist had transformed himself into a lecturer activist, dividing his time between his classes and trade union activity. The island itself was in the throes of election campaigning.

"Christopher!" *Crisstafa*! "Now that is one serious bredda. Him struggle all the while for human rights and justice," the Rastafarian said.

Yardbrough lived in a block of flats inside the University campus. The Rastafarian had the key and let them in. The flat was small, rather spartan, amazingly lacking in books and bookshelves and, judging from the emptiness of the refrigerator, unprepared for a visitor's short stay.

"Him have some union business to look after. So rest your-self, me soon come," the Rastafarian said, vanishing again.

Something about all this – the waiting, the Rastafarian's disappearing acts – was now a source of serious irritation to Hunter. He sat in a chair in his travel clothes, still clutching his travel documents, determined to be welcomed that way by Yardbrough.

Near midnight the Rastafarian returned to announce that Yardbrough would see him the following morning. The flat was at his disposal.

"Some serious negotiations hold him down," he said, twisting his face and making it sound like a wrestling match with Christopher on the canvas hopelessly pinned.

Hunter spent the night on an unfamiliar bed. There was no blanket, no covering sheet; he felt exposed and he lay with his eyes wide open in the dark, his ears cocked to intercept every invading night noise.

His thoughts drifted back to his apartment where everything – his car, his mail, his clock radio, his books, his slippers – remained in a state of constant readiness. No sudden emergencies there to hold you down. People built things that worked; there were seasons, choices, flavors; and always that civil silence, that insulation from other people's obsessions; always the hum of power units running dependably, uncomplainingly, like the re-frigerator in his kitchen, his computer with its crystal blue screen.

To be back there, now! To lift off, leaving Yardbrough on his planet of the oppressed, leaving Bikesman, his Rastafarian lieu-tenant, with his *Bloodfire! Hellfire!* and other incendiary fates for oppressor nations!

In his head he rehearsed scripts of conversations with Yardbrough; when finally they were alone he would look him in the eye and say, softly, *What's happening*? He'd unburden his soul, tell Yardbrough about moments in recent years when a part of him almost died:

"Finishing your Doctorate is one thing. Having to defend it, before a panel of white men with straggly hair and mincing voices…

"You know one of them said to me that my dissertation showed clearly an ability to gather and collate material from library sources but…

"And then the interview continued through lunch. I got the feeling they watching me, observing my table manners before offering me a position at the college…"

Near dawn he fell asleep wondering what was behind Yardbrough's planned move to the U.S. He'd mentioned some-thing about receiving a grant from a Foundation. Had he had enough of organizing the workers? Was he prudently preparing to escape if things got dangerously out of hand?

One could get tired of *organizing*. Tired of defensive strategy sessions, mosquitoes, bony faces. The years slipped away like reptiles in the bush; you wake up one morning and find your hairline receding; the workers are waiting for today's battle plans; you stare across the jungle clearing and wonder why your head hurts so much these days. One could get tired of all that.

15

It was raining when Hunter woke up late the next morning. His first thought was of the day's schedule: a shower, then breakfast – then what?

His first discovery was that the flat was empty, and there was nothing to prepare breakfast with. He was sitting down to a meal of crackers and milk, put together after a desperate search of the cupboards and refrigerator, when Yardbrough's Volkswagen pulled up and the Rastafarian came in.

Hunter was standing in his terrycloth bathrobe, scratching his head. The Rastafarian, dripping rain on the floor, carried a shopping bag; he smiled and feigned exhaustion as if he had braved a rainstorm and a forest of lions to get through to the flat. Hunter waited.

From the kitchen where he was emptying the bag the Rastafarian explained that this was in fact an awkward time to visit; electioneering was in "full swing"; there was violence and gunplay in parts of the city; Yardbrough was still locked in "serious" negotiations; he had "serious" business to take care of.

Hunter looked outside where it continued to rain like the end of the world. He noticed wet footprints on the floor from the door all the way round to the kitchen. What a way for a professor to live! What a way to keep an apartment!

Curious about the contents of the shopping bag, he strolled into the kitchen. On display on the kitchen sink were oranges, corn, sugarcane stalks, vegetables – the good fruit of the earth. As if rewarding himself for his labors the Rastafarian was nonchalantly rolling a marijuana cigarette.

Tempted to ask the whereabouts of the nearest supermarket, Hunter chose instead to grind his teeth; he felt then pure hatred for this Rastafarian fellow, Bikesman as he called himself.

When the fellow came into the tiny living room he found Hunter sitting in his bathrobe, his legs crossed, absorbed in a book, the pages of which he was annotating. The Rastafarian pulled a chair toward him and sat with one foot over the arm. He smoked his cigarette; he hummed a melancholy tune; he gazed through the louvre windows as if divining wisdom in the rain clouds.

They sat this way for a while, not speaking to each other.

Then Hunter got up and made his way to the bathroom. There were gurgles in the pipe, a spluttering from the showerhead, then a piddling trickle of water. That ignited rage. Rain pouring outside, no water in the pipes, no hot meals! He put back on his bathrobe and stormed outside, ready now to scream, to extract explanations.

There was only the aroma of marijuana. Bikesman the Rastafarian had quietly performed another disappearing act.

16

After a second meal of milk and crackers (he refused to have anything to do with the natural foods left in the kitchen sink by the Rastafarian), he was dressed and once more awaiting Yardbrough's appearance, which happened late in the afternoon, during a break in the weather. He came in looking much the same, the thin angular bearded warrior, in blue jeans; perhaps thinner and more bearded, but as youthful as when last they'd met.

He smiled and said he was sorry about everything but these were indeed serious times. In fact, he couldn't stop here long; he'd left the Volkswagen running. Maybe if Hunter came along they could talk on the road. He wanted Hunter to meet his family. Lunch was being prepared.

It wasn't exactly what Hunter wanted to hear, but Yardbrough, his shoulders slack, sounded weary and apologetic; and here at last was the opportunity for motion.

The streets were teeming rivers; the Volkswagen, chugging forward like a river steamer, soon became hot and stuffy, its windows fogging up. The Rastafarian had squeezed himself obligingly into the backseat. Yardbrough was at the wheel peering

139

ahead like a man on a river steamer on the lookout for obstacles in the water.

And Yardbrough talked:

"To understand what is happening here," he said, "one has to consider the whole question of land and income distribution…" Hunter was looking at the wound-up window on his side of the car through which, inexplicably, raindrops filtered and sprinkled. "The key economic sectors, which by and large are controlled by a white creole plantocratic and merchant oligarchy, have assumed a position of total indifference to the welfare of the masses…"

From the backseat The Rastafarian shot in melodiously, "Babylon, yu missile gone soft!"

"In a very real sense, the old plantation-based British colonial structures," Yardbrough said, "have been replaced by an American inspired neo-colonialism…"

"See't there? Selassie I, *the true vine!*" the voice from the backseat hissed.

Still gazing outside at the punishing rain, Hunter began to wonder if his shoes could withstand the mud and slosh taking over the roads. Snow and slush in upstate New York streets posed no problem. Snow was slippery but clean. One could crunch one's way through it with insulated boots. Mud on the other hand was a different proposition, something he remembered with disgust and hadn't come prepared for. It would form a cake on his soles; he'd have to clean it off; it could ruin his patent leathers. He hadn't come prepared for this.

1 7

The Volkswagen turned onto a rain-soaked narrow road, moved slowly, sinking with a thud into puddles and potholes, and finally came to a well-earned rest before a house.

"Come meet my family," Yardbrough said. Hunter looked outside, puzzled, longing to stretch his legs, wary of the mud. The Rastafarian reminded him – in a surprising display of courtly English – that he would be trapped in the back seat if Hunter didn't get out. Yardbrough was smiling as if there was something here of importance he wanted Hunter to see.

They all made a dash for the patio of the house, skipping over puddles of water. The door was opened by screaming children. Hunter spent some time wiping his feet before entering.

It was a small living room, crowded with chairs, cushions, a television set with its rabbit ears askew; and children, a rabbit's pen of children, shouting and jumping amidst greetings and head-patting. Hunter stared back at each child's wondering face. When asked by two snotty noses who he was, he grimaced and said nothing.

A woman came out of a bedroom. She extended a limp hand to Hunter when she was introduced. Her name was Aisha. She had calm round eyes and high cheekbones; her hair was in plaits; she wore an African-style dress right down to her ankles; there was a child on her hip and Hunter made the quick assumption that these squawking children were all hers.

Yardbrough, meanwhile, made himself at home; sitting in an armchair, letting the children clamber over him, laughing, playfully spanking a child; framing a statement, Hunter soon realized: *this is my family, the defenseless and oppressed.*

But what did that statement mean? Was he the father of these children? Had he adopted them? And the woman, her breasts drooping under that dress – had she really nursed and raised each one of these children?

Perhaps Yardbrough would explain later.

There was a call to the dinner table. Evidently Yardbrough had not completely forsaken him. A dining table had been set; steaming food and cutlery awaited him in the next room. The woman with the baby on her hip now invited him forward. He felt embarrassed and wary, but he had been too long the unhappy visitor. A show of enthusiasm, though difficult, was called for at precisely at this moment.

Hunter ate. The rice and the stew steamed up in his face. He ate because his stomach had never before felt so violently empty; he ate because he felt the weight of the woman's eyes on his shoulders, her judgment of him still pending; he noticed that Yardbrough – relaxed, *his elbows on the table* – was attacking his plate with something resembling his ideological passion. Bikesman the Rastafarian had said he would eat later; he was in the adjoining room noisily demonstrating his special way with children.

When it was all over Hunter turned to the woman and nodded and smiled, though secretly he would have done anything at that moment just to be served a jelly doughnut or a quart of Butter Pecan ice cream.

18

It rained again the next day, and gave no sign of ever stopping. Yardbrough had promised to come by (he spoke with an urgency that suggested there were indeed matters of a private nature he wished to discuss with Hunter) but as the hours slipped by and the roof gutters overflowed in that dreary dysfunctional way Hunter was flooded with disappointment and anger.

He tried to read; he fell asleep with the book on his chest; he woke up when he thought he heard the beating of the Volkswagen driving away.

He called the airline office and packed his bags.

Bikesman the Rastafarian took him to the airport. He said something about Yardbrough's "tight schedule" that day, but offered little else. Not even a farewell message. Instead, he sang his redemption songs, lapsing into meditative silence, only to burst suddenly into a bright sure laughter with the same observation each time: "Yes, only one way to the pearly gates."

Hunter was the epitome of forbearance and restraint.

As he waited for his flight call he felt strangely depressed, weighted down by anxieties. His body itched unaccountably. He wondered if his clothes carried the odor of the Rastafarian's marijuana, which might arouse suspicion and create unwanted difficulties at the U.S. Port of Entry.

As he stepped out under blue skies and hurried to the steps of the plane, the weight around his shoulders seem to lift or fall away: the masses, my family, "the ground of the spirit", "the pearly gates" – all the vines and garlands of redemption fell away, leaving him with a sensation of floating, light and free again.

The stewardess at the door gave him the most glamorous smile he'd ever felt on his face. Later she approached him wearing a pretty apron, the same smile, and offering a choice of drinks, meals. He discovered he liked being served; he liked being taken care of by a stewardess. He had a row of empty seats to himself.

He slipped into reverie, then sleep as through a gateway; then a dream.

He'd had a conversation one morning with the man who lived in the apartment above. They were scraping snow off the windshields of their cars. The man was doing his with a violent movement of his arm, his breath expelled in steamy puffs, so that to Hunter he looked for a moment like a hardbitten cowboy of the West having a difficult time saddling up his mount.

How're you doing? the man asked. *How was your weekend?* Did he have a girlfriend to keep him warm these cold nights? Had he heard about mail-order brides, young women he could order like from a Sears Roebuck catalogue? Fine young women, prime cut; quiet, not bossy; from Mexico or the Philippines.

Hunter laughed; the man offered to slip a telephone number under his door.

These interfering Americans! With their stupid interfering jokes. Knocking on your door, offering to fix the plumbing in your house of deepest needs!

Now as the aircraft droned across clear skies taking him home, Hunter saw in his dream someone waiting for him on his doorstep. His mail-order bride from the Philippines! She was wearing a long shiny robe, with a slit revealing smooth thighs, and a wide gleaming smile like that of the stewardess. The airline tags dangled on the handle of her suitcase. She chipped toward him and bowed.

They smiled at each other, happy, satisfied. He opened the door of his apartment and showed her in. She lifted his fingers, put them in her mouth, and said something in her Philippine tongue. She threw her arms around his neck; she slithered to her knees and fumbled with his trousers belt, while Hunter stood there, legs apart, master of the situation.

Fall was a time of renewals like September back on the islands when the school year began again. It was Hunter's first season in New York and he embraced it as a lover his mistress.

He'd learnt new habits, rituals, new words for life-enhancing objects; he bought new clothes. It helped him to discard the past, the monotony of sea and sand, days of sticky heat and perspiration.

He went for short afternoon drives and he marveled at the flourish of autumn, at the trees bright and full of red and yellow leaves, effulgent before stripping themselves. Each morning his skin tingled at the first slap of cold air on his face; he felt a surge of energy as if the cold season was challenging his sunsoaked bones to show that he could take it, daring him to belong.

He stepped easily into work routines, departmental paper work, registration, fresh student faces, blue denim and heavy pink sweaters, foam cups of steaming coffee, the occasional puzzled or disdainful stare (at first they thought he was from Haiti, or some French *territory*; they were surprised he'd never been to Paris). Winter plunged him into its deep end, tested his resolve to adapt and survive. And then came Spring.

It wasn't difficult, therefore, to return from Yardbrough's island, wait for the seasons to turn and filter out of his memory the misery of those days.

Classes were already in session. He was climbing the stairs to his freshman class when he heard laughter from inside the room, then a voice speaking in singsong high-pitched accent. He froze and listened. Was it one of his students? Imitating his professor? Surely, he didn't speak like that? After all these years, after carefully cultivating a manner of speaking, surely he didn't sound like that! Like a man from a day-o-banana island!

20

One day on the elevator going down, he met Prof. Ros Miscuri. She encircled him with a broad smile and told him she had spent part of her summer in Brazil. Had Hunter heard about the hurricane bearing down on the islands? She was concerned, she said, about the banana crops, and those fragile, compact dwellings. How well would they withstand the winds?

Ros Miscuri had drawn closer to him ever since a remark made by one of his colleagues at a Departmental meeting which (only after he'd left the room) struck Hunter as, perhaps, racially offensive. She was now friendly in a fidgety garrulous way that was meant to distance her from others who for all their surface charm reveal their true selves in gratuitous slips of bigotry.

Now she invited him home to a dinner of huge lobsters. "My mother gave me these huge lobsters, I don't think I can eat them all by myself." She spoke the word "huge" in a slightly theatrical way, opening her eyes wide as if she were about to be swallowed, or wanted to be swallowed, by something equally overwhelming. Hunter was put off by her eyes. He made an excuse and declined the invitation.

He followed the progress of the hurricane on the television set. He read about its threat to the Florida coastline in *The Times*. One column described the devastation one island had suffered. A Permanent Secretary in one of the Government Ministries, a Mr. Christopher Yardbrough, was quoted as saying that "despite considerable damage to the infrastructure, the island will rise again like a phoenix from the ashes".

Hunter read the article over and over; he saw the island spinning through a meteor shower of galvanized sheets and tree limbs; with his planetary eye he saw Yardbrough sitting in his new office, alone, his hands to his ears, blocking out the sounds from the adjoining room where his father was huffing and puffing on top of the maid. He saw Yardbrough's lips move as he rocked back and forth in horror, formulating cold, unchallengeable words of sorrow and retribution.

21

Spring '85. A letter arrived from his mother in England. Things were not going too well. His father's health was a problem; he had

145

set out to watch a Test match at that famous cricket ground, Old Trafford; he'd got caught in a downpour, didn't have a hat, got soaked through and through; now he was doing poorly.

There was an urgent need for Hunter's help with something else. His father had been invited back home to receive a national award, but he was "in no condition to travel", his mother wrote. Would Hunter please make arrangements to fly to the island and receive the award in his place?

This raised welts of anxiety. He'd have to interrupt his teaching schedule, take a short leave of absence. It posed no real problem, but at the back of Hunter's mind was the tiny fear it might be read as a faltering in his steady performance. The Dept. Chair had hinted politely at the absolute need to publish. Hunter had assured him he had something in the pipeline. But that was over a year ago. In his absence they might begin to wonder about him.

In any event he made travel arrangements and flew home.

He was expected to stay at the house of a spinster aunt. At the airport a taxi driver grabbed his bag and told him he'd been asked by his aunt to take him there.

As they drove off the man startled Hunter. He said he'd been following his progress overseas. News about his "achievements" had somehow found their way into the local press, in a column captioned *Getting Ahead*.

"You know, I drove your father, Magistrate Valcin, to the airport the day he left for England," the man said.

"Oh, you did?"

"Will never forget that day. I ask him for his parting thoughts on the island. To this day I remember his words: *A plague on both your houses!* And would you believe, my daughter came home from school one day, and was reciting poetry, and she recite the same words, *A plague on both your houses*! I ask her what she was reading… *Romeo and Juliet*! How you like that? …And now, look, I driving the Magistrate's son on his first visit back home. Your first, right…? I tell you, this world is a *shrinking, shrinking* place…"

The shrinking world. Shakespeare from the mouths of magistrates (did his father really utter those words?) and, now, from the daughters of taxi drivers. Fathers leaving, sons returning. The world a babel of languages and subversive dialects. The folding of old tents, the spinning of new webs. So little space left for privacy, for reason and equanimity, if one chose not to *join* anything.

Hunter stared balefully at the island of his childhood flashing by outside his window.

The taxi driver drove him in a brand new Japanese car along the new roadway, named after the Prime Minister, then through the town center which Hunter remembered for its market square political rallies, the odor of fish from the vendors' boats, firefighters lounging outside the fire house, strollers and limers, a canal that overflowed during rainstorms.

He gasped and pointed at a strange new sign, *The Golden Dragon...Chinese Takeout* (a letter had dropped off one of the words). But there were no native Chinese on his island. "We have Chinese here... and Haitians and Africans," the taxi driver explained. *What are they doing here?* Hunter asked. "This island is like a transit point for America... People coming here, waiting their chance... this place is one big waiting area, *oui*."

The taxi driver pointed with awakened pride to new buildings, to traffic lights and parking meters: "At night this place is a ghost town. Everybody gone home to *the suburbs*."

As they pulled up outside his aunt's place – the windows were shut tight, no one seemed at home! – the taxi driver said, "By the way, you bring any speeches?" *Any what*? "Speeches. I like collecting speeches?" The taxi driver was removing his bags. "I have Martin Luther King's speech, *I have a Dream*; and Kennedy's speech, and Winston Churchill, *We shall fight them on the beaches.*"

The front door opened; his Aunt came rushing out, her hair in curlers, her hand clutching the collars of a dressing gown. Hunter was relieved to see her. He paid the taxi driver in American dollars. The man said something to his Aunt in the island patois then he got in his taxi and drove away.

22

Hunter's spinster aunt was a busybody in cultural affairs. Her home was furnished with cultural artifacts to look like a salon for local and visiting artists. Over the years she had developed folkloric expertise, and so she was sent abroad as the island's cultural representative. She was often described in the Women's page of the local press as "dynamic" and "ebullient".

For his visit she had arranged everything: visits to the local newspaper, to his alma mater, to see an uncle in a remote village who wanted to speak to him on an important matter. *An important matter?* Uncle Rommele was thinking of writing his memoirs and wanted Hunter's assistance "in the writing department". And then, of course, the award ceremony. Hunter protested he didn't feel like seeing anyone.

"And you must see Teacher Fostin, your father's dear friend, the Latin teacher," she said. "He had a stroke recently. He always asks about you."

As a compromise – and because he couldn't, as his Aunt said, *stay in the house all day* – Hunter agreed to visit the old Latin teacher.

He put on his jacket with the elbow patch out of sheer habit and he left the house. The moment he stepped out on the streets he felt himself under scrutiny; he thought of turning back, changing to something that would make him blend in – short sleeves and short pants. To be chastised that way, to be sent back home by prurient eyes *to change* seemed ridiculous. He muttered the word *ridiculous* and pressed on.

His Aunt had offered to drive him to Teacher Fostin's place on Baden-Powell Hill but he'd brushed off the idea. He assured her he'd find his way there. She admired his independent will; besides he'd probably meet more people on the road on his own. "You could catch a transport at the market square," she said.

In the town center, near the bridge where years back he took the school bus to the island's college on the Morne, his luck held. A shiny new Japanese mini-van cruising for passengers approached. He signaled; it stopped; he got in the front seat. The engine whined, flawless and new.

They started off, then stopped. Two young women boarded;

they teased the driver for threatening to leave them; they laughed in a coarse suggestive way. One of them wanted to sit up front beside Hunter; he would be cramped. "Mek yourself small," the driver said. She got in, her bracelets jangling, her face ashy with makeup; and immediately she started eating from a box of Kentucky Fried Chicken.

Hunter felt stirrings of nausea. Nothing in the world could be as obnoxious as sitting next to people squirting ketchup on fried food, and tearing at it with greasy hands; people who couldn't wait to get home to a dinner table, who must eat, under his nose.

He threw a glance of helpless appeal at the driver: *This is your transport. Do we have to put up with this?*

The woman sensed his discomfort, his disapproval. To show she had more right to the taxi than Hunter, who looked foreign, she shouted to the driver "*So what's happening, Guinness?*"

Guinness! He wore the nickname with a drinker's pride: the dark hue of his skin was the same as the color of the imported ale. He was a beefy smooth-skinned fellow, fond of fishnet singlets and gold. There were rings on his fingers, a bracelet on his wrist, a chain around his neck – all gleaming gold. Two of his teeth were capped with gold. His mini-van, a trireme on chrome wheels, plied the streets in search of gold.

And Hunter, wedged between the skipper and a finger-licking mate, not sufficiently insulated by his own generous splash of cologne that morning, could only hold his breath and pray for deliverance.

And Hunter moaned: *this is the curse of my life*, this struggle to escape from small places, enclosures that trap the body; flesh pressed on flesh, the spirit suffocating; the heat, the odours – and now the pounding, for Guinness, satisfied with the cargo aboard his craft, was all set to sail up the Morne, and had turned up the volume of his tape deck. Reggae music filled his sails with powerful winds, with drums and wailing songs: the promise of true freedom some good day.

23

Aliter vitium vivitque tegendo.

His father and the Latin teacher were often spoken of as men who had rendered distinguished service to the island. When Hunter saw him again, he was shocked at how terribly Teacher Fostin had declined; he'd shrunk to a mere totem of his former eminence. This was not the same man who silenced his class-rooms by shouting *Order...! Order!*; who sat with his father discussing letters he would send to the local press (he wrote under the pen name Juvenal).

It was frightening to think that this was the fate awaiting island men of distinction: the trembling hand gripping the knob of a walking cane, the bony crossed legs, the cadaverous silence behind which the mind lay unused, no longer appreciated.

Teacher Fostin sat in an old morris chair staring blankly through an open door at a back garden of tomato plants and grapefruit trees and papaw trees; his jaws moved agitatedly as if chewing bubble gum. He seemed to recognize Hunter and he nodded.

His wife did all the talking. She was a neat full-breasted woman, her round face marked with pimples and age spots. She had devoted her life to Teacher Fostin; they were childless; now, as ever uncomplaining, she attended to his needs.

She offered Hunter a glass of lemonade and biscuits. She asked about his father. "Teacher Fostin is not himself these days," she said. She explained he had suffered a mild stroke recently. He was hospitalized for a week, but he was all right now.

She too had followed Hunter's progress in the news-papers (apparently his Aunt had been diligently posting news of his achievements everywhere). Hunter made self-deprecating noises and steered the conversation back to the teacher. A painful story emerged that was to stop Hunter's heart, then send it into palpitations of the oldest fear.

Sitting right there in his morris chair, Teacher Fostin had witnessed late one afternoon to a horrible incident; it had apparently brought on the stroke; he hadn't been quite the same since.

"Happened right out there, near that fence... two fellows took this girl, one of Mrs. Fevrier's daughters, the eldest one... threatened to kill her if she screamed... did this terrible thing to the poor child... Teacher Fostin saw the whole thing from right in here..."

She spoke in a horrified trailing whisper, her brow knitted, her hands smoothing the front of her dress.

Hunter looked out the back door; there were over-ripe papaws on the tree, with holes – you could see the moist black seeds – where birds had pecked and feasted. He looked at Teacher Fostin's wrinkly face, at his jaws working up and down. What shock waves, what hammer blows to the glass encasing his mind!

"Yes, he saw the whole thing... Mrs. Fevrier is living in Barbados now, and the two fellows were given long jail sentences...Teacher Fostin didn't have to testify or anything..."

Hunter folded his arms and tried not to appear hungry for detail. He'd been upended by the disclosure that the old Latin teacher had watched this terrible incident. And then the stroke that rippled through his body – *what on earth had happened here?*

24

Carmina non prius audita...virginibus puerisque canto.

Somewhere inside the house a radio or a phonograph player was broadcasting a church choir's rendition of *The King of Love, My Shepherd Is.* A tectonic shift in the ground of memory and Hunter felt himself back in his father's house, swaddled in those Sunday silences, the crackle and static of BBC World Service; the sea below placid, the light making patterns through the jalousied slats.

Teacher Fostin sat in stony silence; his wife sat with her hands in her lap. Hunter felt uncomfortable, unhappy; he was sitting near the finest classical scholar the island had ever known and he was dumbstruck. Conversation had lapsed. Hunter thought of getting up to go, but he was a coiled spring wound tight with curiosity.

Teacher Fostin's wife got up and signaled to Hunter to follow. In the kitchen, out of earshot, she gripped him by the arm, looked up in his face almost in fear.

151

"I don't understand… day after day he just sits there like that… I don't understand." She gathered herself and smoothed the front of her dress. "And sometimes tears start running from his eyes…*just like that*! When I ask him, *Are you all right, Teacher Fostin?*… he'd shout at me… his face *tight, tight* and his body like it fighting… holding back something… and water streaming from his eye. I've never known Teacher Fostin to behave like this… all these years, never seen this happen."

Hunter listened. It seemed he was expected to offer some explanation, not just words of comfort; after all he was an island scholar; he'd studied abroad. His heart was heavy with consternation. What could he say to her? What could he do for Teacher Fostin?

Then from the living room Teacher Fostin spoke his first words that day: "Gwyneth!" he said, in a raspy trembling voice. "Yes, dear," she answered, hurrying back to his side. Hunter felt embarrassed and followed her in fearful creaking shoes.

She left the room; she came back with sheets of paper. "He wants you to read this," she said. "It's the transcript of the court proceedings."

Somehow they'd managed to get a copy of the trial proceedings, in particular the testimony of the victim. Teacher Fostin had insisted, despite his wife's reluctance, that she do everything in her power to secure these papers.

"Whenever the mood takes him he asks me to read to him," she said.

Quietly, not sure what all this meant, Hunter started reading.

The prosecutor had asked the girl to explain what happened. The girl began her story. She had to pause frequently to allow the Judge to take notes. Often, too, her voice would falter or trail off in a whisper; the Judge admonished her time and time again to speak up.

The embarrassment, the pain, the Judge's insistence that she take her time – *I know you've been through a terrible ordeal* – tell the court exactly what took place; her fear of the court's displeasure, her mother's tight lips, the Police Inspector's stern cautions. Hunter felt the tremors of her distress on the page.

The Latin teacher suddenly hit the floor with his walking stick.

It sounded like a courtroom gavel. Hunter looked up. *What did he want?*

"He wants you to read it aloud," his wife said. *Aloud?* "Yes, he wants to hear you read it."

Hunter tried to shift the lump in his throat. His heart was swelling with fierce pain. He too wanted to know what really happened, but like the girl he was frightened by the old Latin teacher's obsessive silence. He thought of the old school desk and Teacher Fostin hovering over your shoulders with his wild cane and his bad breath. He cleared his throat and read.

Did you scream for help? Of course she screamed, with her tears and her heart, the bush scratching her face, lifting her dress, *I begged them to stop*, the Latin teacher striking the floor with his walking cane; and Hunter looked up at his wife, her head lowered, then he pulled down her panties, the walking cane again, marking time, for something was about to bare itself, *then he push himself inside me from behind*, again and again on the floor; and Hunter looked up at his wife's face, saw a large solitary tear leave her eye, roll down the side of her nose to her trembling lips; and Hunter's face asked, *should I continue? should I stop?* asking the girl to take her time, speak clearly, explain that thing too shamed to explain itself; his wife weeping freely now, for the mystery that had bedeviled the magistrate, the old Latin teacher, was left no choice but to disrobe itself; and Hunter took a deep breath, his heart swollen to breaking point, reading on

REMEMBER
WHO YOU ARE

"But who am I, and why should I remember, Uncle?" I asked, the day after he returned from his vacation overseas. He had gone to London to visit his sister; he had gone to New York to visit another sister.

He was sitting in his easy chair facing the door, looking sad and weary. I had come running down the back steps eager to hear of the wonderful time he must have had. His front door was open and he had moved the chair so that he could see right down the yard to the gate and the street.

I was surprised to catch him that way, slumped and looking out, his chin sunk in his chest. I thought at first he had simply dozed off. If he'd just returned from a trip overseas, why did he look so beaten and exhausted?

"Hi, Uncle. I've brought your dinner."

His chin remained sunk in his chest, his stomach heaving gently. I was afraid to wake him up.

"Uncle!"

He lifted his head, opened his eyes and looked at me for a long while. Oh, those eyes! They were weary too. Weary and sad. What had they seen out there?

"I've brought your dinner," I repeated, climbing the rickety steps slowly. The dish covered with my mother's cloth was warm in the palm of my hands. "How was London? How your sisters?"

His face brightened as if he'd just remembered how to smile; and then the smile faded, as if the memory that had brought it to his cheeks abruptly deserted him. And I thought: *Something terrible happened. He looks as if he's dying.*

His eyes were looking past me. They were the eyes of a dying man, holding on to the light but preparing for places of darkness.

I stepped over his legs and started setting his little dining table,

157

still waiting for an answer. There was a bright travel folder on the table with his passport, a canceled airline ticket, stubs for baggage collection. I cleared them away. In the middle of the room his suitcase and his travel bags – the destination tags still attached, the bags bulging with stuffed items.

What had happened?

I looked at him again. His skin, rarely exposed, so mottled and flabby. He wore a singlet; there were socks on his feet; his travel trousers still had that neat, new look. Poor Uncle! Even the energy to unpack had deserted him. He had come home, dropped everything on the floor, had fallen in that chair, in that position facing the street, and he had not moved since.

"So Uncle, how was your trip? You lose your tongue over there?" I said, prodding him playfully.

His words, in a voice hoarse and faraway, broke through the membrane of my innocence:

"All is vanity and vexations of the spirit," he said. "Always remember who you are."

"Say hello to Juliette…" Mrs. Pidducks was speaking to her four-year old son. We were at the dinner table, the Pidducks family and I, getting to know each other over the fussy use of cutlery.

"Jeremy, this is Juliette," Mrs. Pidducks said in a prodding singsong manner. "She comes from an island in the West Indies and she'll be looking after you when Mom and Dad are busy, do you understand?"

Jeremy nodded. He looked at me with a sour face; then he looked away. "Say Hello to Juliette." Jeremy muttered hello. I didn't think he liked being looked after by just anyone. I didn't think he liked being told what to do.

So I was Juliette from the West Indies. Here in Connecticut I would look after four-year-old Jeremy.

Mr. Pidducks meanwhile was watching all this as if across miles and miles of tablecloth. His professorial manner, the bare movement of his jaws which was his chewing habit – you felt as if a large part of him lay hidden and unknown and that we were fortunate to be graced by his presence at the dinner table.

Later that same evening, as Mrs. Pidducks cleared the dishes, he leaned forward on his elbows and asked: *Which island did you say you're from? Have you lived there all your life?* Searching questions, or just harmless dinner conversation questions? I wasn't sure. I found myself retreating from his long distance eyes.

It seems people here do this all the time: ask about each other as if everyone carried around stories of their lives, in snapshots which they'd whip out to show.

Well, my life was like film rolled tight inside a camera, to be exposed only in dark rooms. My life was not for disclosure at their dinner table; I didn't want them to know about my mother and about Uncle; I didn't care to bring the island and its people right into their splendid dining room with its fine cutlery and the chandelier. I was here and that was enough.

Besides I didn't know how to explain myself to strangers. How do you begin? How could they understand? I was learning, too, not to trust anyone, not family, not strangers, nor friends. With my hands reaching back to grip the bedposts, I remembered who I was.

I would set the table for Uncle and feel that we were family, even though he lived alone in a house behind ours. He'd been separated from his wife, "a wicked woman", my mother called her; she'd left him and was living on another island.

For as long as I could remember I cooked dinner for him and kept it warm in the stove. I would wait until I heard him pushing his motorcycle down the yard; I'd call out to him and tell him dinner was on the way. "Thank you, my sweet," he shouted back. I used to think he stopped staying out late at nights because he didn't want to keep me waiting up.

It was an act of the purest love, this preparation, this waiting for Uncle to come home.

Imagine the ferment in my heart that day I found him sitting at the front door as if waiting for the hearse man in black to pull up at our gate. Something had gone wrong in his life. I started thinking something would go wrong in mine.

As he ate slowly that day I began unpacking his bags. "Don't worry, child, I can do that later." I was twenty, and he still called me *child*! "By the way I brought a little something for you. It's at

159

the bottom of the suitcase." He reached for his napkin and was about to get up. I felt overcome with embarrassment. I urged him to finish his dinner; we would look into the suitcase later; I hurried outside, leaving him alone.

When I came back for the dishes he had returned to his chair, solemn and tired as ever. The gift he had brought me was on his lap but I was too pained to open it. I wanted to know what had happened to him overseas.

Growing up, that sweet little child, Juliette, would sit beside him often on his front steps listening to stories: ghost stories, full moon stories, *be a good girl* stories. I perched now on the arm of the chair and put my arm around his shoulders and I waited.

"I'm alright, you know," he said, his jaws working up and down. "Don't worry 'bout me. You're a sweet lovely child. But life out there not kind, let me tell you. People have hearts like green guava, hard and bitter." He took my hands and squeezed them, his dry fingers trembling with kindness and worry. "Always remember who you are."

"Since when you so full of wisdom," I said, trying to nudge him into a lighthearted mood. He sighed.

As it turned out, the story of what happened out there was told to my mother who later relayed it in gossipy bits to me. This I could not understand: his choosing to tell my mother *the story*, while I was left with mere words of wisdom.

Had I grown too old for stories on his knee? Was he trying to spare me boring details? Had something happened that was too distressing for even a twenty-year-old to understand?

I think it was all of that and none of that. I think he was trying to protect me. His wish was to arm me with the truth as clear as the blue rings in his eyes. We were bonded by a homegrown love, my mother, Uncle and Juliette. More   important than the story, was its lesson. He hoped I would take that with me, like a ring slipped on my finger, wherever I went in this world. *Remember who you are.*

Uncle was a proud self-made man; happy with his job, happy with his life on the island. This vacation abroad was his first trip outside the island; it celebrated his retirement after years of service at the Government printery.

He had written his sisters explaining his intentions: a trip to New York to see one of them, and then to London, England to visit the other. I had never known his sisters but in the years before his retirement he started talking about them with a new pride and excitement.

They'd kept in touch with him. He would send them newspapers, copies bought and wrapped up unopened, then posted off. My mother was impressed with his devotion to his sisters. She had no such devotion to her family.

I used to think: how wonderful this island life: you chose someone or something, at home and abroad, you poured all your energy, all your trust into filling up their lives. You lived connected to the outside world by a generosity of feeling – sending newspapers, receiving Christmas cards. My mother and me, Uncle and his sisters, the joy and fulfillment of living for each other. This sweet island life.

We were brought into this world, my mother used to say, to give of ourselves. Sometimes we chose badly the object of our gifts; sometimes we received nothing in return. But the giving – not the stingy holding back, the rationing of ourselves – *the giving* was what counted. Back then whatever my mother said I embraced as gospel truth.

One evening sensing my reluctance to bare my past, mistaking it for awkwardness or shyness, Mrs. Pidducks, in between urging Jeremy to eat, steered the conversation toward blue waters and white beaches and sunshine all year around – "I can't imagine why anyone would want to leave" – and hurricanes which sometimes passed through the islands and popped up on their television set.

I felt more relaxed and offered a few postcard descriptions.

I felt Mr. Pidducks' eyes watching me, adjusting the focus of his attention now that I'd begun to open myself a little; clearly interested in what I had to say. At the time I thought he was still trying to decide whether I would cause problems, whether having me in their home as an *au pair* was the right decision. When I couldn't take any more of this scrutiny I looked him straight back in the face – Mrs. Pidducks was at that moment distracted with Jeremy – and my eyes asked, *What is it you want from me?*

He was overcome by a fit of coughing, as if something had suddenly stuck in his throat. He lowered his head and reached for a napkin.

Rightaway I felt I knew him. I had seen him somewhere before.

People are all the same under the skin. And men, my mother would whisper harshly, even though she has only traveled to neighboring islands, are definitely the same all over the world. Here among these good people of Connecticut you have to listen closely, watch closely, to understand what they really mean. At some point you stumble upon their skeletons; a tremor runs through your body; you know you've touched the seabed of their souls.

I'd seen Mr. Pidducks before, only then he was Mr. Papo, and he was with my mother in my mother's bedroom, thinking they wouldn't be disturbed. I had seen him later at our church where I played the piano and he led the choral group. I had looked him in the eye and, as through a moist window, I had seen into the depths of his soul.

I was surprised and frightened at the confidence with which I did this, and for a while I would deliberately avoid looking people in the face, fearing what their eyes might show me.

That evening, as Mr. Pidducks and I declined to have coffee, as we sat at the end of the meal, minutes before the scraping back of chairs, and the flight to where we all preferred to be, in separate rooms, in that moment Mrs. Pidducks turned to Jeremy:

"And did you enjoy dinner?" she asked, coaxing him to fill the silence with a child's innocence. "Oh, just look at the mess you made… you'll have to learn to manage your spoon better than that…" Carrying on that way while Mr. Pidducks, his face impassive, looked at his son as if studying this perplexing result of his and her sexual calculus; for they were both in their thirties, Mrs. Pidducks had said, and had delayed having children *until they had established their careers.*

And while she continued urging Jeremy to respond for all our sake, Mr. Pidducks toyed with his professorial beard, sensing some sort of victory, for already the child looked more like him, a brooding child, weary of this world; much more like him, not like his mother.

162

I smiled a polite reassuring smile. Juliette of the West Indies, caregiver, pure goodness in her soul, would soon get to work looking after Jeremy of Connecticut, child of their separate careers and passions.

I threw one passing glance at Mr. Pidducks which he caught and returned: telling me he was aware I had been down to the seabed of his soul; he had felt the jarring contact; he'd made a mental note of it; he'd be in touch.

Like Uncle, my leaving the island to travel was a kind of reward for services faithfully rendered. At least this is how Mr. Papo explained it to my mother.

"She has given sterling service to the Church. She is a fine example of selfless dedication. I think she should be rewarded with a vacation."

Mr. Papo was lord and master of our church. He rehearsed the church choir; he delivered the sermon. A mountain of a man, with a booming pulpit voice, his broad shoulders bulged under his spiritual garments with the vanity of a road laborer. His words came crashing into your heart and left debris of biblical truth. He'd pause and we'd say *Amen* and he'd lift a large white handkerchief to his brow as if asking God forgiveness for sweating like a pig.

So here he was putting his arm around my shoulders, his fingers squeezing with a strange searching pressure, and he was saying, "How would you like to take a vacation? A trip to the States?"

I didn't answer rightaway. His hands were now rubbing my back in a way that was meant to encourage me. It gave me strange feelings. I was praying they didn't show on my face. I waited to hear what my mother would say.

She made uncertain noises; she spoke of visa problems and places to stay; she didn't seem too eager to embrace the idea. Mr. Papo removed his hands from my shoulders.

I left the room on the pretext of checking the stove where dinner was in preparation, and for awhile there was silence in the house. The silence of conspiracy and lust. They were looking at each other; they were seeing in each other's eyes the nights and days ahead, of bedroom passions with me out of the way.

163

I bit my lip and held back an impulse to cry, *No, no, I'm not going anywhere!* Swelling inside me was the feeling that I was being cast out into the world; that this vacation was contrived to get me out of the way, for I was considered an obstacle to their secret passion.

And with that feeling came strange thoughts: *This is how you came into the world, Juliette: a man and a woman, their loins on fire, exchanging glances, wanting each other, not wanting you. This is how you came into being, a child of careless circumstance, sheltered and shielded for twenty years. Now they're sending you away because old carnal fires are raging. You were conceived in grimaces of passion, not in love.*

At that moment, alone in the kitchen, hearing those voices in the adjoining room, I felt the snip of the cord, and I came crying again into the world, astonished and angry and new.

All right: I would go, I would travel. After years of dedication and service I would take myself away from this house.

And so months after Uncle returned from his trip abroad, his heart bruised and broken forever, I departed.

On the plane droning through the sky toward cities of excitement, toward beefy-faced relatives waiting at airport terminals with smiles of welcome, I fell to thinking about Uncle. He had hugged me fiercely as he said farewell and he'd whispered in my ear his dying man's last words: *Always remember who you are.*

The story of what happened to him fell on my heart in scattered pieces. I put them together this way:

"They put me in a seat over the wings. I ask them *expressly* not to put me in a seat over the wings." He'd buckled in his seat belts anyway, then removed the Texas cowboy hat he'd decided to wear (the sister in New York had sent it for him: he liked wearing it during Carnival week and at the cricket ground during a Test match).

"At first everything was fine; they were happy to see me; they asking for everybody and her auntie back home." Within days he began to feel like a prisoner.

In London if he felt like walking about the streets – "You know, just taking fresh air" – he was told angrily to stay inside. "She took me once to see Buckingham Palace and the guards. Otherwise I was locked up inside this stuffy little room, and she gone to work." As if ashamed to show her old island relative to the people of London city!

He fled to New York, bitter but hopeful. There his sister was even uglier in her fears. He had mentioned to her his old age problems: his hypertension, his bladder problems. Her reaction was astounding. "I hope you didn't come up here to die on my hands," she declared. It threw him into a sad rage.

To die on her hands! He would rather return and die on his island. He would rather pass away quietly and alone in his house on his island! The thought of dying was never on his mind when he'd left. What did she mean? Why this sudden fear he would die on her hands?

He came home feeling half the man he was. I believe he had begun to die the moment he opened his front door, dropped his bags, and lowered his travel-worn body into the chair.

At the airport Mr. Papo's relatives were waiting for me. They had been told to expect this young lady, Juliette. For two weeks they were to show her around, make her feel happy.

Poor Uncle!

I went in search of a restroom; the fluorescents were bright, the mirrors large. I studied my face in the mirror. For the first time in my life I applied lipstick. I combed my hair back tight, baring my forehead. I slipped on sunglasses and studied my face again, *What a pretty child, Juliette.* I was all set to step outside to Mr. Papo's relatives but my legs, spongy and nerveless, refused to walk. I sat down near my bags and waited.

Poor Uncle!

I heard someone paging me on the public address system, summoning me to a telephone at the courtesy desk, my name echoing throughout the building, *Juliette, we looking everywhere for you, child, looking for you all this time.*

More than an hour passed and I imagined Mr. Papo's relatives giving up, *she must have missed the flight,* going home.

I stepped outside the building in quick, stiff strides.

No one came up to me, no one waved, *Over here!* The city of indifferent noise, shiny car tops, rushing hearts, criss-crossing dreams ignored me. The air was cold. I felt I had to keep moving,

165

otherwise panic would claim me, my legs would weaken, I would collapse. I fled back inside the building and walked the carpeted floors until my heart ran dry of courage.

Then I noticed Yomarys. She was sitting in the airport lounge, chubby faced, her legs crossed; blue jeans, straggly hair hanging down her shoulders; not traveling; in fact, I never found out know what she was doing at the airport that day.

It would be tempting now to believe the Good Lord had sent her to my rescue.

In struggling to be brave, to hold myself from falling apart, I had not *looked* at anyone as closely as I did then. I noticed the book in her lap, her curved shoulders, her tiny granny-style glasses.

She looked up and caught me staring.

"You seemed completely lost, like you were running away from home and didn't know where to turn next," Yomarys told me later. "I smiled at you, wanting to help, but you looked away."

She looked out of place in the airport, somehow shutting out the noise, somehow transforming the lounge into her private reading room. I wanted to be near her, to be like her, secure, self-absorbed and alone.

"Excuse me," I said. "Could you tell me if there's a YWCA near this airport."

Yomarys laughed as she recalled: "*A YWCA*? What is she talking about? All I saw was your face about to burst into tears and I thought, *Oh my God, she needs help!*"

I was trying not to appear helpless: brave Juliette, crumbling inside, getting ready to jump for her life, no parachute, grasping at pieces of the sky.

I heard Yomarys say, "Listen, you can come with me, stay at my place for a while if you like."

She said it gently, her voice bracing to catch me as I fell. I vowed to ask her one day: were you waiting too for a flight? were you waiting for an angel to fall? Or was it just the right place and the right moment to read a book?

Four years old, Jeremy Pidducks was being raised to enter a future of computer technology. He was born prematurely, Mr. Pidducks said, and he suffered from asthmatic complaints. Jeremy was at that moment tapping the keys and firing at a zigzagging line of menacing objects on the screen. It was not his destiny to be a football star, Mr. Pidducks explained, tousling his hair; but he would be the man at the controls bringing order into a football-loving world.

It was shortly after ten in the morning. Mrs. Pidducks was away teaching math in a high school classroom. Mr. Pidducks, a college professor, wasn't going out until later that afternoon. "I'll be in my study in case you need me," he said. I sat flipping through a magazine, ready to respond to Jeremy's need for distraction, wondering if I'd ever have reason to need Mr. Pidducks.

Sometimes Jeremy would knock on the door or rattle the doorknob of his father's study. Mr. Pidducks would emerge, his orange moustache bristling with annoyance; he'd look at me, then speak to Jeremy in a slow precise English, without a trace of emotion. Then he'd look at me again, saying in effect: *you ought to be doing a better job of keeping Jeremy amused.*

"Jeremy, your daddy doesn't like you playing near that door," I would say.

"Jeremy, do you want me to read you a story about Fozzy Bear?"

Outside the trees were shedding leaves; I made a mental note to buy lotions for my dry skin.

Whenever Mr. Pidducks was about to leave he would talk to Jeremy with a clear affection, answering questions as he fixed his scarf. It amazed me at first, these father-son exchanges, Mr. Pidducks speaking as if Jeremy was mature enough to understand every word. "No, Daddy has to leave now otherwise his students will begin to wonder what has happened to him… No, there's not too much congestion on the roadway at this hour." Words spoken almost distractedly as to a stranger, with an eye on the watch strapped on his wrist; then stooping to receive Jeremy's hug, Jeremy's words of love for his father, his R's not yet conquered.

I'd take Jeremy to the window and pull back the blinds. He watched intently as the car backed out the driveway. I tried always to get him to wave to daddy; he'd stare outside at the wind bowling the leaves across the lawn; I sighed and put him down.

The days when he stayed home were not very many. Usually

167

a yellow school bus came to pick him up, to take him to a special school in the area. I was at the door at two o'clock when the bus brought him back.

Those hours alone, in between Mr. Pidducks leaving for college and Jeremy's return from his school, were my saddest hours.

I wandered around the basement trying to get used to living and sleeping under the earth. Through the basement window with its burglar bars I could see the driveway, the pipe to which Mr. Pidducks would hook up the green garden hose in summer – all of this startlingly at eye level. The boiler gave a click and the furnace roared. Everything was safe and warm and extraordinarily quiet. I would curl up in bed, overcome by farawayness, feeling the cold in my bones despite the boiler. And I would drift off to sleep.

I had these strange dreams: my mother, a giant hen, *clucking, clucking* as she searched for her twenty-year-old chick, Juliette: roaming the yards of her neighbors and her friends and asking over and over in the same desperate clucking tone, *where is my Juliette? where is my Juliette?*

It used to be safe and warm and quiet, too, in our island home, though there were morning noises (cocks crowing to each other) and night noises (grasshoppers in the weeds); and it was comforting to walk under the wings of that giant hen, knowing no harm would come to me; knowing that the feathers of those wings would protect me from the glare and the stare of dogs and dogfaced boys and dogmatic men.

Mummy loves her little girl.

I reveled in all that attention and love. I rubbed it like an ointment on any bruise, any hurt I suffered as a child. It salved my worries about our fatherless home. It rescued me from the embarrassments of menstruation. It answered all the questions of an adolescent who shuddered and wondered about nasty-minded boys and whispering snotty girls.

Sometimes I was awakened from these dreams by the telephone: Mrs. Pidducks calling to say she might be late, speaking fast, sounding harried, issuing reminders about Jeremy's needs.

As I waited for the doorbell and Jeremy's bus I would see my mother again. Not the giant protective hen of my dreams. My mother as a once attractive woman, with a dancer's sensuous body and a not too pretty face: the woman who brought me into this world, unplanned; the woman lured into lust by a nameless lover. Once her dancer's belly had flattened back into place, she swore it would never happen again; regretted bitterly the mistake; swore to love with all her guilty heart the child of that mistake.

Turning next to the church, my mother became evangelical about saving floundering souls, about saving weak bodies, lustfooled hearts. My weekends were filled with prayers and songs and many social functions to Jehovah.

Some afternoons Mrs. Pidducks returned in a state of disarray. She greeted Jeremy as if she'd been kidnapped for years and had been released just that minute. She scrambled around in near frenzy asking questions, scattering love. There were tears in her voice, nervousness in her fingers.

At such moments I felt relieved I was not Jeremy, or Jeremy's father, or any relation to Jeremy. I folded my arms and waited for the storm to pass.

If Jeremy was asleep when she came in Mrs. Pidducks went straight into the bedroom and closed the door. Sometimes I would hear sounds, a terrible muffled howling, coming from that room; I'd retreat quietly to the basement; I could not bear to hear these sounds.

On the island people cried that way only when someone close to them had died: a heart-wrenching bawl, followed by heaving silences, then another heart-wrenching bawl. But no one had died for Mrs. Pidducks, which made it all the more frightening to hear.

When she came out her hair looked brushed and fixed some-what back in place. Her face was drawn as if she had used it to wring herself dry of that mysterious grief; but she was back to her normal active self and I pretended I'd heard nothing.

Life went on.

One morning I overheard her on the telephone speaking in whispers she must have considered hushed, though her words carried all the way to my astonished ears. "She's doing fine… I'm impressed with her intelligence. I mean, we were hoping for

169

someone from the Midwest or another European... but it's turned out pretty good so far. She seems intelligent, at least bright enough to stimulate Jeremy."

Ah, child, always remember who you are.

"So how do you like your little den?" Mr. Pidducks asked, one hand in his pocket, the other gripping his pipe. He was watching me dry the dishes.

"It's alright," I said, like a good island girl, willing to respond to any question. Not wanting to push the conversation too fast, beyond the point where my social skills were hopeless.

"You must be good at *something* you haven't told us about... besides taking care of kids," he said, fumbling in his pocket for a lighter to light up his pipe; unsettling me with that question out of the blue, and acting as if the answer was not really important. Waiting, anyway, for an answer.

I didn't want him to think he had scared me with this harmless question, this gratuitous poke at the logs of my life.

"I was a Secretary. I went to a Secretarial College after high school."

"Oh, that's *gooood*." Still unable to light his pipe.

He was not going to get anymore out of me that day.

The next day: "There is a Business College in town. They offer classes in Computers? Evening classes... I could talk to someone, arrange for you to sit in... Computer skills could help you wherever you go... What do you think? You're not doing much in the basement at nights anyway."

I told him I'd have to think about it. *You must be good at something... not doing much in the basements at nights anyway.*

Well, I was a good secretary because my mother brought Juliette up reading and speaking proper English; and the manager of the tourist hotel where I worked came from Germany, and he told my mother I was perfect because I cleaned up his not so good English, and his correspondence read very well when I was through with it.

But it was December in Connecticut and I had settled quickly into the house routines at the Pidducks'; and maybe Mr. Pidducks now felt a need to do more for Juliette from the West Indies, opening up for her doors she never dreamt she would enter. I did not then know what his true motives were, and I did not much care.

Watching Jeremy at his video games, I thought I caught a glimpse of his future, of the world his father was avidly preparing him for. It was sullen and sedentary; it was self-absorbed and given to tantrums and fits of generosity; much like his father's.

Then one evening, Mr. Pidducks again: "Well, have you thought about the computer classes…? I spoke to this friend of mine…?" I was about to say, yes, I'd be willing. He sucked on his pipe, and threw me a lightning bolt right out of his dry blue eyes; I felt a tremor run through my body, and I knew what it was Mr. Pidducks had wanted from me all along.

When it seemed that winter was finally on its way out, leaving brighter skies, green leaves, the flowering of cheerier days, Mrs. Pidducks started taking Jeremy and me for drives.

Maybe she was responding to yet another suggestion from one of her friends. They had hitherto encouraged her to do aerobic exercises with a video, to ride the exercycle she kept in the basement, to switch to a vegetarian diet, practice meditation – all this after she had had Jeremy and had complained of unrelieved listlessness. All of which she tried and eventually gave up. In any event here she was taking Jeremy and me out for evening drives.

I told myself: she wants time alone with Jeremy, away from his computer, his brooding father, all the feverish parenting in the house during the winter months.

We drove on the highway for miles, turning off only to visit the mall. She insisted I hold Jeremy's left hand, while she held his right, and that way we strolled through the crowds. We bought Jeremy ice cream with sprinkles. We went to the cinema and for an hour and a half we hoped Jeremy liked the show.

One afternoon, thinking she had left the iron plugged in and imagining her house on fire, Mrs. Pidducks turned around and for thirty minutes jeopardized our lives with the most obsessed driving I had ever seen. We got home intact, but from that moment I was convinced this woman was slowly going out of her mind.

Sounds ridiculous, I know, but it seemed I was in the middle of some sort of tug of war between the Pidducks. Here was poor Mrs. Pidducks on one side straining and pulling with all her tense energy, some days sliding forward to certain collapse, at other times winning the war as Jeremy appeared to draw closer to her heart.

"How's your sister?" she would ask, snapping the silence in the car.

"Oh, she's fine," I would say, thinking of Yomarys.

"Why don't you invite her to come up for a visit?"

"I've been telling her to do that," I lied. "She's always too busy."

"I know how it is. I've been to New York. Manhattan can drive anyone to tears."

These were frantic moments for me. Mrs. Pidducks always seemed on the verge of opening her heart, baring all her troubles with Mr. Pidducks, maybe hoping I would take her side. She might have been testing the waters for empathy levels, wondering if it was after all wise to involve this *au pair* in her problems; wondering if the *au pair* was *aware* of those problems. Had she *noticed* anything? Should she nonetheless confide in me?

Frantic moments, too, because I had invented this sister who lived in Manhattan, to whom I paid weekend visits once a month. To keep her alive I was forced to invent more lies. In fact, I had become so good at lying and deceit, it worried me. But I told myself it made my life less complicated. It buffered Juliette from the looks of stony eyes, the questions of stony voices.

Yomarys was now my sister in New York. In truth she had become the translator of everything alien and forbidden in New York. To her, I would say, I owe my new lease on life.

"*Juliiiieette*! How you *doooing*!" she would shout, the moment she saw who it was at the door. I'd smile shyly; we'd kiss each other like true sisters.

"I'm doing fine, thank you, just fine," I said, "I'm learning all about computers."

"Arrright!"

"And how's the actress? Still *Broadway bound*?"

This was Yomarys' dream, to make it in the theatre. She was taking classes in the Theatre Arts.

She would strike an actorish pose, toss her head, arch her back

172

and say in a shrewish voice, "This girl is Broadway bound. Wait till I become a star, you'll remember I told you so."

Some of her brashness, her almost mannish drive began to rub off on me. Bit by bit I became more assertive, learning ways of breaking out of my island shell. I didn't want her to think I would remain always that pathetic wet kitten she had rescued at the airport.

Yomarys was twenty-one, born in New York. Her parents came from the Dominican Republic. She shared the apartment with Sarah who was twenty-six, born in New York, of Jewish parents. They worked during the day, Sarah as a teacher's aide, Yomarys at a Health Club where she earned lavish tips. What they had in common was this crazy dream of becoming stars on the New York stage.

Lucky people! To be fired that way with ambitions! I don't think I had seen this fire in anyone back home. There was not much you could get fired up about on our island, except Jehovah and His heaven, and the bodily fires He unwittingly started among some of his worshippers on earth.

My visits to Manhattan were usually occasions for celebrations of a sort. Yomarys called it *having fun*. We sauntered out at all hours of the night into streets astonishingly crowded, with well-lit shops and places you could sit, drink, talk, and forget what time it was.

Yomarys chided me for my seeming inability to use swear-words like *fucking*. "You'd be amazed what that word can do for your spirits in the city," she said. She led me through department stores as if on a mission to reclaim my wardrobe from too many long pastel Sunday dresses. She appealed to Sarah for help, insisting I needed a new look – stockings, bracelets, leather, tight jeans, different *things you could do with your hair*.

We were a sight to behold as we walked the streets at night: Sarah tall and gawky, like a basketball player; Yomarys deterring would be male molesters with words like *Fuck you, asshole!*; Juliette, the silent one, chipping to keep up with their strides, reminded not to look back at the "freaks" and "assholes", even though I didn't think they meant us any harm.

I couldn't resist sneaking glances over my shoulders: that

chubby black girl wearing a blonde wig; that white girl dressed from head to toe in black leather; those little boys who had no business in the streets at this late hour, who nevertheless walked as if they were conducting business; all the fireflies and runaways drawn to the flames of city streets. You noticed them once; you never saw them again.

"C'mon, Juliette. Stop looking over your shoulders."

Sarah was as loud and fearsome as Yomarys. I have to thank her for the *au pair* arrangement with the Pidducks. A friend of hers, an Irish girl, had been with the Pidducks for a year; she was leaving; was I interested? It was as simple as that. What good luck! What good friends to stumble on in any city!

I started wondering if there would ever be a fire inside me, an obsession, something that would give my twenty years a sudden bright focus. Twenty years on my island had not stuffed my soul with the kindling you start fires with. I   overheard Sarah saying to Yomarys one day, *Give her time, maybe she has a lot of things to work out.*

Yomarys and Sarah talked as if every day was an experiment with their life. Regardless of what it was, an encounter on the subway, on the streets, something witnessed or overheard, they brought it home. It tested their character. They talked about it and searched for what it might mean to their lives.

When they spoke of their parents it was with fondness and irritation. Sarah's father had died when she was fifteen; her mother lived alone now, and was appalled at the direction of Sarah's life: her choosing to rent her own apartment, her unmarried status. Yomarys' mother was divorced and lived not far away, in the Bronx. She went back home to visit, but that was as far as she cared to go.

And Juliette? What of Juliette's parents?

I'd feel cornered; I groped for words to explain myself; I told them there was really no mystery, no challenge about islands. Everything was small; everyone knew each other; there was the sea and the hills and carnival; there were no seasons; the days and nights had a numbing way of simply repeating themselves.

I smiled and tried to sound nonchalant as I explained all this. Actually I managed to conceal chunks of the truth.

I'd broken off contact with the island. The impulse had come to me that first night I had met Yomarys and, wet with panic, had asked directions to the YWCA. What I wanted was a place to hide away.

I sent a postcard or a letter home now and then saying I was fine, there was nothing to worry about, I would explain everything later. I gave no return address. I imagined everyone worrying them-selves to death, but I encouraged no response. I wanted distance from the old attachments; wanted miles and space and unfamiliar things; I wanted *out* of the bubble back there.

On the road going back to the Pidducks, staring out at skeletal trees, the snow-layered landscape, my body shivering at the cruel loss of its sun, I would sometimes wonder: *Juliette, girl, where would you be now had you not met Yomarys that day at the airport? What chain of circumstances would have led you into the city and into what end?*

Count yourself lucky, girl, a voice inside said to me, though how long would this good luck last? *Remember who you are,* another voice said, but who am I, and why should I remember?

When Yomarys and Sarah – in the apartment, after midnight, sipping wine and nibbling cheese, giggling a lot, pretending to be drunk – spoke of men, it was with a mixture of sadness and contempt.

Yomarys seemed not to trust the species anymore. She'd had an abortion after her high school boyfriend had got her pregnant. She'd found him *fooling around with other women* while urging her to have his child. She'd had the abortion to show him he couldn't make a fool of her.

I was shocked by this revelation, the cheese suddenly salty, the wine bitter in my mouth. A high school romance souring into bitterness and hate, the ripping out of a foetus in revenge, her eternal distrust of all men: shocking beyond belief.

As for Sarah, she had not much to say. *Boyfriends?* She had known no such creature. "Boys were intimidated by how tall I was. They didn't want to date someone they had to look up to," she said. Now in her late twenties and still boyfriendless, she could think only of her crazy dream of Broadway and a mother for whom she still cared never mind her nagging.

175

Juliette? Well, for a long time Juliette lay tucked away safe and secure in her virginity.

Her mother would put her to bed, calming her fears about menstruation.

Her mother would tell her that sex was the trap men laid for foolish gullible young women – young crotch-fondling men, wolfish no-good men, and older married men worried about their waning frequency.

We would be standing under the awning of the big department store in town, handing out WATCHTOWER booklets to passersby, my mother smiling that promise of new peace and security, the coming of Noah's day; and she would say to me, feeling that her warnings were not enough:

"Look around the island. Do you see what's going on?"

I looked around the island, and I thought, my mother is right: foolish young women did fall into traps; the prettier ones, like the girls working in the banks, walked coquettishly into these traps. Some schoolgirls, flattered by the attention paid to their forced-ripe breasts and bodies, forgot about ambition. A whisper, a smile during Carnival season, and soon enough they were swollen with child and a foolish sense of womanhood.

There was one boy with a monkeyish face at our church who stared and mooned over me. He was a shy, helpful and utterly harmless sort. I couldn't imagine him as a trapper of women, and I certainly did not encourage him.

And that was as far as Juliette went with boys.

"One day," my mother promised, "you'll meet a nice fellow. And you'll get married and have children."

"But what's your secret, Ma?" I asked her once.

"*My secret*? What do you mean?"

"You know…your way with men, so they don't hurt you."

She searched my face, puzzled by what seemed a precocious readiness to learn. She wasn't sure if I was truly ready. Then she leaned close to my ear and she whispered harsh words like sharp razors she would now let me have.

"I never let them kiss me," she said.

It sounded like a sensible prescription: keep all two-legged

176

predators at bay until some nice fellow comes along; then marriage, a child or two. I was content with it.

Meanwhile sex was a stupid blind surrender that led more often than not to pregnancy and disgrace; the folly of islands with little neon and plenty bushy places; the poking and grunting inside shuttered dwellings in villages with no electricity.

Juliette was kissed and tucked away under the covers of her virginity.

Of course, I never revealed all this to Sarah and Yomarys. But the time came when those parts of the story, held back so long, started worrying me for meaning, for someone to whom I could tell. And the day came when Mr. Pidducks,   convinced that I now knew what it was he wanted of me, made his trip down the basement stairs, and what followed also cried out for meaning and for someone to whom I could tell.

The change of seasons, from winter to spring, brings along with the budding of seeds the release of other subterranean yearnings. Islands have no seasons; we plant then we cut the banana and the sugar cane; hurricanes threaten us but usually with little more than their new names; we do not know those fickle shifts from arctic cold to desert heat.

One morning you wake up and discover a suspicious lump in your life; you don't know where it came from, or what to do with it; no season of wind and cold had prepared you for it. It pushes on you decisions of a sweeping kind.

I woke up one morning in the basement of the Pidducks' and through the window I could tell – the wind whipping up the skirts of April – that winter had not quite gone away. Shivering, for I had put away my sweaters, I heard Mr. Pidducks preparing to come down the basement steps to where I lay waiting.

Since that first evening at the dinner table, seeds of yearning had moaned underground. Now despite the season's uncertainty, or maybe because of it, something was about to spring a life of its own.

Mr. Pidducks had found no reason before to come down to the basement, at least not while I was there. Mrs. Pidducks, always discreet and polite, ventured downstairs only if it was absolutely unavoidable. She showed me how to use the washing machine and on Saturdays she brought the bundles to be washed. Mr. Pidducks had always stayed away.

At the top of the stairs that day his feet hesitated; his shoes squeaked on the kitchen floor as he turned back, searching for a pretext to come down.

I got out of bed and searched the drawer for a clean sweater; then I pulled on a pair of jeans; then I realized I was getting ready to receive him, and my heart scurried around like a squirrel and I sat on the bed wondering how to disguise my fear.

Juliette's mother had taught her to say an absolute *No* to the overtures of men. She had given her an enchanting glimpse of the future: her wedding night in the gentle arms of some worthy young man. She had not explained how you handle moments like these, the back and forth shuffle of Mr. Pidducks' feet, the back and forth swells of Juliette's desire.

My mother had taken me to see a doctor in Barbados where the doctors were said to be more professionally advanced than on our island. We had gone there because my periods had become more painful and unbearable. I was sure something terrible was wrong with me.

It turned out to be nothing serious. I had some vaginal growth known as fibrosis. The doctor had to perform an orthoscopy. It all sounded very neat and easily cured when it was explained; but there were whisperings in his office between the doctor and my mother; and much later on the plane going home I was told there had been this delicate question of rupturing my hymen.

The doctor was of the opinion that since it was still intact, maybe my mother might have wished it to be ruptured the natural way: *Didn't Juliette have a boyfriend? this sort of thing was sometimes so important to a young woman; no, he wasn't for one minute suggesting some promiscuous one-night stand.* My mother could barely contain her outrage: *he was sorry he brought the matter up, he just thought perhaps,* so it went on.

Now as I heard Mr. Pidducks making exploratory steps down the basement stairs, a stale anger crept over my body. I told myself: *Girl, no one shuffling on steps over your head or whispering in a tiny office is going to decide that moment for you*. I was ready to deal with Mr. Pidducks should he try anything.

And there he was, finally down the stairs, apologizing for the intrusion, wondering how I was keeping up, was it warm enough down here. Here he was proprietarily looking around his basement, thin as dry stick, polite, coughing dryly; then fingering a few books, a chair, and saying how the weather had played a dirty trick on us, doubling back like that.

And there I was shaking like a leaf, words snagged in my throat as I watched him out the corner of my eye, watched his long legs restless as a pony's wandering here and there, but closer to where I sat on the bed; until I wondered if I should have said, *Would you like to sit down?*; until it was too late; he was sitting beside me on the bed.

And the walls came tumbling down; or rather the walls began to melt away.

Strange how these things happen. I had no idea how these things did happen. You erect these walls to frighten people off. You erect them so high no one dare try to scale them. Walls of abstinence, walls of virtuous disdain. Those *Don't even think about it* walls.

Yet at that moment, in that overheated basement, even before Mr. Pidducks touched me, even as I clasped my hands and prayed he wouldn't touch me, I felt my own nakedness – the wall suddenly not there – my desire trembling and exposed.

I expected him to be bold, to grasp my shoulders, gently push me down on the bed; instead he seemed to lose his nerve; he got up, put his hands in his pocket and started talking again. I said to him: *Why don't you sit down?*

He patted his pockets as if searching for his pipe; he must have felt suddenly helpless without it; he knew that if he left the room to get it, still dry-mouthed and burning, that would have been the end of his day.

He sat with his legs crossed tightly and he looked as sad as a flat tire. I felt sorry for him, I must admit.

Then I thought: *But, Juliette, you can say for the first time in your life an absolute YES to this man.* And it dawned on me: *why not here, why not now, why not Mr. Pidducks, squirming and boiling with the purest desire?*

179

I must have been staring at the tiles on the floor, distracted, my shoulders hunched. It gave him a surge of new boldness. In the next instant he was beside me on the bed, quite close this time, holding my arms, touching my neck, pulling me towards him, reaching down with his hands to my breasts; so bold and determined this time; his hands so cold on my skin. I trembled.

All good girls are supposed to stiffen, coy and reluctant. I tried to stiffen. I discovered I didn't like the feel of his soft hands on my skin. But the walls had melted away; I wanted it to happen; I wanted to get it over with as quickly and amazingly as it could happen.

Now I know this: you don't ever *get it over with* quickly unless you're some clock-watching prostitute; unless the man is in a hurry and inept. Each act will take its name and take its time from the circumstances, and memory like a wicked child eavesdrops on your most careful preparations.

I pushed Mr. Pidducks away firmly; then with my back to him I began removing my clothes.

What would he think when he saw my golden apple breasts? I wasn't built like Mrs. Pidducks who despite her drained haggard look, had a broad-hipped post-maternal body. *What if suddenly he changed his mind? Could someone really want my body?*

When he began making love – apologizing first for removing only his pants and underwear, saying something about pains in his chest and the devilishly cold weather – it was to a Juliette he might have wished all his life to possess. And what happened was none too quick and just short of amazing.

Maybe we were both too riddled with anxiety and expectation. Maybe there was not enough affection between us, just this cold curiosity and need; a little fumbling under the blanket, a muttered *Sorry*; and then *Shit!* the word hissed out as Mr. Pidducks rolled off in disbelief.

Shit! Not a word you would easily find in Mr. Pidducks' vocabulary. It had been Mr. Papo's word, too, when I surprised him and my mother in her bedroom. The same word, that same vexed sound, the same cry of surprise and frustration.

It was the middle of the afternoon and I had come home from school earlier than usual. His car was parked outside our gate but the house was locked tight and my mother should have been at work. To walk around to the backyard I had to pass her bedroom window. How careless of her to leave the louvers cracked open like that! Anyone could break in; anyone could look inside. I looked inside; just stopped and peered through the louvers.

It was when I moved again, my feet making a crunching noise on the gravel below the window, that Mr. Papo, his bare bottom amazingly smooth, his long-sleeved shirt still buttoned at the wrist, seemed to freeze: he said *Shit!* he threw a panic-filled glance at the window. I saw his face, round and shiny and wet, *so wet*, with big bright beads of perspiration.

Oh, how quickly like weeds your understanding of these things grows. A glimpse through the window of your mother *naked with a man* and your mind leaps over mountains to the highest plateau. You see so clearly everything.

I crossed over to the neighbor's yard, disturbing a mother hen and her brood, and I waited behind a breadfruit tree until Mr. Papo's car started up and drove off. Dizzy with resentment, wanting to go inside and use our bathroom, I thought about what I had seen: my mother on her back, her legs in the air, her legs like the arms in the air of a carnival flag-waver.

It wasn't the position that intrigued me, though I had never once seen my mother flat on her back like that, with some sweaty bare-bottomed beast crouched over her like that. Nor did I feel, then, betrayed by this mid-afternoon tryst.

It was the wonder: what had come over her all of a sudden after all these years, after swearing to me no man would ever touch her again? Had her body pleaded with her for one, just one, last sweet time? Had Mr. Papo cast some sexual spell over her? Can desire be locked away in a convent or a dungeon forever, never to return?

In Mr. Pidducks' case I think I know what happened. His professor's brain, always shadowing his body, got into the act; before he knew it he was making schoolboyish noises as he climbed on me, all tense and anxious; suddenly he lost his nerve and there he was once again going soft like a tire losing air.

This crisis we had not anticipated. His lying beside me waiting for inflation I did not want.

"Sometimes you've got to rev them up, help them get started,"

Yomarys had said, telling us what she did next, while Sarah and I smiled and exchanged horrified glances.

I reached over and groped between his legs, staring up at the ceiling so as not to suggest any perverse delight in what I was doing. Eventually I got him started. And there I was, my legs in the air like the arms of a carnival flag-waver, my head turned to one side so that I could see through the basement window the driveway, and the front wheels of the Pidducks' car.

No one was going to interrupt us. Mrs. Pidducks and Jeremy would not be back for hours. No one could see us. The basement in this house under winter's still grey skies was like the deepest hollow in any cave. We could have screamed and howled like happy wolves.

Instead a part of me was watching all this, waiting for something volcanic to happen. A part of me was listening to Mr. Pidducks as he started to wheeze and huff, the exertion too much for his thin chest. I felt him softening inside me; he was slowing; and just when it looked as if he would sputter and go flat again, collapsing in frustration on top of me, I pulled his head forward and bit him on the right shoulder.

With teeth marks smarting on his shoulder Mr. Pidducks became a raving wolf, doing violence to my body, saying the vilest things to that body, his eyes shut, his neck stringy with stretched veins.

Yomarys wouldn't have thought of doing that. My mother wouldn't have done that either. This was Juliette taking control, feeling pain, astonishing pain where she had always felt a quiet yearning; growing anxious lest she wasn't doing enough to be loved; wishing it had never started; wanting it quickly to be over.

When at last his small chest stopped heaving, when his body stopped shuddering its gratitude, he touched my face and whispered, "That was unlike anything that has ever happened to me. You'd never guess how long it has been since I've felt this way."

I thought of Mrs. Pidducks. How long had it been since she'd made him feel that way? I began to wonder what in fact went on inside that bedroom from which Mrs. Pidducks usually emerged ragged and tired.

And then I didn't want to know and didn't care to guess. I

182

was feeling cold, naked and cold. I got up and reached for my clothes.

No more talk. No more intimacy for Mr. Pidducks. I would not let him crouch over my heart.

I dressed slowly, my back toward him. I think he understood I wanted him to leave. He came toward me, hesitant, wanting right then to bless the earth under my feet, sorry for the things he'd said in his passion. He touched my shoulders. I started removing the rumpled sheets. I heard him climbing nimbly up the basement stairs.

The grass, the leaves, flowers, roof repairs, people in shirtsleeves and short skirts – spring is here! You greet the old faces as if they were new faces, you marvel at bare arms and heavy calves, the fresh coat of paint that's needed over there. Our lives, worn heavily all winter, turn inside out.

I started taking walks, but something was missing: the places where I used to walk, the sunset hours, the streets through which I ran errands as a child, the narrow road up the hill to school, the beach; the old familiar earth under my feet was missing.

It shouldn't have mattered, but the streets in Connecticut near where we lived with their neatly spaced houses, their proud homeowners out on aluminum ladders, the streets said to me: *Hi, there, brown legs. You're new around here, right?*

In Manhattan where everything moved constantly, and people walked tight-lipped and tight-bodied, I began to miss my sky and sea, the harbor, the smell of the fishing boats, vendors in the market square.

I bought a pair of sunglasses. From my window I watched the streets below.

Spring made me see its hard-edged corners, made me feel its pounded surfaces. There was never enough overhanging light. Maybe the risk I had taken so wildly with my life had run its course. There was no place left to go.

One evening I wrote a letter to my mother. I said: *I know you've been worrying about me. I want you to know that I'm all right. I am staying with friends in the city.* I offered no explanation for my strange behavior. I put a return address on the back of the envelope.

183

Weeks went by with no answer from the island. It left me sharply distressed. Now that she knew my whereabouts I expected my mother to reply. Nothing. Not a word. I wasn't sure what to make of it. Was my mother gravely ill? Had people been trying to contact me all this time?

I wrote another letter, putting down in detail everything that had happened to me. Going on and on for pages. It was so bulky I couldn't get it sealed properly in the envelope. I tore it up into small pieces. I'd never felt so miserable, so completely cut off.

It might not have been so bad had not the circumstances begun to change around me, forcing me to see life as a fickle thing, like the seasons, bringing out in us strange deviations.

I had imagined that with spring Yomarys, Sarah and I, less confined by the weather, would draw closer, venturing out to new places. But now Yomarys was sullen; she complained and snapped a lot. The last time we went out she had said something about us looking like *loosies*. Increasingly she withdrew, finding excuses not to join us.

What did she really mean by calling us *loosies*?

My mother had taught me to despise loose women on the island. That could not be what Yomarys meant. My mother had preached the value of aiming one's life like an arrow upward to Jehovah. Yomarys now made it seem as if we had been climbing a mountain; suddenly there was slack on her rope; she was falling; she was loose. Was that what she meant? Dangling loose over some precipice?

One day Sarah said Yomarys was moving back to the Bronx. *What had happened,* I asked? *Was there anything we could do to help?* She needed time to work things out. *Work what out?* She had met her old high school boyfriend. *The one whose child she aborted*? They were seeing each other again. I didn't know what to think.

Then one day her room was empty. She was no longer one of us.

Sarah asked if I wanted to move in with her, share the apartment? I didn't know what to say. With Yomarys taking off, everything falling apart, I really didn't know.

Back in Connecticut things began to go awry. I was awakened one night by furtive movement, urgent whisperings, the slamming of the screen door, and Mr. Pidducks' car backing quickly

184

out the driveway. They were rushing Jeremy to the hospital. They did not stop to explain this to me and for the rest of that night I slept fitfully.

They returned the next morning after an all night vigil, still saying nothing to me. I heard them in the kitchen making coffee, saying nothing to each other. Then they went into the bedroom. The house fell into a deep churning silence.

When I saw her again, bumping into her in the kitchen, her face still looked drawn and weary, as if her life and her body had been at it again, hands at each other's throat; but she'd washed her hair and it was hanging down her shoulders handbrushed and fresh. She wore a dressing gown sashed tight at the waist and I could tell there was nothing under it. With Jeremy away her body seemed set to romp in fields of a strange new freedom.

She fixed herself a cup of coffee and took the frozen meat out of the refrigerator. She asked, sipping, with one arm folded across her tummy, how I was doing. She told me Jeremy was doing just fine and should be back home soon; she lapsed into a dreamy state, sipping her coffee, staring at the floor; then she returned to the bedroom.

These were the weird days of early spring. I was having dreams like intruders on my empty nights.

I dreamt I had flown back to the island, repentant and eager to explain everything. I was met at the airport by my mother who made a violent scene, slapping me across the face over and over, and dragging me by the hair past the astonished eyes of the customs officials.

I dreamt I was back home, locked in a room, grinding my teeth until they all crumbled like biscuits and fell out my mouth, leaving me to face the world with only my gums. I would wake up in great fear and put my fingers in my mouth, making sure my teeth were all there.

On the day Jeremy came home I helped bake a fruitcake and string a paper sign in the living room that said *Welcome Home, Jeremy*. He looked frail, his cheekbones were shiny, but you could tell he was happy to be back. Prompted by his mother and father, who stood close together shooing him forward, he made a short run and threw his thin arms round my neck.

185

I sensed the Pidducks watching us, their son back in the loving arms of Juliette. Delight and approval lit up their faces. Right there and then, just as Jeremy disengaged his arms and rushed inside to his computer, I decided I was not going to stay in Connecticut another year. Something turned inside my stomach like a memory. I was sure I wouldn't stay.

I heard Mrs. Pidducks behind me, her thighs packed tight in blue jeans, say "We're taking him to see his grandmother tomorrow. Wouldn't you like to come along?" The following day we set off to visit Jeremy's grandmother.

We sat at the four corners of Mr. Pidducks' Volvo in a strange silence. Mr. Pidducks pretended to concentrate on the roadway after I'd caught his wandering eye once in the rearview mirror. Jeremy was in the backseat beside me absorbed in a handheld computer toy; it made a tinny sound that irritated everyone, but we said nothing to him. Mrs. Pidducks sat erect, staring out her side of the window.

I leaned my head back on the car seat and wondered what to do about Sarah's offer to share the apartment. Moving to Manhattan was a good idea. I would have to find a job. In all this shifting around I felt a need to talk with Yomarys. I could not imagine going ahead with my life not knowing what she was doing with hers.

I'd thought we were on our way to visit an old lady living alone in an old house. As it turned out Jeremy's grandmother was staying in an old people's home. She was Mr. Pidducks' mother and as we swung into the driveway Mrs. Pidducks muttered something about how expensive it was merely to upkeep the lawns. Losing his composure Mr. Pidducks said to her, "Listen we've been through all this before…"

The words hissed through his teeth with irritation and Mrs. Pidducks, fearing she had started something that could engulf and embarrass us all, turned in her seat and, the loving mother again, told Jeremy we were here.

So Jeremy's grandmother was a problem for them: what to do with her, how much to spend looking after her. The Pidducks were playing a tense game, eviscerating each other with quiet

186

ferocious strokes, over Jeremy and Jeremy's grandmother, the very young and the very old. It was unbearable for any *au pair* to watch. It seemed a good time for this *au pair* to move on.

We got out the car, the family pride a little ruffled but intact, and we went in search of Jeremy's grandmother.

We found her sitting in a rocker on a patio. She was wearing a floral patterned dress, a cardigan, and she was staring across the lawns at the trees, a picture of comfort and abandonment. It was hard to tell what she was thinking as suddenly we surrounded her and made our presence known.

"Mother?" Mr. Pidducks said, in a surprisingly soft tone, "we've brought Jeremy to see you… How are you today? You look rather well… Here's Jeremy. Jeremy, say hello to Grandma Pat."

We were standing in front of her, smiling, waiting to be acknowledged. Grandma Pat looked at us, unsmiling, a little regal despite her curved shoulders, silvery wisps of hair playful on her head. And I thought: *she doesn't recognize us, she doesn't know who we are.*

Apparently she knew who we were. She turned her head from Mr. Pidducks to Mrs. Pidducks, receiving their smiles with stony face. She turned to look at me. "And this is Juliette from the West Indies. She's helping us with Jeremy."

The smile on my face froze under the scrutiny of her eyes, hard and old and blue like the judgment of a generation past. And I thought: *she doesn't like me, she definitely doesn't like me.*

She turned to stare at Jeremy who had said, "Hello, Grandma Pat" in a trailing voice, as if he didn't know this lady in the rocker and didn't really want to give her a hug. She looked at him a long time, making us all uncomfortable now for she still hadn't spoken a word of greeting; just that turn of the head, the chin shriveled and disapproving, and her measuring eyes.

Her hands gripped the rocker; she was preparing to get up. "Well, it's about time you got here," she said in a raspy old lady's voice. "I've been packed and ready all morning."

"Mother, we came to *see* you. You aren't going anywhere. How are you? Are they taking good care of you here?"

"This is not my home. I can take care of myself. I'm ready to leave as soon as you are," she said.

187

Silence. Jeremy seemed the only one who didn't understand what was going on. We all turned as he pointed to a squirrel that appeared out of nowhere and scurried across the lawns. We couldn't have been more relieved at the distraction. "Would you like to catch the squirrel?" Mrs. Pidducks asked. It seemed at that moment an exciting prospect.

Mr. Pidducks was pulling up a chair. I gazed at the lawns and wondered what it felt like simply to walk across the freshly mowed grass, away from Grandma Pat in her rocker; a quiet stroll on the lawns, as no doubt the residents here did on occasion, within the secure borders of the trees and the wall.

I said, *Excuse me*, and I slipped away; first in the direction Mrs. Pidducks and Jeremy had taken, searching for the squirrel; then veering off on my own, walking away, my head bowed, as if I were neither visitor or resident; just someone from the islands who'd slipped off her shoes and found the grass under her feet as delightful to walk on as the beach.

I had left the island late in the afternoon. It had taken us one hour to drive to the airport. I sat in the backseat of Mr. Papo's car taking in those last minute instructions from my mother and Mr. Papo, until I grew tired of their solicitude, their excited chatter which I saw as nothing more than the sharpening of their appetite for each other's bodies once I was safely up and on my way; I could see the talcum powder on my mother's back, which was her habit after a shower, but which now hinted at sexual enticement.

And I felt a faint resentment, first, then sadness and fear, for I was moving out of that circle of family and familiars I had known all my life. And I would soon be alone, despite the careful preparations waiting for me outside the airport terminal.

Resentment, sadness, fear – we were halfway to the airport now and the glances and reminders from the front seat had dwindled to silence – and then a surging wish to forgive my mother for what she was doing.

Maybe, I started thinking, she deserved these slutty flagwaving moments with Mr. Papo. Her body, so long disciplined, so heavily fortressed against the return of desire, wanting so much a heart it could trust; her body might have pleaded with her one night for release, for a furlough in a heaven of her making. Surely

Jehovah could forgive her that single lapse, forgive her the transgression she'd feared and fought against all these years.

Juliette!

Mr. Papo hit the brakes and jolted me back to the island, the road dusty, the sun throwing pink glows on the scrawny hills; and there, walking on the side of the road, not near enough to the verge to avoid mishap, was an old woman: a villager in drab clothes, worn shoes, a basket hooked on her arm; walking a little unsteadily, compelling us to maneuver carefully around her. And as we came abreast of her, Mr. Papo slowed to her walking pace and called out, *Aunt Iris, how you do?*

Juliette!

The old lady stopped, looked at the car with suspicion, wondering if her frail life was in peril; then she looked at Mr. Papo and smiled, her face creased and lined and shiny. *You want to hit me down, eh?* she laughed. And Mr. Papo laughed.

The old lady looked in and said hello. She must have been long past seventy years; you would think she had no business on the roads. Her speech was slurred but fierce with surprise and mock anger; her front teeth discolored and twisted.

We were holding up traffic, a mini-van honked impatiently behind us, so Mr. Papo promised to drop by Aunt Iris on his way back from the airport. I remember turning in my travel clothes to look at her, standing off the road now, still smiling, a little wary now of vehicles creeping up on her or roaring by.

I strolled across the lawns; I saw those broken teeth; I heard that old lady's screech of amazement when she recognized Mr. Papo. And I thought: a home for old people is not a good idea. They're not for me. When this is over – this wild spending of my saved up years, the panic, the flight from panic – when the time comes to count the pennies of my last days, I'd like to be back on the island, an old lady walking the dusty road, a headtie of soothing leaves, a basket full of mangoes and memories. I would live for the surprise and delight of meeting someone by chance on the road.

But the first step would be to move away from Connecticut. I would tell Sarah, yes, I would share the apartment with her. I would have to let Mrs. Pidducks know.

I thought I heard someone calling my name and I turned to see her coming toward me, tripping a little in her haste across the lawns. I couldn't see Jeremy anywhere. Her knees had this funny way of knocking each other as she walked which gave her hips and her behind a sensual sway she never intended. It seemed the right moment to tell Mrs. Pidducks what my plans were.

As she came nearer I realized she had been calling my name. Her face looked aggrieved once more and bitter. Something about her stride, its arrow straight flight right toward my heart, made me tremble, made me stoop to put my shoes back on, wondering if it was time to go, telling myself, as memory and bright wish went soft in my stomach: *she knows already; she has heard every whimper of longing, every howl of pleasure in their house; she knew all along.*

BATTY BWOY, DIVERT!

Some places you avoid like the plague in this city, in this world, though it took me a while to start feeling this way. Back on our island there were no places like that, no township or village you'd never be seen dead in. My mother had relatives everywhere and, thanks to my absent father who had a need to spread his seed, I had half-brothers and sisters scattered in villages as far apart as Morne La Paix and Falmouth.

Soon after I came to NY city I started riding the subway to the end of the line on weekends when I had nothing to do. I'd pretend I was Columbus; I'd emerge from underground and wander through the streets of white neighborhoods, black neighborhoods, Spanish or Italian neighborhoods; marveling at the buildings, smiling at people on stoops; skirting round youths with sullen bony faces playing stickball; feeling no fear for I was only passing through. Cruising, as they say.

This was how I came upon the store that sold African fabrics in Brooklyn. It was on Empire Boulevard, on a block with shops and stores jammed one next to the other, and troughs of cheap merchandise spilling onto the sidewalk. It had a sign, *Gold Coast Inc.*, and it was boxed in between a Chinese takeout and one of those Spanish Delis, its shelves crammed with a million tiny packaged items.

The owner sat on a stool behind his counter pouring over a newspaper. He did little business, as far as I could tell, and he was always reading.

He was a tall, dignified man with a round fleshy face, a square jaw and owlish eyes with dark half-moons under them. He reminded me of Miss Lewders' Moor. Miss Lewders was my English teacher and when she taught us *Othello* she tried to describe what a Moor in the streets of Venice looked like. It had to be someone like this fellow: bigskinned, solitary, chest swollen with suspicion and pride.

He had an itchy pugnacious nature; he couldn't stand people coming into the store just to look around. When I strolled in one evening – to get away for a while from stamping my feet on the cold sidewalk – he must have counted to ten, then he declared in a deep bass voice, "This is not a book store. If you come in here to browse, you in the wrong place." He made *browsing* sound like a criminal offense. Shifting his tone, just in case I was a legitimate customer, he said, "Can I be of assistance?"

Some people had a way of wandering inside and fingering his fabrics. These two fat women, for instance, who sometimes waited for the B87 bus, would put their heads together and giggle and comment on everything; but they didn't buy. A child might knock over one of his polished sculpted pieces, chipping a nose or an arm. The child's mother made a big show of distress; she'd apologize and slap the child twice; the Moor would calmly fold his arms and wait, his eyes bulging with rage. The mother would declare it was an accident; she didn't have any money to pay for the damage!

So day after day, waiting for business to pick up, he sat on his stool reading the newspapers or a book. The last book was about Kwame Nkrumah.

I got to know him very well because the B87 bus stops right outside his shop. On warm summer evenings, the light still bright in the sky, he'd stand outside the storefront smoking a pipe, wearing a fez and a dashiki, stone-faced like a brooding Othello.

Sometimes, starved for conversation, I'd ask him, "How's business?" He'd look me over, wondering if I was trying to be sarcastic; then he'd suck his teeth and rail against the buying habits of *his people*: they spent money on greasy Chinese food; they couldn't stand the smell of collard green; they bought crotch-squeezing blue jeans that risked reducing their sperm count instead of wearing a breezy Nigerian *agbada* with ample sleeves, ideal for summer weather; they wore hats with logos for the NY Yankees, the LA Rams, while he had nice kente cloth hats that would look much more dignified on their nappy heads.

I grew to understand why he was so angry all the time. His name was Mr. Collymore. He didn't look like a Collymore from the islands, but apparently he came up here from Barbados back

194

in the fifties intending to go to college and study Economics. Something went mysteriously wrong in his life that left him scarred and bitter. In any event he decided to go into business for himself.

We became friendly because I listened with sympathy to his outpourings, which came in installments as I waited for the bus. There were days when I half-expected him to turn on me and denounce my jeans, sneakers and leather jacket dress habit. And on Friday nights I made sure he never caught me hurrying home, tired, with a paperbag of takeouts from Kentucky Fried.

Suddenly one evening he was no longer there. The store front was shut tight and padlocked, a corrugated gate stained with graffiti pulled down over the show window. I thought, maybe he'd lost the lease; he might have had a stroke; or he simply gone back to Barbados. People and places have a way of disappearing in this city.

The store stayed locked down for weeks. When it reopened, the new owner was a lightskinned Rastaman selling nature foods: coconuts, cane, ground provisions, some creamy looking stuff in bottles with names like *Irish Moss* and *Strong Back* that promised to cure everything from asthma to sexual impotence.

He had the loud speakers of a sound system positioned at the door as if to advertise his culture as well as his merchandise, so that as you waited for the bus you had this reggae music pounding away on your eardrums. Then his friends would gather at the doorway, two fellows with dreadlocks and tams, winding their waist and doing that hop-and-drop reggae dance. And singing along to lyrics like, *Nobody move/ nobody get hurt, Nobody move/ nobody get hurt.*

Talk about moving from one extreme to the next – first, Mr. Collymore's store, cluttered with stuff, so quiet and depressing when you stepped inside, all those staring polished African heads, the faint-colored striped fabrics, all the faraway gloom of the forest in this Brooklyn store; and now this young Rastaman with his nature foods, not doing any better, just playing loud music and standing slackhipped at the doorway, twirling his beard strands and reasoning with his dreadlocked friends about the evil ways of the Babylon system.

They must have been doing some kind of business, for next thing you know the dreadlocks were the owners of a shiny brand new Japanese car full of extras and trimmings. When they weren't lounging outside the shop, they sat in the car, going nowhere, just displaying *pride of ownership*. They even got traffic tickets which they left under the windshield wiper to show they tougher than tough and didn't care about the Babylon system.

I would be waiting for the bus, sometimes for twenty, twenty five minutes, trying not to show how amazed I was at their sudden prosperity: the stylish Timberland boots, the thick corduroys, the tricolored cords in place of belts. You look at that situation and you wonder where they get the money to buy a Japanese car; you begin to suspect these fellows into some shady business.

It never once crossed my mind they might have been curious about me until one evening I overheard this conversation.

"Batty riders fi' dead."

"You na see't."

"Batty bwoy fi burn in hellfire."

"'Gainst all natural law."

"I never tell you how I fix that batty bwoy on Flatbush. Me see him walking one night in him tight leather pants and him jerry curls."

"Me know who you a-talk bout. Me know that batty bwoy. Me see him regular inside the McDonalds on Flatbush drinking coffee."

"I tell you, blood rush round my head like scorpion. Me turn to Chalice, me tell him, *lewwe beat this batty bwoy*."

"'Gainst all natural law. For the wicked shall suffer the wrath of the righteous."

"So we jump 'pon him. Beat him till 'im bawl. Kick him in his balls. Him curl up like a little girl, and the more him bawl, the more we stamp 'pon him, mash up 'im face."

"Me had to pull the dread away, else him woulda kill the batty bwoy."

"Him lucky. If I had my gun I woulda push it up 'im backside… and… *boosha*… *boosha*."

Island people must be the best in the world when it comes to simulating gunfire. I had been trying to appear as if minding my own business, gazing down the road at the B87 which I could see ploughing its way slowly through heavy traffic and lights. The dread called Chalice was sitting on the dumpster outside the shop, swinging his legs like a little boy pleased with himself. The fairskinned Rastaman was twirling his beard and quoting Bible verse. It was the other dread, with a narrow face, dark glasses, matching boots and leather jacket who had enacted the jumping, the kicking, and the beating of the "batty bwoy". He was a one-man show there on the sidewalk doing his gunfire simulation, with a pumping and recoiling motion of his arms. One afternoon I was startled to find the gun pointed straight at me.

It might have meant nothing at all had I laughed or otherwise shown my approval of the violent climax. But my eyes must have given me away, or it might have been my way of holding myself apart, wary of any gratuitous assault on my person. In any event, I sensed him watching me, even as the B87 rolled up; watching as I moved to the door, then stepped back to allow a passenger to get off; still watching as the bus pulled away.

I looked back, wanting to confirm whether he *knew*; and there he was pouting his lips as if sending me a kiss, only his arms were moving once more, pumping the shotgun, and I could hear the *boosha...boosha...* the blasts so strong they could shatter any glass, make your soul run ducking for cover in any city, in the mean streets of this stalking world.

My mother would send me old newspapers every three months or so. It was her way of reminding me to keep in touch with her, with the island. She knew I was no letter-writer; I had to be jolted into writing by bad news, or a request to send money. But just looking at the package – at the five or six island stamps honoring this time the Governor General and some island flowers – and the brown wrapping paper was enough to make me homesick for everyone back there.

I could see her stopping by Mr. Harmon's shop on the Chausee, and explaining that the papers were for her son in New York. I could hear her telling Mrs. Lemieux at the Post Office that I was "doing well for himself, God willing", even though she had no way of knowing how well I was doing.

She bought the papers week after week, folding them carefully; then when she'd collected enough, she wrapped them in brown paper, tied them with string, using rubber bands just in case the string broke, then applying Scotch tape to hold everything together.

Sometimes the ink lettering of my name was smudged suggesting it had rained on the morning she'd made her way to the post office. She always took the trouble to mail a letter on the same day she sent the papers. Usually the letter arrived first telling me the papers had been posted. All of this left me in knots of homesickness for the next seven days.

I didn't read the newspapers right away. I took a shower; I got into my pajamas; I ate dinner; then as the belligerent noises of the city faded into background I began reading myself back home.

I read them one after the other – my mother was careful to arrange them in the correct order of the dates of publication – then I put them in paper bag for garbage collection the next day.

Our island is a small place; newspapers are published twice a week. Politics, carnival preparation, *bassa bassa*, a road accident, local boy doing well overseas – there isn't much you couldn't pick up yourself in the market square. Here in NY city when the package arrived, I felt obliged, considering all the money my mother had spent on stamps, to read everything.

Occasionally a news item would upset me. The fire that destroyed Liliendaal's Grocery Store for instance. I read that news story with horror and disbelief, dwelling over the details. That store had been on Valmont road long before I was born. My mother sent me there, rain or shine, to buy cassava bread. Now it had gone up in flames!

My mother wrote about the neighbours, about who pregnant and who dead. Lately, she said, terrible things were happening across the island. The "drug business" was taking over and some people were committing horrible violent crimes, kicking down doors, shooting people in their beds. When the Government tried to put a stop to it, they kidnapped the son of the Minister of Education!

This sort of crime was unheard of before. She didn't know what the place was coming to. And young people were picking up the worse habits. She thought it was time they brought back flogging with the cat-o-nine tails.

If I were back home these happenings won't have bothered me much. They shocked you for a while but life went on. Here in NY city this hunger for news was my fear that island life was changing in mysterious ways; that, even as I turned the pages of old newspapers, strange forces were at work.

This was how I found out about the first man to die of Aids on our island. The news came as an assault on my past, on my house of memories.

His name was Gregory Gregoire. He was our man about town; popular and good looking; worked with an insurance company and changed his Japanese-import car every two years. He was a high school drop-out; a light-skinned saga-boy who sported a gal-a-rush-me hairstyle; and he was the master of ceremonies at the Queen Show during Carnival; he could have any girl he wanted.

There's enough there to explain why I resented Gregory Gregoire, why most young men from poor black families spoke about him with a mixture of envy and resentment.

The news of his death came bit by bit, in issue after issue, so that I read first a gossipy article about his "mysterious illness"; then ten minutes later in another issue there was a photo of him, smiling, but looking gaunt; he had "issued a statement of indignation" denying rumors about the cause of his illness and threatening to sue the paper for slander and libel. Finally about half an hour later I read that he was dead.

Back then not too much was known about Aids on our island. Catholic priests talked about it from the pulpit as God's way of punishing the fornicators of the world. The news reporter gave the story a gossipy slant, dwelling on Gregoire's reputation with women, then speculating about possible liaisons with homosexuals. It ended with a question: was the real Gregory Gregoire hiding in the closet all these years, behind the slips and skirts of his women all these years?

I put away the newspapers and thought about that. I even hoped it was true. That's a terrible thing to admit but I saw it as a kind of retribution for all womanizers like Gregory Gregoire. As my mother would say, they got what they deserved!

My mother's letter came the next day. I opened it expecting to find the whole story about Gregory Gregoire's day of reckoning. Instead she told me in the second paragraph that Antigua Clemendore had died.

A hurricane couldn't have wreaked more devastation inside me. I read her letter over and over. My house of memories was ablaze.

In the middle of the night I searched for the garbage bag with the island newspapers; I read again the articles about Gregory Gregoire; I read again my mother's letter. Something was not quite right. Why hadn't the newspapers reported the death of Antigua Clemendore? Had I missed the news item somewhere?

Antigua Clemendore had died, too, in a mysterious way, quite suddenly, after months of weight loss and seclusion. He was my mother's dearest friend, but there were things she couldn't possibly know about him, things which now led me to believe that he, not Gregory Gregoire, was probably the first man to die of Aids on our island.

Thinking about them – the one I admired and loved, the other I despised – bringing their faces up from the past, I realized they had quite a lot in common. At the same time they were men of opposing instincts and obsessions, which might have made them deeply resentful of each other.

For instance, at Carnival time Gregory Gregoire was always chosen to introduce the Carnival Queen contestants. It was the high point of his life, presiding on the stage before weary noisy crowds: wearing a cream-colored jacket and a cravat, the booming echoes of his voice at the microphone touching every corner of the island; always kissing the girls, smiling his handsome smile and asking for "another round of applause" for the contestants.

On the other hand Antigua Clemendore was a man of the streets, a flamboyant man of the streets. He smeared his body with paint and shoe polish and played eccentric characters on J'Ouvert morning; he was Mother Sally at Christmas, dancing and striding through the streets on stilts; he organized a kiddie carnival band. Nothing gave him more pleasure than this street sweating and street dancing, the shepherding of children in his band towards the Judges' stand.

200

This is what endeared him to my mother, this "devotion to the children". In some ways, too, he became devoted to me.

They don't talk of role models on our island, but there was a time when I wished I could be more like Antigua Clemendore. Later we developed an attachment, you could say. In truth he was the one responsible for me leaving the island and coming to New York.

Antigua Clemendore taught me to accept my difference, his difference, everybody's difference. That was no easy feat. Back then to be different on our island – too black or too bright or simply ambitious – was to attract killer bees of resentment and spite.

My instinct was to conceal my difference, though it was something everyone couldn't fail to notice. At school it aroused comment and frequent laughter, from a beleaguered teacher, from classmates. My brother used to tease me about it; my father in his drunken moods would rail at me and *my tendencies*. I used to think that was the reason my mother moved out his house, taking me with her. She was shielding me from his scorn, his random abuse.

Far from burying his difference in shame and withdrawal, Antigua Clemendore flaunted it, celebrated it.

He was a shabine, "a red nigger"; he showed no interest in running down women; he walked with a slight sway in his hips and spoke in a "cultured" accent, sliding easily between correct English and patois.

Despite all this he always carried himself with dignity, walking the streets in leather sandals, in bright Hawaiian shirts, a straw hat on his head at a rakish angle. He used to wear his hair in braids and locks long before the Rastas made it fashionable.

He was in his thirties and I was in high school when he started visiting my mother. Fellows at school noticed that and gave me a hard time.

– Look like Auntie Clem checking you these days, they said.

I was having enough problems with my image. The last thing I wanted was to be linked in any way with Antigua.

I overheard him once telling my mother that instead of sitting on toilet seats it was better to perch or squat. My mother laughed;

201

he sounded serious; it was the best way, he argued, to "vacate your waste". That was the most disgusting thing I'd ever heard. I tried to picture Antigua squatting like some ape on his toilet seat, his hairy arms folded across his knees, *vacating his waste*! For that reason I chose to have nothing to do with him.

You try hard to run away from something, it surprise you around the corner as in a dream. Antigua and I became close friends on a day of high anxiety when I badly needed friendship.

I had taken the high school overseas exams set by Cambridge University. My next move – a good job or higher education – depended on the results. Like so many others on the island I sweated through July and August, until the day word got out like escaped mice that the results were back on the island.

My mother had connections with the Ministry of Education. She would find out my results long before I did. I lived in fear she would come home one afternoon and I would read my results on her furrowed brow, in the tone of her voice when she called my name.

One day went by, then another. Nothing. She left the house; she came home for lunch; she went back to work; she returned in the evening. Something was mysteriously holding up the release of results. There was nothing I could do but wait.

Meanwhile I looked over the question papers and, trying to remember what I had written, gave myself scores. Good scores, lower scores, honest scores. No matter how generous I was I had this sinking feeling the news from Cambridge, England was bad.

All of a sudden one afternoon she started pestering me about a finding a job.

– But Ma, I waiting for my O Level results, I said.

– Your brother didn't wait for his results, she argued back.

Which was true. He'd taken his exams three years before, then he'd gone straight into a shirt and tie job as a bank teller. I had no such ambitions. Why was she harassing me this way? It turned out her connections had slipped her my results. They were bad. Very bad. She was disappointed and angry but for some reason she couldn't bring herself to break the news to me.

The results were eventually published in the weekend issue of the newspapers. People searched for names and grades and gossiped about everybody's fate and future. I was ready to drown myself in shame, to hide in a cave for centuries now that the whole world knew how badly I had failed the Cambridge exams.

This was how Antigua found me – ashamed, hiding, a Cambridge exam failure.

He showed up at our gate riding a motorbike. I was sitting on the back steps. I heard him come into the yard and couldn't believe my eyes: the motor cycle, the white short pants, white American sneakers, fancy American tube socks. A change of costume, a change of pace, and *bam*! his life was on a brand new road.

– What happened, you locked out? he asked in his singsong voice.

– No.

– Your mummy home?

– She went out.

– Somebody do you something?

– Not really.

He checked his watch, slackened the band on his wrist and massaged the wrist.

– I hear exam results out. What Mr. Cambridge do you?

I told him. He looked at me as if somehow I'd let him down. Then he sighed.

– Lambs to slaughter. Every year, fresh lambs to slaughter. And Mr. Cambridge never set eyes on these islands.

He spoke softly and sympathetically. He seemed genuinely distressed. That sound of compassion I'd never heard before. Usually when older people talk to young people on our island, they preach, they bully, they pummel you with words. Antigua spoke with such real feeling I had to look away and hold back tears in my eyes.

– I pass Miss Lewders' subject, I said.

– English, right? he said. Maybe Miss Lewders could find a job for you in the library. It nice and quiet there. What you think?

I shrugged. It didn't sound like a good idea.

– I still don't understand how I fail so many subjects, I said.

– Look, forget about Mr. Cambridge. You can't moan and groan the rest of your life. Listen: lock up the house, lewwe go for a ride.

I felt my spirit swell a little like a sail in rising winds, but I hesitated. To be seen with Antigua on a motorbike, to be pointed at on a day when all the talk in town was about high school students!

– *Garcon*, it's a good time time to break away from all the doom and gloom around town, he said.

– Alright, but I'm not passing by the Square, I told him.

– Not to worry, *garcon*! There are highways and byways out of town.

I knew I was taking a big risk, but I wanted to stop thinking about Mr. Cambridge and my mother and a job. I wanted to ride on the motorbike, to be taken far out of the gossip-filled town, far out of my own misery. It was so easy – locking up the house, climbing onto the pillion, roaring off, feeling the wind in my face as we rode away.

On the roadway, going up the Morne, Antigua turned his head and said:

– Listen, when you riding with me, you take the bends with me. Don't lean the other way. Your fear is you might fall. Lean into it. Always lean into your fear.

Soon we were racing up the hills, passing through villages. My fear of falling slowly vanished. I learned that day to lean with him at high speed round the bends.

I felt reassured by the warmth of my thighs against his thighs.

– You have to decide where you going to work, my mother said to me one day.

– Leave him alone. Give him time to find out what he wants to do with his life, Antigua pleaded.

He was now taking my side, shielding me from the blasts of my mother's impatience; making it appear as if the matter of *what he wants to do with his life* was too important to be settled in some frenzied way.

I took my cue from him and wandered around town, pondering about my life. Other fellows had made, or had been pushed into making, quick decisions. Some had taken jobs; others were moving on to "higher" education. A few had disappeared.

I spent most of the afternoon near the harbor watching the tourist liners maneuver to turn around, the propellers stirring a cauldron at the stern. I wondered what it was like being the captain of those ships, navigating seas around the world.

Sometimes the fishing boats were in. There was one fisherman I liked to watch; he wore a bright yellow mackintosh and a cone shaped hat; usually he was besieged by women carrying baskets, picking and choosing; he had a great way of holding them at bay, jangling his scales, laughing and joking and making fast change from a fist full of dollars.

Water was all around us. I couldn't see a future out there for me, whether charting the seas with tourists or trawling for fish.

One morning, coming down the hill, I heard someone calling my name from a house. Antigua. He told me to wait, and soon he joined me.

– What happened to the bike? I asked.

– Broke down. It cost too much to fix and I ent no mechanic. In any case these roads don't need more machines.

Another change of pace. This time he carried a walking stick; a canvas bag hung from his shoulder; an unlit pipe was stuck in his mouth. He was "a seeker of truth".

Suddenly he stopped, put his hand round my shoulder and invited me to take in the view. It had rained most of the day. The sky was still overcast. I gazed with him at the city below, at the roofs of miniaturized dwellings, at the placid sea, the damp shiny vegetation.

– You say your prayers this morning? he asked.

– My prayers?

– Look carefully. Meditate on the beauty, the handiwork of the Creator.

He made a gesture with his walking stick, like Moses waving his staff. I couldn't hold back laughing. He wasn't pleased with that.

– Look again, *garcon*! God is the greatest artist. Smell the air, fresh and sweet. Look at the coastline, the skyline, clean and sharp, etched by the hand of the Creator.

I didn't know what to make of all that. I wasn't in love with Nature. There was too much bush and vegetation around for me to stand back suddenly and take notice. His hand on my shoulders squeezed gently, firmly. I didn't want him to think I was stupid but right then I didn't know what to say.

205

What I saw as we continued down the hill were three goats foraging in the garbage people dump by the side of the road; then I heard loud cussing between two women, their hair in early morning disarray, over some man; then I saw a little boy, tearful and obstinate, being struck and pushed by his older sister. I felt the contact of my feet with the road surface, the dipping wobbling sensation of going downhill.

Antigua walked ahead, his chest puffed out, swinging his Moses staff as if the handiwork of the Creator was still everywhere around him.

– What does 'Tigua do, I asked my mother one day.

She gave me a strange look.

– He's an artist. You aren't going to be an artist. You got to find a job or a trade!

Gregory Gregoire, as far as anyone knew, did not pass his Cambridge exams. Yet there he was – with a little luck, and help from his old man – selling insurance. And screwing women. And playing God with a microphone in his hands.

Antigua Clemendore, from what I heard, didn't pass his Cambridge exams either. How he became an artist, my mother couldn't explain. I got the impression it was some kind of a calling.

He sort of drifted on a homemade raft, so to speak, doing several part-time jobs: earning a little money here, making frames for people with paintings, playing the flute with a jazz trio working in hotel lounges, designing costumes for the carnival season. And always, somehow, getting by.

Antigua cut a figure of color and energy around town, but I couldn't be like him. I didn't have the courage to be like him. I couldn't conduct myself like that and have people calling me names. Besides, my mother, much as she admired Antigua, would have caught a fit if I even hinted at following in his footsteps.

I found my calling the day Antigua dropped by to visit with a new friend of his. He introduced my mother one afternoon to Pete, a chubby fellow with a rich red beard, who had just arrived from Canada.

Pete was some kind of volunteer sent by the Canadian Government to teach Motor Mechanics at the Technical College. His palms were soft, his eyes twinkled boyishly behind glasses, and his manner was as gentle as a lamb.

Somewhere amidst the laughter, Pete's nervous silence, and my mother serving lemonade and mauby, attention turned to me, my jobless empty future.

Antigua declared:

– Maybe you could send him to the Technical College. Pete will take care of him, right Pete?

My mother looked quizzical; Pete breaking out of his silence grinned and asked me what I liked doing best; my mother wondered if she knew anyone at the College.

– And when you graduate maybe you could fix my bike, Antigua laughed.

Just like that, with everybody blowing bubbles and making it sound like some rainbow of an idea, the tracks of my future were laid down. I didn't have the nerve to protest. In September I started classes at the Technical College.

My mother was more relieved than thrilled. It wasn't a job but at least there was the promise of employment when it was over.

It didn't turn out too bad. On the first day Pete stood before us like a harmless smiling bear and charmed the class into becoming auto mechanics.

– We're here to fix cars, he began. We're training to be car doctors. We'll learn to operate on the sick machines they wheel in. We'll put them right, make them well again, and send them back on the road.

He was rubbing his soft palms and smiling with blissful eagerness. The fellows found him strange but they liked his friendly manner, his genuine interest in us.

– Judging from the state of the roads, he added, the machines will soon be sick again, but that's all right, we'll put them right, and send them out to run again.

I liked the way he talked, making everything so simple, so full of adventure and fun. Like Antigua he was different, gentle.

The years went by: our seasons of Christmas, then New Year's Eve, then Carnival, and in June more victims were sent off to be slaughtered by Mr. Cambridge.

I met Miss Lewders several times; she still taught English at the college, still wore those tight-fitting skirts and *lapas* and walked in slimbodied quicksteps. And she was still unmarried. Always she expressed surprise I had turned into an auto mechanic. Always she told me how pleased she was I had passed her subject. She'd rub my back and squeeze my shoulder, preparing to rush away, and leave me with her favorite wisdom words, "The world is your oyster" or "Carpe diem!"

I graduated from the Technical College. I got a job with Mr. Prospere's Rent-A-Car business. The work was not too demanding. Tourists, finding our roads slightly perilous, drove with great caution. I kept the cars in good running condition.

Gregory Gregoire, looking younger than his age, kept telling the Carnival crowds, "It's show time!" He got a pretty stewardess pregnant and for a while he was seen driving around town with the mother and child beside him in the front seat, sunlight falling through the sunroof on their heads like a sacrament.

Antigua kept dropping by, though now he'd worked out a routine with my mother. He would show up escorting tourists – usually during the Carnival season, or the Christmas season – longhaired, smiling white couples in sneakers, their skin peeling from sunburn. My mother would invite them in to lunch under the breadfruit tree in the backyard; she served local dishes and drinks; Antigua gave little lectures on local herbs.

The next big change had to do with Antigua's conversion to Rastafarianism.

Antigua braided his hair, though in a clean stylish way. He wore a tricolored belt, African dashikis, and sometimes a blue track suit pants. My mother teased him about all this:

– *Aie, aie, aie*! You look African from the waist up, and a basketball star from the waist down. Is where you really belong? she said.

– I'm a citizen of many worlds.

– And since when you become this big Rastaman?

– What big Rastaman? You hear me talking about Haile Selassie? Or going back to Ethiopia?

– All that hair on your head, Lord have mercy!

– Is *hairstyle* you looking at, not *hair*! Besides, I have nothing against shampoo.

– Well, I have to be careful. Next thing I know, you smoking ganja in my living room.

– Now, hold on! Let me tell *you* a little secret. You see that glaucoma you worrying yourself about, I could cure that problem right now with a little herbal preparation.

One evening I came in and found him lying on our couch; he had a high fever; he had picked leaves from our soursop tree and had spread them all over his chest and on his brow, drawing out the fever.

– Better than aspirin, he said to me, his white teeth gleaming. I thought he'd gone crazy.

This interest in Rastafarianism was the turning point in his life. The last great change I was to witness; the final act before the curtain.

For one thing, the local Rastas were angered by the way Antigua seemed to flirt with their religion. They were serious fellows, our Rastas. They hung about the market square with their dreadlocks and their bibles scowling at passersby. Sometimes they sold oranges and sugar cane and water coconuts at street corners. They were easily provoked into arguments about Selassie or the Pope or Bob Marley.

But nothing vexed them more than the sight of Antigua riding by – the bicycle was now his mode of travel – sporting his dreadlocks, cutting style with their religion. They shouted after him about the sins of Sodom and Gomorrah and promised him a special hellfire of unending pain for his wickedness.

It was round about this time that I began seriously thinking again about my life, comparing myself with other people, feeling restless and fed-up with everything. I wanted a change, a new season. I couldn't explain why. I just knew I was tired of the same old same old on the island.

But where to go? What to do?

On our island young people don't bring up their deep problems with other people. When things reach a breaking point, you do something rash like getting a girl pregnant, or getting blackout drunk at weekends. Or selling drugs. Anything to deceive yourself into thinking your life not sinking day by day in quicksand.

Maybe I wasn't desperate yet for any of the above. I decided to talk to Antigua. After all it was he who had helped me over the first roadblock, that day of destiny with Mr. Cambridge.

Just when I needed him most I couldn't find him.

– 'Tigua been round lately? I asked my mother.

– He visiting his mother in Bamboo Village, she said. She not feeling too strong these days.

His mother! I'd never thought of Antigua having a mother, like my mother. I mean, he'd always struck me as someone independent, someone who had cut away from family. Needing no one. Too busy inventing new roles for himself. He was the artist always planning ahead for the next kiddie carnival. He had no time for old ladies in the country.

I should have known better.

He showed up eventually and I caught myself staring at him, seeing him for the first time as some old lady's son.

But now he was a sight to behold. Physically he had shrunk almost to skin and bone; his dashiki hung limp on his shoulders; his arms and his face looked anemic; his energy was still there but it wasn't the fierce bubbling energy we knew him for.

Before I could raise my problem he asked if I knew anything about drumming. He needed a drummer rightaway for his Dance Theatre Company, a group he had formed two years ago. They practiced every weekend, African dances; but recently his drummers weren't showing up. He invited me, urged me, his thin arms flailing in distress, to help him out at least for that weekend.

As it happened his drummers returned that night, saving me much embarrassment. I decided to hang around until the group was finished. This caused me some discomfort. It wasn't easy watching about twelve or fifteen girls in leotards shaking their breasts, stamping their feet and shuddering their hips.

I have this image of him sitting in the dimly lit schoolroom long after the dancers had left, his long legs outstretched, his face gaunt, his body exhausted. He must have been dying bit by bit, minute by minute, and all he could say, muttering to himself, but intended for my ears too was:

– Don't understand why I feel so weak!

210

I thought at the time he was taking the Rastafarian avoidance of "worm-infested meats" too far. Oranges and vegetables were all right if all you did was read the scriptures and meditate on the evil ways of man.

I wanted to tell him, see a Doctor; but I was caught up in admiration of his strength, his absolute refusal to be slowed by any common complaint. He was after all someone different, a man changing shape as the fire inside moved him.

He was always telling my mother how much great artists suffered, how despite raging fever or pounding pain they wrote or painted or composed. Our island had its artists. It gave them little room and time for greatness, he said.

We walked home that night, slowly; he was wheeling his cycle; there was a cool breeze coming off the ocean; most people had turned in for the night; here and there a dog barked. It was to be the last night I spent with him.

Antigua said things to me I'm still afraid to repeat. Never before had anyone revealed so much of his life, things I'd feel compelled to hide from other people. We're not used to opening our personal lives to others. We're afraid of the wrong response, laughter behind our backs, betrayal.

He must have sensed something was happening to him that was irreversible, even though he had no name for it, and couldn't understand why he of all people had been afflicted. So he talked about himself and his mother, about the island and the world, about why he chose to stay, and what might have happened to him if he had left. That night alone with him changed the rhythms of my life forever.

I remember flashes of anger, for instance, at those balding journalists who curry-favored certain politicians, who couldn't tell the difference between "artists" and "artistes". He poured scorn like vinegar on our Minister of Tourism, Mr. George Pone, who *had the nerve* to tell him he should make himself *useful*: to suggest that he and his *masquerade boys* could dance and play music at the pier to welcome the tourists when the liners docked.

He spoke about roaming the hills and the beaches as a boy; about his love for the children at carnival time; his search for a way to embrace the hard, living beauty of this island; his love for the sea on Sunday late afternoon; for the island after midnight shut tight in dog-barking sleep; his love for me.

And I remember clearly this: we were approaching the market square. It was deserted but for two vendors selling water coconuts and cookup rice. Antigua was talking about his dance group. Most of the girls had not done too well at Mr. Cambridge exams. Like me they were adrift and unsure. His Dance Theatre was a place they could bring their bodies "for discipline, for care and for culture", a place to harness their wayward emotions, wait for storms to pass, set a new course for their lives.

But things didn't quite work that way. Some of the girls got pregnant and dropped out. He spoke about this with bitter feeling as if there was a conspiracy directed at him and his Dance group.

– They join the group. After a couple of months, they get plugged and drop out.

He described it that way, the girls getting "plugged", and the villains were young men like Gregory Gregoire who could not view the bare limbs of women without pulling at their crotch and planning some carnal entrapment.

Gregory Gregoire was responsible for one of his leading dancers, the most talented of the group, getting "plugged" and giving up.

– I swear, if God don't punish Gregory Gregoire for his sins, there will be retribution here in this world!

At this point I joined him in the silent hope that Gregory Gregoire would one day get what he deserved.

We were passing the coconut vendors. I threw a glance at the flambeau flare, at the coconuts piled up on a crocus bag, at the machete waiting for the next order. The vendors were two Rastas; scratchy reggae music came from a transistor near their cart.

One of the Rastas said in a low menacing voice:

– Woe to the evildoers. Those who stray from the paths of righteousness and practice unnatural fornication.

I didn't think the remark was meant for us until we'd passed them, and I realized that Antigua had fallen silent.

– Batty bwoy, divert! the voice reached after us again.

And I thought: he's used to all this, these righteous fellows rushing out like guard dogs to snap at his ankles, snarling from behind Selassie's palace gates at his wayward soul. No need to panic. We'd hold our heads high and ignore them. Bible spouting rabble!

Antigua kept walking, his shoulders curved, his head bowed in troubled thought. The deep voice pursued him with its scriptural warning like a hand slapping the back of his head.

– Jah go lick you with diseases, batty bwoy!

I had always seen Antigua as master of his private world, always in control, over himself, over petty nuisances like this. Right at that moment he did something I'd never imagined him doing. He turned and looked back; and in a voice ferocious with the fever of his dying, still hoarse from instructing the dance class, he said, *you fellas… you children of Zion… you so quick to punish, so ready to judge. I don't mind you waiting for ships of salvation to take you home. Just leave me alone.*

THE WALL

There will be an official report of what happened: carefully typed, full of facts and dates and verbs like *proceeding* instead of traveling; making it easier for someone in authority to read before he hands in *his* report to his superior who must, of course, adjust his tie and bring his lips closer to the microphones of the press.

There will be something in the newspapers, written so that readers on buses and subway trains would have no problem making simple connections: a story about a man from the islands and a tragic accident in the city; or a tragedy of the islands and a man in the city.

Since reports like these do for our souls what a breakfast cereal does for our bowels, we might wish to find another way: the route that brings to that other microphone, our heart, the parched lips of those who died and those who wished they could be born again.

Here is what we know:

There was a multi-vehicular accident off the Southern State Highway. It happened at about 4.00 in the afternoon, so the light was not a factor. It happened on a section of the road where for brief seconds motorists lose sight of what is in front of them, or assume that whatever is in front of them is *moving*. In this case there was a stationary car in the center lane. The first car to come around the curve saw it too late, swerved, ran off the road and overturned; four more cars came after that, saw the same car sitting in the highway, attempted to avoid it by swerving or braking, and ran into each other.

Multiple injuries, some critical, cars at twisted angles, their polished steel crumpled or torn off.

By some odd miracle the driver of the stationary car escaped injury. His car was not even touched; he seemed unaware of the carnage around him until a young woman climbed up the embankment from the first car, tapped his window, and asked if he was all right. What happened next has everyone baffled. The

217

young woman apparently got into the car, and it drove away from the scene.

Now as for what we *don't* know, here's a Q & A from the usual suspects: both sides now:

Q. *Maurice dead*!

Those were his first words to me.

His hands still gripped the steering wheel with the consternation of a man holding the still warm body of a newspaper headline, refusing to accept its judgment. His fingers were dry and wrinkled, and his eyes stared through the windshield, pained, unblinking.

And I thought: he has been struck by lightning, or the whiplash of sudden grief. I know how to give comfort. If I put my arms around him, let him cry, listen to him as he howls and clings to me, if I give him what every woman knows a man in his state needs, he'll get over it; put it behind him; blow his nose, wipe his eyes in his shirt sleeves and get over it.

So I walked around to the other side of the car, tapped on the window, signaling him to open the door. Then I gave him a sharp command like a slap on a baby's behind:

Drive!

A. Well, I can't explain what happened unless I borrow old cliches like *struck by a bolt of lightning* which is probably the most telegenic way to put it.

I remember the fingers tapping the glass, sharp knocks, frightening at first, a sound like stones bouncing off your windshield. I remember lifting my head, or lifting Maurice's head, for before he died they'd told him to face the wall, and at some point he must have pounded his head on the stones asking over and over, *Is this really happening?* and *Where are my comrades? Where are the people?*

How could something like this happen on my island?

Lifting my head, turning to see this woman's face at my window, hair strands blowing loose from under her blue winter beret; wondering what she wanted, then thinking she might have walked or driven all the way from the island;

218

skating across frozen seas, one hand behind her back like some winter Olympian, bearing news to strangers broken down on the highway.

I rolled down the window a little. The cold November air put its knife to my throat.

What I said was: *Maurice dead*?

Q. Actually I didn't materialize from *nowhere*, though, as I told him later, I come from the island where Maurice had been told to face the wall.

"You from Mesopotamia?"

"No, but my aunt was born there."

"You know, when I tell people here I was born in a place called Mesopotamia they look at me as if…"

"I know, as if it's a joke."

"And they'd look me straight in the eye and say, *Isn't that somewhere in the Bible belt*? And I'd say to them, Isn't Paris in Texas? Isn't Lisbon in New Jersey? Cuba in Kansas? Mesopotamia is a village in our island. The world is a blue heart, contracting and expanding. These days a satellite fork could lift you from your living room and plunk you down into a raging famine or a civil war any time in the world."

"You sound like a man who watches too much TV."

"Of course, that's the wrong thing to say, if you're in *their* living room. Too serious. Spoils the mood. We're supposed to be immigrants, right? With nothing to share except tales of escaping with your life!"

I was in the first car that missed hitting him. We smashed into the divider and spun around before rolling down an embankment. Maurice was at the wheel. His first impulse was to hit the brakes. Someone else might have thought of steering around the obstacle; but I know my Maurice. Split seconds before the crash I felt his body harden, bracing for impact, heard his feet stamp the brakes, the gap closing quickly and sideways, the tires screaming like a burn victim as the rubber peeled off, for Maurice relished little human contact much less a collision like this.

By some miracle we missed the car. We spun in a skater's delightful slide on ice. We hit the divider with a crunch, and spun

219

some more; then we rolled slowly off the road into the grass. And there was this heavenly silence.

He looked at me, dazed; he looked at his hands as if they'd just performed some life-saving miracle; he looked out at the sky, blue and bright and chilly. Then he reached for the door handle.

And I thought: I'd better get outside too, find out if I could still walk, if my body could feel the cold wind and other sensations of being lucky to be alive. And for no reason I could think of – except perhaps I didn't want to stand and survey the damage done to *his* car, hear him swear then turn to me wondering, *What do we do now?* – I walked back to that other car, tapped on the window, heard him say, *Maurice dead*; knowing he couldn't have meant my Maurice, but in any case he'd got it right: it takes something like this to break up the ice in your veins, send gorgeous blood rushing.

A. "So, where are we going?"

"Where were *you* going?"

"I was just driving."

"Like back on the island? A Sunday afternoon drive?"

"Something like that."

"I don't too much like driving in this country."

"What about… what happened back there?"

"Back there? I don't think anybody knows what happened."

"Okay, let's just drive for the time being. Pretend you're heading for Mesopotamia."

So I kept driving. And since nothing had really happened to me – except that I had stopped just in time before the car hit the wall, and now out of nowhere this woman – I stayed in the center lane, ignoring the road signs that generously give you time to change course: take any exit off the highway, then the boulevard, your driveway, garage, cell.

Amazing, how smoothly your hands go on automatic pilot, so that you feel safe and fearless in left lanes at any speed while something else engages you: in this case, Maurice facing his wall, at Fort Rupert – or was it Fort Frederick? – *"which had been bombarded with mortar fire from rocket launchers and heavy machine fire lasting for about fifteen minutes,"* the news report said.

He must have flung himself to the ground; must have heard

someone outside ordering the troops to man the barricades, the sound of feet running by and trumpets calling men to arms, for the island was about to change hands again: the Dutch firing from ships in the harbor, or it might have been the tricolored French with shaggy-haired drummer boys and new names for the villages. In any case, what could he do but keep his nose to the ground, lifting his head to shout, *Brothers and Sisters* – as musketry and cannon tore through the valleys, and banana leaves flapped like white flags – *Where are our children, where are the ones we love?* And this extraordinary sound, more deafening than roars from the stands at cricket matches or at party rallies, this twentieth century cataclysm, *mortar fire from rocket launchers*, must have moved him to scalding tears or prayers, nose to the ground, fingers reaching down into the earth, asking the long gone dead to pull him safely under, take him away from the stupid mistakes, the multiple sclerotic things suddenly going wrong.

"So you knew him?"

"Knew whom?"

"This Maurice you're speaking of… There are tears in your eyes. Why're you crying? Anyway it's hard these days to *know* anyone unless you can figure out the combination to their hearts. Unless you let their spirit knaw at your soul like characters in good fiction – that's what my Maurice says."

Know him? Yes, I knew him. Though not in the way the whole world knows him now after those twenty second clips on TV and radio where he's framed as the good guy or bad guy, depending on the nation's GDP or the state of your marriage.

I knew him like a twin brother. We went to school together. My name followed his alphabetically and in those old college days of corkhats and *He who would valiant be, 'Gainst all disasters*, we were monitor and deputy monitor, Head boy and deputy Head boy; we were buddies, as they say in this country.

"Were you *companeros*, as they say in Cuba?"

"No, we were never *that*. Never *companeros!*"

"Do you often cry like this? Here's some tissue."

I don't cry at all. I was astonished at what was happening, the tears welling up from some hidden spring, as if someone else was crying through me.

I mean, I'd heard the news of what had happened on the island. They'd mentioned his name – some names they're not used to pronouncing here, like Colin, which usually comes out Colon. They talked about the dust and the chaos that usually follow the collapse of any house built on compassion for the masses. I heard the news, swallowed the facts, but the capsules must have been timed to disintegrate inside me over days or weeks, for suddenly on the roadway back there I felt this pain in my chest; I took my foot off the accelerator, wondering where I was, the car slowing, you've got to keep your speed up on these highways. I looked up, the sign overhead said BABYLON, NEXT RIGHT, and then it hit me: Maurice was facing the wall; I could feel his head banging against my ribcage; I stopped the car and started crying just like that.

Q. Well, they'll be looking for us, someone to blame for leaving the scene, a scapegoat to help them sell tomorrow's newspapers or bring back the good old days.

They'll never understand what came over me, what made me say to Maurice, *I think your wife knows about us*, as the car radio did something bewitching from Brahms – *It helps me relax*, he told me once – which sent me back to the basement and my *au pair* duties.

Maurice is probably the most civil person I've ever met: those thicklensed glasses, the pipe wedged in his mouth, his socks and shoes when he's buttoned to the wrist, the fingers playing with the hair on his lips – and *voilà*: the Professor of melancholy, one leg trapped in a tranquil marriage, one hand reaching out to tousle the hair of some wild dream.

"What in God's name are you talking about?"

"You heard me – and please don't swear like that – I said, I think your wife knows what goes on when she's not there."

"I don't think that's funny, Juliette."

"I'm not *trying* to be funny."

"Naomi couldn't possibly *know*… I mean, she isn't *there* to notice anything. We've been very careful, very discreet, haven't we?"

"I suppose so."

"You *suppose* so!"

"I haven't said anything to her."

222

"I hope you're not implying… I hope you're not suggesting for one minute that I might have given our little game away."

"Have you given our little game away?"

"Don't be ridiculous. Look, if you don't mind I'd like to concentrate on driving."

Silence. Brahms *allegro non troppo*. Cars passing us fast in the right lane.

"A woman can tell these things."

"How would you know? You're not exactly an expert on women's passions, least of all my wife's… I'm sorry, I didn't mean that… Look, could we drop this?"

"But don't you think she'd notice if you've slept with someone else?"

"How could she possibly notice, Juliette?"

"I don't know. Something about you is bound to change. Something about any man. A wife could tell the next time you slipped into bed beside her."

"So now you're an expert on marital infidelity!"

Infidelity. He was the one who uttered the word. Not until that moment in the car did we ever consider the whole thing as infidelity. It was just something that *happened*, though at one stage I blurted out, *You're old enough to be my father,* giggling, not wanting to hurt his feelings. Not missing a beat he said, *And therein lies the pleasure, my sweet… You never knew your father so what's the difference.*

But what if she knew? I know, *whatif* and *whatif*, all the way down the rusty chain! Yes, I know, nobody's got time for these games. We're driven souls, focussed on the ONE WAY road ahead: our quiet revolutions, our daily bread, our *O My God*! nights of perfect sex. But what if?

A. Easy for anyone to say who hasn't felt the loss of a loved one – which compels me to admit my love for Maurice, admit the obverse side of this feeling of loss. What if, indeed, he hadn't played Mark Anthony that year in our school production of *Julius Caesar*?

That was one of his finest achievements, Mr. Puddephat, our English teacher said, and he should know: retired, back in Shakespeare's England where he probably heard the news on the BBC.

223

Must have sucked the breath out of him as it flashed across the television screen, and his wife – bad hip, walks with a limp, childless, loyal till death – must have looked up from her knitting.

"What is it, dear?" she must have asked

"It's Maurice. It's about his island. There's been some awful mess. They say he's dead."

"Maurice?"

"You remember Maurice. Best Mark Anthony we ever had at the college. A born leader. A natural. Poor devil seems to have got himself in a mess."

"I don't remember any Maurice."

"You don't remember much these days, do you?"

"I can only recall that very rude young man who told you he wouldn't renew your contract. *We won't be needing your services*, he said, *we're taking over now*. Becoming *Independent*, he said. Our own flag, our own national anthem, all the rest of it. *Won't be needing your services*! Well, if things are in a sorry mess now, they've only themselves to blame."

"No, no, no that wasn't our Maurice!"

Born leader. A natural. Our Maurice. That he was, indeed, and maybe he took things too far, surpassing himself, which is often the temptation of the brightest, the scholarship winners.

But what's a natural born leader to do?

I resisted his appeals to take a part, not born to conspiracy, wary of crowds in the square. I volunteered instead to be prompter, hissing lines the players might forget, though the fellows rarely forgot anything, except Cassius. I had to prompt him once: "Do not presume too much upon my love." Had to say it again, he didn't hear me the first time, wondering if the audience had heard me hissing from backstage.

Do not presume too much on anyone's love, not least the love of the masses, the love of your beloved, that's what I'd hiss to any crowd in the square! But nobody listens to the prompting of a soul backstage these days; it's all done for the cameras: adjusting the tie, *my fellow Americans, Jamaicans, Croatians, comrades, colleagues, do not presume*: the fast fading glow of today's headline news.

So what's a fellow to do but watch from the shadows, envious a little, wishing sometimes it was me speaking those lines, bewitching those crowds from the podium; wishing it was me remembered and hailed by England's Puddephat as a born leader.

On the final night I had to prompt Cassius again: "That you have wronged me doth appear in this." Maurice was standing in the wings in his toga, a white sheet borrowed from his mother's dinner table, waiting his cue; he'd been hushing the masses backstage who were told not to peer around the curtains at the audience in the dark: *They can see you peering*, Mr. Puddephat had said.

I might have warned him – had I known then what I know now – that on any island *wrongs* are more often than not imagined; we're not that quick at dissembling, not shrewd at disguising hurts; disagreements turn rancorous, a scratch festers into sore temper; then allegations and denials flying left and right, jackasses braying in the press, and once the revolution starts spinning there's nothing more weighted with suspicion and fear than a slighted comrade, one who feels or imagines himself betrayed by the other he'd trusted to the hilt.

    – *You wronged me!*
    – *Do not presume*
    – *But you wronged me, man!*
    – *Too much! Too much!*
    – *But you wrong, man!*
    – *Do not presume too much upon our love!*

Q. If all that doesn't sound like a man wrestling the jaguar of his conscience, I don't know what does.

We were moving slowly now along the roadway, men at work, three lanes merging to two, time to take stock of what other people in their bucket seats can afford to drive, bumper stickers – *Unless you're the head buffalo, the view is always the same* – and we're thousands of miles from homes ravaged by monsoons, killer volcanoes and other holocausts. You could feel guilty, rolling along the highway safe and dry in your spiffy machine, not wet up to your underwear in some rainsoaked rice field.

When I thought about it, he had a point.

Harder than standing on a stage or on a solidarity platform and making speeches to the masses who are ready to accept anything

225

you promise as long as there's bread in the shops, good stiff bananas, and a chance at the lottery or the football pools: harder than *that* is keeping the romance between Brutus and Cassius going once they've taken their revolutionary vows.

Maurice and I were lovers with a high-temperature fear of love. We discovered this one evening while his wife was giving their four-year-old an evening bath. We heard the child squeal with delight as his mother carried him towel-wrapped into the bedroom, and there he was telling me about himself, baring his soul, so to speak, while I sat unable to conceal my delight that he should entrust me – not his wife, Naomi – me, the *au pair* up from the islands, with a tale of what made him so unhappy.

It seemed their revolution was in trouble. He was dutiful and considerate, though after a while you sensed that was all there was to their marriage: this attentiveness, remembering her birthday, kissing her goodbye, *Could you change the oil on my car this weekend?*, the boy's dental appointment – all that obligatory stuff.

He might have mentioned his struggles with O'Neill as she snuggled up to him, nibbling at his throat, the boy tucked in and fast asleep, both of them *not feeling up to it tonight.* Might have said he was sick and tired of teaching students – those huddled masses wading ashore from Mexico or Haiti – how to write English. I mean, what use all those years studying the life and work of Eugene O'Neill, his Ph.D thesis, what use *all that* when what the struggling masses needed was help with their daily basic syntax? Naomi, silent, *knowing how he feels*, letting him go on. I mean, what is happening to this nation, to civilization as we know it?

All of which must have dampened any smoldering lust fires, putting them out for weeks or months on end.

And then his article on O'Neill published in a scholarly magazine. Shot down in the next issue by stalking scholars with high-powered prose, staking their claim to O'Neill territory. Saying in effect he doesn't know what he's talking about. Skewering him because that's the way it goes, people waiting to pounce on your stuff like raw meat for the maw of their careers.

To which Naomi must have kissed him, *Never mind, try to get some rest*; turning on her side. And by next morning the boy's awake, and there are things to attend to, the facade of caring, other clock-ins that pay the mortgage and keep us busy like workers in a bakery each morning kneading fresh loaves.

Poor Naomi. Married to Maurice. Vows. Till death. And poor O'Neill, who wants to climb into bed with them. Poor Maurice unwilling to say, firmly, *No, not now, Eugene, not now!*

What's a woman to do under all that weight? What's the other woman to say – the *au pair* up from the islands, who'd never heard of Eugene O'Neill?

"To tell the truth, my reading stopped after high school. I mean, serious reading," I said.

"I ought to lend you something by O'Neill."

"That would be nice."

"Have you heard of *All God's Chillun Got Wings*?"

"What's that?"

"It's a play O'Neill wrote, I think it was in 1923."

"I wasn't even born yet."

There was always in his fisherman's eyes a wide patience with the ocean of ignorance he must sit on every day. Now, it seemed, someone was tugging on the line, though my remarks accompanied by foolish island giggles might have struck him as silly, not worthy of his time.

But a girl can tell there's something squirming at the other end. I suppose it's all those empty nights in the basement; it could get cold and quiet down there. When the lights are out and the whole house is locked up tight, their island revolution starts coming apart each time they turn on their sides. A girl listens and understands these things. She discovers where the fires have gone and like a moth she's drawn to the wandering flames.

"What does he write about, this O'Neill?"

"He doesn't write about any one thing. I mean, he's written many many plays. One was set in the West Indies! I suppose if you tried to squeeze it all into one central concern, that would be, I think, the soul inside our bodies, what happens when faith is lost."

"Sounds interesting. How did you get hooked on O'Neill in the first place?"

"That's an interesting question… and a long story. I've never told it to anyone. I don't think I ever explained it to Naomi."

227

Ah, something held back from Naomi! A secret squirreled away all these years! Isn't that how conspiracies start?

Had he let her into his secret she might have squirmed a little under the bedspread, her bedtime sadness turning to sweet need, then pinned a medal on his chest, for he'd earned a night of passion with that tale. So that suddenly one night there's turbulence over my head – *O my God, like that, yes, like that!* – and it's Naomi, who rarely screams, who's always tight-lipped in the throes of her pleasure.

But how many medals can you earn? How many stories could any Maurice invent to raise these sudden squalls?

I listened. I might have have smiled often, or giggled too much in that simple way of island girls. But the telling became a confession from his soul.

There was Maurice, young and adventurous again, on a road in the Carolinas; his car broken down, so he's walking to the nearest gas station; heat, dust and sky the clearest blue engendering awe and fear; until a house way back off the road seemed to beckon him, weary. There might be someone there who knew about cars.

The house: sun-bleached and wood-framed, built with an owner's love of open spaces and solitude. The grass took his footprints and gave back soft warnings. It was near sunset; he had to get his car fixed before an unfamiliar dark set in.

Closer. A dented parked truck. Trees that loved clean shafts of morning light. Then a man and a woman. Blacks. No time for distrust now. Closer. The man was sitting between her legs. She was scratching his head with a comb, oiling his hair, fingers twisting it into braids.

Smiles. Erasing the strangeness of strangers.

The woman young, *a dusky belle*, with slender bare arms. The man, much older, could have been her father. She had the finest teeth. Pearly white. And her dress pulled up revealed the smoothest ripe brown thighs.

She caught him staring, even as he stammered and pointed helplessly back down the road. She must have heard the rushing of his blood as of a nearby stream. The man knew what to do, of course, *Just a minute, I'll get my toolbox, make yourself comfortable, care for some lemonade.*

228

Caught him staring again, his helpless desiring blue eyes. And Maurice tried to tear his eyes away, struggling with the rush of desire.

The car miles back down the road. Many more miles away his apartment with its locks and smoke alarm and neat bookshelves and humming computer; and here, immediate and powerful, that clear face like lilies in his stream, those thighs, the man sitting dry-docked between those ripe brown thighs.

As the man sloped off to find his tools and the keys to his truck, sliding away from between her thighs – which remain open, not taunting him, the dress tucked in a little carelessly since she wasn't expecting company – in that moment he wished he were in his car, driving by, seeing her, statuesque, in a passing flash, so that there was no need to engage those eyes which did not want him, which knew his world, and could tell in a flash his yearning.

Something caught in his throat. He searched for disarming words: *I would do anything, I would be your slave, if only you would let me.* Eugene O'Neill.

She might have sensed his discomfort. *Want me to do yours?* she asked.

Those words. Their transparent way with words. That moment.

He'd wanted to tell someone about those words, about the way her eyes did not waver, the tremor of desire in their laughter.

Naomi and the boy were out the night he told me this story. When he was finished I had stopped smiling. I stared into his icy November blue eyes, now moist with relief, and I thought I saw the soul of a runaway slave.

Awkward silence. Maurice about to fall from his narrative perch to his knees. The sound of something ripe tumbling through the branches. I asked him if he'd ever eaten a mango. I presumed he knew what I was talking about.

A. "Where are we going?"

"Oh, so you're feeling better."

"What do you mean?"

"Once you start asking questions like that, it means you're back to normal. You've shook off the octopus oozing slime all over your conscience."

"Who are you?"

"Me? I'm just an *au pair*, up from the islands, a little disoriented at the moment…"

"An *au pair*? We don't have *au pairs* down there. And you don't talk like a girl from the islands."

"Oh? How do girls from the islands talk?"

"As if their minds are somewhere near their bottoms."

"Boy, you're really in fine form right now. You can take the next EXIT and drop me off anywhere."

"*Anywhere*? But where are we? And what are you going to do?"

"Find my way back. Maurice has probably recovered by now. I think he'll be relieved when I show up."

Feeling better? Octopus oozing slime? *Au pair*? She didn't know what she was talking about.

She wasn't there as Maurice, dressed down in that neat collarless outfit designed to put an ordinary-prole face on the leadership, inspected the guard of honor, dressed up and stiff at attention; he walked through the ranks, and took the salute, and must have wondered how valiant (to borrow a Latinate word) they truly were, what kind of warriors (in the tradition of the Zulus) they would make in defense of the revolution.

For they were ordinary young men, the people's army, straight out of high school or the powerlessness of the people; conscience hardened by the sun; cropped heads filled with the cinema heroics of U.S. marines led by Clint Eastwood, bodies built on cassava, plantains and rum; stern and glamorous in uniform; menacing on duty.

Surely the Cubans or some political adviser named Ernesto must have warned him, must have told him they were prone to excesses, the result of no beaches to swarm ashore, no *Sierra Madre* to fight through until the triumphant ride on tanks into the city; they were just *fellas* with big guns, who like to joke about women, chew and suck sugar cane, and tilt their hats back on late-night guard duty.

So that when the order came, the enemies of the revolution identified, facing the wall, ah Maurice, you must have felt you had a chance. All you had to do was turn around, refuse the blindfold, say, *Fellas, hey, allyou stop this firing squad nonsense, hey Vincent,*

230

Lester, hey, Cosmos your pants fly open, boy! Listen, we pass that stage!

Last chance: all he had to do was stare down that upstart Lieutenant who used to play outside left on their high school soccer team, compel him to reconsider as he read the "Execution Order" and the fellas lifted their heavy duty machine guns.

One last chance: maybe if he fell on his knees; though, if they spared his life he could never live down the gossip and the kaisos about how the Revo leader went down on his knees and beg for mercy.

One last *last* chance, then: the people could save the revolution like a last minute goal, storming up the road to Fort Rupert, waving banana machetes and grass scythes; but all he could see was clear afternoon sky, the sea below passive; and he didn't have to check his watch to know that the market was closed for the day, and those head-wrapped vendors were heading home before dark and the mosquitoes, for there was dinner to cook, and some little boy was going get a serious cutarse because he won't listen.

"The shooting lasted for about ten minutes and while the bodies lay on the floor where they had fallen, the soldiers again opened fire on them. Bits and pieces of flesh and blood splashed about the square," the news report said.

Ten minutes of stuttering ecstasy, gold-ringed fingers squeezing the triggers, the shudder of all that fire power; the body on the ground jerking and twitching, the fellas making sure he really dead.

Ten minutes of echoes ripping across the island, kiskidees aflutter in the trees, taking off in horror for other islands; cows, goats, chickens sensing tremors as fresh blood soaks the earth; propellers churning, the revolution changing course; some grizzled old geezer fond of island history shaking his head, *Executions at dawn, they used to execute people at sunrise, not sunset, bechrist, these Revo fellows don't know nothing.*

O, Maurice, what did you hear? What did you eyes behold in those ten minutes?

The afternoon light, as the sun goes down, colors melting on the horizon; the afternoon sky you used to contemplate from your verandah overlooking the careenage, a book waiting in your

231

lap, a prayer like a boil on your lip. They say your whole life does flash before you, every living second parading past at blazing speed. It must have danced before your eyes like fireflies.

O, Maurice.

Q. I didn't think he was feeling *better*. Fellas feel *good* after they've pulled the trigger and emptied their souls of sperm. Not better.

The nerve of him – to suggest I don't know what I'm talking about! I know what it is to be desired, to be opened up, to be pounded and pounded for ten minutes, wild birds screaming in that forest. And just because I don't strut and shake my moneymaker and spread aphrodisiac feathers doesn't mean I don't understand human loss and appetite.

I could tell you a thing or two about loving, which in a way is like killing, if you consider that something dies each time lovers assume positions and execute their love. I could explain how things fell apart, Naomi eventually overthrown from her pillowed plumpness under the canopy of the high four poster.

You didn't have to be a coiled spring in their mattress to understand the pretence, the careful attention to each other's feelings the *not feeling up to it tonight, darling*, while murder must have simmered in Maurice's heart each time he didn't quite get there, deep down in the hot Carolina swamp, where that other woman still sat with spread thighs, offering to polish his knobs.

He took me back there one evening; the ghostly hand of Eugene O'Neill led the way.

I had to find a juicy mango, shipped all the way from the Dominican Republic. Maurice has this attachment to knives and table napkins. You'd be amazed how he cuts through a morning orange, making neat sections, then peeling away the rind, so attentive to detail, so careful with knife and fingers not to make a mess.

Naturally I had to show him our island way: you don't peel back the skin of a mango as you would a banana; bare teeth sunk deep into the pulp; a squirt of juice in your face, and away you go, sucking and squeezing and squeezing, until we've cleaned that mango back down to its white seed. Of course, some of it trickled down his beard and onto his sweater, which distracted him with worry for awhile. Didn't want to leave anything for Naomi to pick up on, *What's this stain on your shirt, dear?*

The day came when Naomi and the boy set out on a long drive across state lines to see her mother. There was so much preparatory fuss and chatter, *Did you gas up the car?* making believe they truly care, the gift for grandma on the back seat. And I was doing everything not to meet Naomi's eye, knowing something would happen, something already happening as the seat belts locked her in and she lifted her head, *Have a safe trip*, for Maurice's kiss.

I was watching from the doorway.

Did she glance my way over his shoulder after that kiss? Was the smile still on my face? Should I have waved at the boy one more time? Isn't there something about all this that gives the game away? Each side sensing something's up – the propellers churning, the revolution changing course – not quite sure where the signal's coming from?

I waited in the basement. He sat in the living room all morning, the pipe wedged in his mouth, reading. I had some tidying to do down in the basement. He went out. He came back. I watched television and planned a trip into the city the next day. He came down and asked me if everything was all right and did I mind coming upstairs, share a lobster with him.

"I don't think I can manage all this."

"Course you can... Here try the dip... What are you drinking?"

"I don't drink."

"You don't drink? Well, tonight I'll introduce you to something new and extraordinary. A Chablis. Have you tasted Chablis before?"

"You trying to get me drunk tonight, eh?"

"And how about some music? What would you like to hear?"

He wasn't really trying to get me drunk, though it wouldn't have taken much encouragement to turn me inside out. It was a different Maurice at the dining table, cheerily breaking lobster legs and pouring his Chablis, hair rumpled like an Emperor's, a boyish grin on his face; no time for paper napkins, nor Naomi who'd promised to call as soon as she'd arrived at her mother's.

A different Maurice, alone at last, lord of his castle. A different

233

Juliette, too, the *au pair* come up from the basement, casurinas of desire in her hair, with each sip of wine something breaking free from those hairy pincers of habit and fear.

And what happened next you can call fun or fornication or whatever you like, but I was thinking: *Girl, the island where you lived all your life is back there, this Chablis tastes dry, I like the sensation of lobster on my tongue, he looks so romantic snapping legs, lifting his glass to propose a toast, here's to all islands where we once lived.*

"Do you believe that deep inside our bodies, something struggles to breathe free?" I asked

"What makes you ask that?"

"I don't know. Maybe it's all this wine and lobster. Right now I feel something inside me making me want to dance."

"O'Neill wrote about the soul under skins. At the core of our being. Pining, screaming, praying for release from every prism or prison."

"Oh? Tell me more about this O'Neill."

"I'll tell you what we could do. I'll pretend I'm one of his characters. I'll speak his lines. Let's move away from the table. Leave everything just the way it is, we'll clean up later. Come into the living room where it's comfortable."

Two bodies soaked in Chablis? You shouldn't think it had anything to do with too much wine going to our heads; I was aware all the time of what was happening; I was ready as never before – free of fear, free of mother, free of patriarch islands. The moment ripe for revolution.

As for Maurice, he was like a schoolboy actor ready to go on, the first night performance.

No doubt about it, he knew his lines. He had taken over O'Neill, or maybe O'Neill had taken over him, either way the words... *We'll go away...where a man is a man, where people are kind and wise... the soul under skins... I don't ask you to love me... I want only to be near you... to serve you, to be at your feet like a dog.*

So close to me, I could see moisture on his lips, his hair flat and damp on his head from some mysterious sweating; and his eyes, the glasses put aside, filled with a sudden myopic need to be taken at his word. So close to me, his hands reaching under the sweater

234

for my twin julies, his soul at my feet like a dog, every word licking my face with tenderness.

The telephone rang. I jumped to my feet. His hand circled my waist, his fingers gripped my buttocks with the fiercest longing. I touched his damp hair. I saw Naomi, standing erect, one arm folded over her belly, waiting for someone to pick up the phone. I felt his head against my thighs wanting to give its life and its blood.

Whose Maurice was this? Naomi's? *No, mine!* I didn't have to ask him to love me. He was at my feet. The telephone ringing. The moment ripe for revolution.

And Juliette, sweet Juliette, at once timid and certain this was what she wanted, this was what she'd feared and wanted all those years, the pleasure of lifting her sweater over her head, the baring of her julies, the labial squeezing *like that, yes, like that.*

Moments like this hang for a while, then ripen. Mangoes detach themselves in time, then tumble through the leaves.

I slipped to the living room floor; no reason to think that anyone would hear us; these clean walls had never seen such wreckage, our clothes strewn everywhere, a little anxiety, there would be sticky stuff on the rug, we'd have to scrub it away before Naomi got back. These walls had heard only the polite offer to fix Naomi a drink, or on occasion a mezzo soprano who'd spread her arms and in full throat do tricks from a walnut cabinet in a corner. These walls would hear for the first time the howling and the dying, our bodies sloshing through muddy swamps, the revolution in full cry.

When the telephone rang again, Naomi very much worried, glancing at her watch, *maybe he just stepped outside*, when it rang and rang, Naomi quite sure now there was someone at home, Maurice panting, my legs locked around him tight as a blindfold, it was all but over; not quite, the telephone ringing again, *maybe he went out to secure the car*, Maurice on my back like a dog, all over the rug, all over the house.

Please, one more time! This will never happen again.

Ah, Maurice.

235

Q/A. Where are we, in any old U.S. Main street outside the city once you've come off the highway, what do we do next? where do we turn? Well, I've got to find my way back, things have been rather quiet lately, and someone's bound to throw a fit asking questions, "She showed no emotion", nothing stays the same, though you must admit you feel a lot better, I mean, it isn't as if we can do anything about it now, despite what those friends of the revolution advise, *Don't mourn, organize!* everybody turns away and gets on with it, the lousy job, the philandering spouse, there's enough to keep you busy, smaller pains to hide *the pain*, fresh memories to block *the memory*, you really think it's that simple? of course, it is, see that gas station, there's bound to be a surly acne-blemished attendant who doesn't care for blacks and is more than willing to direct you out of his neighborhood; then what? well, there's always the six o'clock news, did you hear that in China during *their* revolution in the '60s thirty million people died? I mean, imagine that, *thirty million Maurices dead*, no, no, not *my* Maurice, we should count ourselves lucky we came up against the wall, touched it, lived to see this day, and you can let me out here, I'll find my own way back, thank you

CAMACHO'S
KISS

The day his daughter was born, March 31, 1986, he'd always remember because forty eight hours after he had to take them home from the hospital in the tow truck, and as they neared home he spotted this car with New Jersey license plates broken down on the highway. He could tell the driver was in trouble, he stood staring at the machine as if it wasn't supposed to break down, and usually they don't.

But there they were, Camacho, Banuchi and the baby Cherokee, cruising home on the south-bound highway, and over there on the north-bound, three lane traffic beginning to slow and merge, he could see a commuter in distress, a Japanese man in a blue business suit, his wife standing beside him in a neat white dress, hugging herself from the cold, chastened at this sudden public exposure on the roadway under a chilly March sky.

Abruptly Camacho stepped on the gas, the call to action, the wild dash to get to the scene before any other tow truck operator. This time Banuchi screamed, *What's the matter with you?* for the jolt almost woke the baby, *Where the hell are we going?*

It seemed unconscionable; they were going to stop by his mother's place first to show the baby, then they'd pick up a pizza and go to their apartment.

But Camacho had seen that look on the face of the Japanese man, the panic and rising terror, for he would have to abandon the car on the road with the hood raised; and just across the highway the peeling facades of derelict buildings, harbor of felons and idlers and rats, after all this is NY city; they trap you at traffic lights and wash your windshield for quarters; they watch and wait for a situation like this, you walking away to get help for your stalled car.

This Japanese man would want his BMW towed away at any the cost, all the way to New Jersey: *Sorry, Banuchi, got to go to work!*

239

Banuchi not really understanding, *Camacho, you're supposed to be taking me home. I've just had a baby!* But already they swing off the highway at Third Avenue, run through two lights, turn onto the north-bound; a glance over his shoulders as they merge, no other tow truck in sight, his orange flashers spinning, and Camacho knows he's won, no one can beat him to the stall.

When they arrive the Japanese man is still standing beside his car, waiting for the miracle he must have prayed for, that pulls up in front of him on oversize wheels.

Banuchi still can't believe this is happening, but she loves Camacho and although the doctor had told her they were not to *do* anything for eight weeks, she'd love to go to bed with him as soon as this was over. Camacho has a gentle reassuring manner, doesn't talk much, kind of shy and quiet; good looking, smooth hard biceps and a cute pony-tail; just watching him hook up the BMW makes Banuchi forgive him this crazy shit.

The Japanese man is impressed too. Camacho looks clean and trustworthy, wears a black T-shirt even though it's a cold day in spring; and he wears a body-builder's belt. He twists the rearview mirror and runs a comb through his hair before he jumps out the truck and gets to work.

Soft-spoken, courteous, Camacho urges them to get in his truck; the Japanese man is apprehensive at first; he looks at Banuchi who jiggles the baby and says *Hello.* Anxieties evaporate when they see the baby, another miracle on the roadway, this must be the Year of Small Miracles. It's a tight squeeze in the cab of the truck but Banuchi makes herself small, moving her hospital bag to her feet.

They drive off: the Japanese man glancing back at his car, shocked at the way it looks hooked up and disabled; his frail wife smiles at Banuchi's baby as Banuchi makes herself smaller, feeling embarrassed. Camacho asks the Japanese man to bear with him, he had to make a little detour first off the highway, not far, so they could drop Banuchi and the baby off at his mother's, then they'd be on their way.

He checks his gas gauge for the long ride to New Jersey, and he thinks: it would be great to have more babies, maybe three or four, in quick succession; they'd all pile into the truck like this, go for Sunday afternoon drives.

That day with all its drama was often recounted by Banuchi when her friends dropped by to visit and play with the baby. She'd embellish the story a little saying, for instance, that the Japanese lady – turned out they were Korean – *almost freaked out when she climbed into the truck…almost had a heart attack* when they stopped outside the building where Camacho's mother lived.

The day her daughter came home was also the day she felt Camacho begin to drift away from her.

It might have had something to do with those weeks during which, following the doctor's instructions, they were not supposed to *do* anything; it might have been her imagination but Camacho was staying out late at nights; she didn't trust these Spanish-speaking schoolgirls with their bracelets and their attitude.

He'd show up at odd hours of the day carrying shopping bags and sounding off like a deer hunter just back from the forests; he'd play with the baby, grab something to eat, then he was off again, shouting up at her from the streets, *Banucheeee, do you need anything?* He liked waving at her as she stood framed at the window with Cherokee at her hip.

He gave the impression he was on the road all day rescuing broken down Korean commuters in BMWs and towing them to safety; making dollars, *make you happy babe!*

It gnawed at her heart, these absences. There were days when she cried.

One day the bath tub overflowed and there was water everywhere, and one afternoon Cherokee won't stop crying and was turning blue. *Camacho, where the fuck are you, man?*

They shared quiet weekends in front of the television set watching rented videos. They sat in the living room which was bare but for a rug. Their bedroom on the other hand was furnished to the ceiling like a love nest, with an old fashioned four-poster, side tables, a vanity mirror, silk window curtains. Banuchi loved the illusion of space in the empty living room.

Camacho would bring back Chinese, or pizza from her father's shop. Later in each other's arms, she tried making love to him; she thought he'd like rolling around during the commercials, pawing and kissing like baby lions; he didn't; he didn't like being kissed.

His love-making before they'd moved into the Bronx apartment was usually in choky narrow places: the bedroom at his mother's place, a telephone booth, the school's gymnasium; he liked taking risks, *If you don't take the risk, you miss all the fun.* "But this is crazy, someone might see us," Banuchi used to say, pulling down her jeans. Crazy shit like that excited him.

Now in the living room of their home, she'd get as far as unbuckling his belt then she'd give up; go inside to change Cherokee; she'd hear him shouting, *Hard core, fucking hard core, man!* during the action scenes on the television set; she'd wonder if this was what life would be like with Camacho forever and ever.

But Camacho was her love. They'd stuck with each other through high school. They called each other by their last names in mock imitation of their teachers.

Camacho was a wizard with cars. Banuchi worked as a receptionist in a dentist's office. They had plans. Vague faraway money-needing plans. They were saving up. Initially Cherokee wasn't in their plans but once she was on her way they decided to bring her into the world.

And Camacho was her hero. He'd saved her from herself, from her family. They'd saved each other from the traps and dead ends in the world. The temptation of drugs. Clinging to each other, loving and shielding each other. Doing crazy shit against the world.

How could she ever forget the night he turned up outside her bedroom window and said, *I have come to take you away*, making a frightening face with Count Dracula teeth. Her brothers had known he was coming; waited for him all night at the subway stop banging their baseball bats against a railing and checking every Spanish-speaking nigger who came up the steps and headed down their block; hadn't a clue what he looked like but they were ready to beat the shit out of him.

Stupid idiots, with their swagger and slick hair; stupid *guidos*, thinking they owned the block; swearing no Spanish-speaking nigger was going to come into *the neighborhood* and talk to their women, *who the fuck he think he is?* Banuchi got so scared she called Camacho, told him not to come after all; got so angry she told her brothers he *would* come the following night; he'd bring a Spanish-speaking crew onto the block, *beat the shit out of all you stupid guidos*!

Then on Friday night, way past midnight, a tap on her window, a strange face, *his face*, his fingers wiggling impishly at her; she couldn't believe this; it's two in the morning, drizzle streaking down the window pane, and there's Camacho smiling and telling her to open the window. She didn't know whether to laugh or swear but her belly was on fire; she wanted to grab him by his belt and haul him through the window, take off his damp clothes, dry his hair in her lap, *you dumb bozo*, drag him to her bed and squeeze him in the coils of her legs.

I've come to take you away, he said, like some crazy vampire. Was he serious? *O Camacho, you're full of crazy shit.* But how did he get here? He'd fought his way up the block, hurling his enemies into sidewalk trashcans with the sword of his love. In that instant she knew she loved him, loved his face all wet and fearless, wanting her to leave with him right now.

Like this? she said, fingering her nightclothes, *I can't come like this!* He smiled like some prince of darkness. She knew right then that she would go anywhere with him. It was the first time she'd ever left her home without using the front door.

You don't forget something like that. You figure it must mean something. They were born to run, Camacho and Banuchi, *we were meant to bloom together*, like lovers in those poems Mrs. Dellacamera, her English teacher, made her read, *Had we but world enough and time*, and they had time, she would give it all the time in the world.

He'd even encouraged her to go back, once the die was cast, make up with her family who had turned their back when they found out what happened that night; her brothers cursed and didn't care; too scared to go into the Bronx and bring her back; her mother upset each time they sat round the dining table, Banuchi's chair vacant; her father who loved her more than anything in the world, ate silently, told the family, *leave her alone, she'll come back,* believing a father's love was stronger than any young man's passion.

Camacho drove her to her father's pizza shop, six months pregnant, in his tow truck; let the old man see what a decent guy he was, had a job, would take care of his daughter.

And Papa liked him; didn't embrace him the way he hugged Banuchi and cried and asked if she was all right; liked him, anyhow; *he seems like a nice guy*, he told the family; soft-spoken, with a head on his shoulders, and hair on his head, not like his two sons who cut their hair off, bald like Kojak, stupid jerks. Told Banuchi he wished they'd get married now that the baby was coming, it would make her mother happy.

Camacho her hero, her love, father of her child.

Days when she hated him, or thought she did; days she told him he was nothing but a *schmuck*, a mean selfish man from a mean little island of *barbudos* in the Caribbean.

Those eight weeks of *not doing*! They'd pass and she would have him again. She hated thinking like this, as if the only way to hold him was within the vise of her thighs.

Christ, Camacho, you're turning this heart into a lake of bitterness, hard and cracked.

And Cherokee, *ah Cherokee, my love*: frothing up her milk, her baby fist clutching the air, her face staring up from the crib as Banuchi powders her; she'd smile releasing dozens of butterflies, and Banuchi cooed and sang and forgot what pain time aims and shoots at impetuous hearts. *Ah, Cherokee, you are my love!*

Camacho had in fact begun to drift away though he didn't think of it as drifting.

It was just the way things were, the volatile rhythms of his days and nights, waiting for accidents to happen, prowling streets and highways in search of raised hoods, the adrenaline surge as his radio crackled and he took off for the accident scene.

Sometimes needing a break he'd head back to the old block where his mother lived, run an errand for her. When he was done she had the table set and a meal prepared. Outside his homeboys lounged in the shade, lean and handsome, in bright sneakers; and the young women he grew up with, who had boyfriends, but

244

glanced his way wishing for just one night in his arms, for Camacho's got the juice.

He didn't fight back when Banuchi fought with him; took her hits like a man; helped her change Cherokee, his big shoulders hunched; let her steam and rage until it was time to hug her, *no, don't touch me, man*; told her he loved her, should be spending more time with her and Cherokee, but the way things were, the tow truck and everything.

He offered to take them on Sunday afternoon rides but Banuchi refused, fearing another emergency like the one with the Korean man. Besides she didn't think she'd enjoy riding around in a tow truck on Sunday afternoons when everyone else was out in polished cars enjoying the first weeks of spring. *When are we going to get a fucking car, Camacho?*

Then it was time for Banuchi to go back out to work.

The tow truck took the baby to his mother, Banuchi to the subway; bills to be paid, the apartment to be cleaned, they began to feel like married folk, tired at the end of the week, not much time for lovemaking, and when it happened it wasn't quite the same. Her body had changed after Cherokee. It would never be the same. The milk-warming breasts, the thighs, the tumescence – was she getting fat? had Camacho stopped liking her?

Camacho said it was all right, unwilling to complain; told her he loved her, turned on his side and went fast asleep. Banuchi just a little suspicious, now that the craziness had gone out of their young love.

Slowly she reconciled her life to the change. *You've got to learn to live with it*, her boss, the dentist had told her, *learn to deal with it*. She popped his words like pills into her overheating heart.

She'd put the key in her door, drop her bags and tell herself, *I'm doing all this for you, Cherokee, my love*, while Camacho took everything in stride, one day at a time, moving with the flow, the flow of traffic, the flow of his thoughts.

Those eight weeks of abstinence, Banuchi home with the baby, had not really altered his character, though sometimes stuck in a traffic jam he'd be lost in thoughts about himself.

He discovered he liked being on the road, working; he liked the thought of Banuchi at home taking care of business; he liked coming home to Banuchi and the baby; and dropping in on his mother who was always there for him. This notion of people he cared for being in fixed places while he prowled and raced and rescued was most satisfying to him.

At times his face would tighten as a wandering sadness passed over like a cloud, and his thoughts strayed to his father whose bones lay buried somewhere in California.

In junior high school one day he'd been asked to write about someone he admired, a role model, and while everyone else on the suggestion of Miss Waldrop chose Martin Luther King or Roberto Clemente or a basketball star, Camacho chose his father.

"My father," he wrote, "lives in California. Every summer he drives all the way from that state to New York to see my mother. He stays for a week or two, then he drives back to California. He'd leave in the morning when I'm asleep. I'd wake up and he'd be gone. But those two weeks are the happiest days of my life. He brings me presents. He takes me to Coney Island. We have wonderful times together."

I'm sure your father is a wonderful man, but this wasn't exactly what I wanted. But his father was the man he most admired.

Why not someone we all know and consider a hero? His father was someone he knew and considered a hero.

Miss Waldrop couldn't understand. English teachers were nice, they spoke proper English, but they didn't understand shit!

His mother understood, but she warned, *You're not going to grow up to be like your father, you promise?* What she wanted was his promise never to leave her, the way his father did, even though he sent her money and she learned eventually to live without him, learned to wait for his visits. He was the only man she'd ever love. She liked the notion of belonging to one man of all the men in the world; bearing his child, the flesh of his flesh; letting him take her body like no other man ever would.

She kept all the pain and loneliness out of Camacho's life, so that her son grew up to know and understand only what he saw: a silvery haired man, over six feet, his face ravaged by the good Californian life. *When are you going to stop drinking? It's no good for you!* wearing cowboy boots, and blue jeans that gave him a bowlegged gait.

246

He'd come rolling into New York in his 1960's Cadillac, an old beautiful workhorse of a car with a license plate that read NOW, BABY; bearing gifts; his smoker's raspy voice filling the apartment; and for two weeks his mother glowed with happiness.

Camacho: knowing and loving the man who rode into the city and then disappeared; so that when he heard of his death it seemed like just another disappearance; he heard his mother telling the woman in apartment 5B his father had been killed in a highway accident, hit by a truck, his beloved Cadillac crushed and crumpled, on the I-95 back to California where there was another woman; and no one dreamed of contacting her except some drinking buddy who remembered the way he talked about his woman in New York, and found a snapshot of Camacho and his mother, and an address, and thought they might want to know everything had been taken care of, *we gave him a nice funeral, he was one hell of a guy.*

Camacho: choosing to treasure the fiction of his father, staying away from his mother's stifled grief, her swollen red eyes, the fevered watering of pots of cacti on the window ledge; suspecting he might never see his father again though one day – who knows? – the Cadillac would come rolling into the city, astonishing everyone, *he's back, he's back*, wearing a white suit, shoes and tie, a Cuban cigar unlit in a mouth full of gold-capped teeth, *he's back in the Bronx*, beers from the *bodega*, stories about the San Diego Padres, and the conga drums deep into the night.

On hot summer nights under the awning of the *bodega* he sat with Manuel, one of his father's New York pals, and played the congas. Manuel was an old baseball player who'd come from Cuba hoping to make it in the major leagues. He never did; he settled instead for playing drums in an orchestra. This is how he met Camacho's father, on summer nights, daylight saving time, apartments stuffy; they drank six packs and sang old Cuban love songs; mopped their ageless faces and talked about women they loved.

Manuel still wore those lacy Guayaberas and an Afro hairstyle from the sixties; and Camacho who knew little about playing music decided one evening not to go home to Banuchi and Cherokee; he'd hang out with Manuel and play the drums.

247

He'd grip the drums between his thighs, lift his head in that rapturous way his father did; he'd whack the skins with his palms and sing the refrain of *Guantanamera* which was the only Cuban song he knew; and Manuel told him he was the spitting image of his *papi;* maybe he'd be just as lucky as his father, a man who had achieved the lifelong dream of any man making his own way in this world, with his car and his women and the conga drums.

Three years can pass bringing not much change to the city: three Christmases, three July 4ths, three seasons of baseball games; the same cries for winners and losers. Then a building is razed after seventy years of housing memories; a man dies after two decades as a lifeguard on summer beaches. In the meantime new immigrants are knocking on doors; the supers throw out old furniture; desperate lives hunger for new tenancy.

In the three years it took for Cherokee to start walking, to speak English (with a little Spanish and Italian thrown at him when she was uncooperative) Camacho's mother took to wearing tight fitting clothes. She'd pat her stomach and joke with her neighbors about her sexy body. A few men offered to take her out to dinner, taxi drivers with fat wallets, younger men who used too much cologne and tried to impress her with their languid handsome bodies. She chased them all away.

Something, perhaps the birth of her grandson, compelled her to return to the days before she met Camacho's father, when she knew she was beautiful, and when the right man had not yet come along.

She turned her house into a childcare center; young working mothers paid her to watch their children while they went off to school or caught the subway. She proved to be good at this; it brought the glow of happy young womanhood back to her face; kept her busy; gave her back some pride now that she didn't have to wait on welfare checks.

Banuchi had lapsed into a mood of resignation after several attempts at weight loss programs. She told herself she would be forever plump; she didn't think Camacho would leave her; she ceased to worry about those Spanish-speaking girls with their anorexic bodies and foolish high school dreams of becoming models.

It was the dentist she worked with who brought complications to her life.

He kept confiding in her all through his divorce proceedings, which were long drawn out and apparently very painful. They had lunch together in Manhattan restaurants; he'd insist on paying the bill, causing Banuchi much discomfort, for now she felt compelled to take his side, absorb the anguish in his whispered stories about the selfish demands of his wife, the divided feelings of their six-year-old daughter, Samantha.

They'd return to his office; he would put on his white coat and get back to work as if nothing really bothered him.

Banuchi was thrilled he'd chosen to entrust her with intimate details of his life; she grew fond of him; never before had any man led her into his painfilled heart. She admired his handsome dark-haired face – he looked a lot like Mr. Picinnini, her high school science teacher, on whom she'd had a crush for one whole year. She liked the soft-voiced ease with which he slipped back into his professional role, reassuring his patient the needle wouldn't hurt one bit.

She thought she understood the turbulence at the bottom of his soul, and she wondered about Camacho whom she lived with, whose child she bore, whom she *knew* though not in the same deep sympathetic way. To Camacho she was a high school sweetheart, now plump, and maybe less desirable; to the dentist she was a confidante, a soul companion, a friend for life.

So that one evening after he'd cleaned her teeth and she'd rinsed her mouth and they were locking up the office, his hands touched her bottom, and what happened next surprised her but didn't fully alarm her. She told herself it was bound to happen, all that confession and trust building up inside, a chance spark in the cubicle setting off an explosion.

She heard his voice crack and she panicked a little; she let him embrace her, thinking that was all he wanted, a little physical affection; she threw her arms around his neck, meaning to hide her surprise, to suggest it was alright; he reached under her skirt; he pressed her against the wall in a determined frightening way.

She could have pushed him away, could have looked him in the face, shocked and dismayed; telling him this had gone far enough, he was behaving badly; but everything had begun to flow a long time back, the sympathy, the baring of his hurt; and it all seemed a little crazy, their bodies wedged in the walkspace of the tiny office; crazy and desperate, his wanting her now, this minute; not really bullying her, so that the slightest murmur of objection from her lips, *where the hell are you, Camacho*? might have put a stop to it.

Instead she closed her eyes and prayed he would restrain himself, not go through with it; she lay back, flat as a doll; he seemed so intent, muttering his need, saying to her, *please, help me*. She was afraid to say anything, do anything; then his stiff hurried penetration, so foreign; an uncontrollable shudder as if he were about to dissolve in tears.

She had to push him off. He seemed momentarily not aware of his weight on top of her; then as she tidied herself, afraid to look at him, he grasped her hands, his pants still around his ankles, and he swore to her, still on his knees, it would never happen again; staring into her face, pleading to be understood as never before, *I don't know what came over me!*

Shut up, she hissed.

It was too much, his whining, his half-dressed sloppy remorse, hair over his eyes, looking up at her puppy-like, saying she had every right to be angry, asking to be spared her anger.

On that day the face of the world changed for Banuchi. She felt she had reached the end of her youth, the end of all romance with the world. A cold hard lump now moved inside her: not resentment, not anger; a swelling new certainty about herself and what she wanted for the rest of her life.

She wanted Cherokee to be happy, to grow up and make no mistakes; to understand that men find themselves in messes of their own making; they were not to be trusted; they were always to be controlled.

Intimacy meant keeping them at a safe distance until you felt *that* need for them; watching them curl and writhe in the stew of their own anguish; your hand on the knobs controlling the flame.

Above all she wanted now to marry Camacho; she felt a need to be anchored in marriage to Camacho.

Cherokee's third birthday was coming up. It seemed a good

moment for celebration, a time to take stock of their lives. Camacho had talked of buying her a big teddy bear, an ice cream cake. She would throw a little party for Cherokee and her friends. After they'd put her to bed, she would say to Camacho, looking straight into his face, her finger nails like talons in his waist: *I think we should get married.*

As for Camacho, after three years, he had acquired a sports car.

It had something to do with Banuchi's refusal to be taken on afternoon drives in the tow truck. *All right,* he thought, *I'll get a fucking car.* Sometimes you had to give these women what they wanted, ornaments, jingle jangles, all the shiny shit they craved, otherwise they'd chip away at your soul.

Then: *Whose car is this?* He told her.

Then: *How the fuck did you buy this car, Camacho?*

It was a long story. The car really belonged to Camacho's brother, Carlos, who did short spells in the city gaol on Riker's Island to the everlasting shame of Camacho's mother; came out and hung with his homeboys on the block; got busted, went back in; came out this time with a scar above his right eyelid and a tattoo on his arm; disappeared for awhile to New Jersey where his girlfriend lived.

To make a long story short Camacho was holding the car for Carlos, though it was Carlos who'd walked into the showroom with a brown paper bag of notes, talking of *getting me a Trans Am.*

So what was the problem, didn't Banuchi like the car?

Am I supposed to like the car, just because you've got a car? Besides it wasn't a family car; and how was Cherokee and the car seat supposed to fit into this car? *O, Camacho, what's inside that thick skull of yours?* She pinched his cheeks, sounding a lot like her mother.

They went to visit her family in the car.

Banuchi's brothers were impressed. The elder brother, Nicki, with one arm in a sling, he'd been in a fight, took it for a spin around the block. He disappeared with it for an hour.

Restless, dangerously moody, waiting in the Banuchi's overfurnished living room for Nicki to bring back his car, tired of Banuchi's mother who, he realized with alarm, had the same

251

shoulders, the same bulging breasts as Banuchi, Camacho stepped outside. When Nicki came back he got into his car without a word and drove away.

During his working hours the car was parked in front of his mother's building, a showpiece of block pride.

It was watched over by the homeboys on the block. Precinct cops rolled by and eyed it with suspicion. It was washed and waxed and little boys were chased away when they tried to sit on it. It was embellished across the windshield with the words NO FEAR, to match the words painted on the side of the tow truck, GO GET 'EM, BOY

And as the months went by, and it looked like Carlos wasn't coming back to in a hurry for his car, and Banuchi became less thrilled with it, Camacho discovered how hard it was to please women; how lonely a man can feel some-times; how deprived, fixed to the earth; no horizons to aim for, no wider purpose except what bound him to the job and the bedroom.

Car like that, you need to take it on the road, his homeboys told him. *Was built to run, not sit in the shade all day. You gotta blow it out man. Use it like a golden sword. Ride the wind. Conquer the fucking world, man.*

One week before Cherokee's birthday Camacho met Mercedes and a wind of fortune swept over the plains of his heart.

He had just towed a car home, its right side smashed in, its owner riding in the cab too distraught to talk. The man had left a paper bag of mangoes on the seat. Camacho realized this on the way back to the city. He decided not to turn back; then he spotted Mercedes and her Chevy Camaro.

She was sitting in the car on the shoulder of the Southern State highway, smoking, staring straight ahead. The hood was not raised; there were no obvious signs of distress. What caught his attention was the way she straightened up as Camacho raced by caught; he pulled off the road and watched her in the rear view mirror. She appeared to crane forward looking at him; she threw the cigarette away. Camacho threw the truck in reverse and backed slowly onto the shoulder.

It was just after ten o'clock, a bewitching time of day. The roads and highways take on an appearance of being almost deserted by vehicles. People are elsewhere, in buildings conducting business, at a table drinking coffee. But here was Mercedes, standing by her car, watching him run a comb through his hair before stepping out; knowing, she would tell him later, that something like this was bound to happen, the tow truck dispatched by her guardian angel.

– Need any help? Camacho asked.

– What does it look like I'm sitting out here for my health? Of course I need help. The fucking car just died on me. One minute I'm moving along, the next it shuts down on me. Brand new car! *Fucking dies on me.*

– How long have you been waiting?

– What difference does it make? Can you do something?

Pretty, abrasive Mercedes, glancing at her watch as if she had an appointment. He didn't care for her Long Island white girl attitude. But he had to admit she looked good, leaning against the car, hands folded, dark glasses, cutoff jeans; head tilted so that you noticed a sharp jaw line.

– What do you want me to do?

Abruptly she turned and walked away as if she'd had enough of this world of stalled cars and stupid tow truck operators; then she turned back and came right up to him.

– Would you please hook up the car and take me home? she said.

Riding beside him on the short trip home she lit up a cigarette, relaxed and rattled on about her car which wasn't supposed to break down; a bit like life itself which ought to roll along free of breakdowns on the road, didn't he think so? Camacho smiled.

Her father was a writer for a West Coast magazine, she said; she was just returning from working out at the gym when *this* happened; also she was trying to decide whether to go back to college; in the meantime she worked as a pedicurist.

What the fuck was a pedicurist?

Her father was backing out of the driveway when the tow truck drove up. Camacho saw a balding man wearing dark glasses; he had the same sharp jaw line as his daughter. He waved and asked if she was all right then he drove away.

And it should have ended there: out the truck, unhook the car, get paid, another satisfied customer, even if she did talk a mile. But Mercedes came up to him, her dark glasses raised to the crown of her head; she planted her body, gym-trimmed and slender as a young man's, in front of his, and she asked:

– Would you like to come inside? I haven't got sixty-five dollars. I might have to write a check. You take checks, right?

And Camacho hesitated; he looked into her eyes, lucid blue, quite pretty eyes, and he thought: *she's not as happy as she pretends to be... take a check? No problem... nice neighborhood, nice lawn... no problem.*

She wouldn't let him wait outside in the driveway; he wasn't sure he wanted to come inside; but there he was standing in her living room, looking around at the furniture, the potted plants, paintings on the wall, a bookshelf for her father, the writer; feeling uncomfortable with every passing minute, his hands stuffed in his jeans; wanting to get back quickly to his truck.

She had his check all written up; now she wanted to be sure she'd spelled his name correctly. She had a teddy bear cuddled in her arm and she sat on the living room sofa, not quite ready to let him go, lifting her leg and planting her dirty sneakers on the leather sofa with a nonchalance that startled him.

– Is it all right, she asked.

– It's fine. As a rule I don't take checks but I guess in this case I can make an exception.

– It's a good check. Don't worry, you'll have no problem.

– Thanks, he said, turning to go.

– Where do you live?

That pulled him up like a jerk on his leash; and he told her where, *in the Bronx*, spoke the words with that drawling homeboy pride, though he suspected she'd never passed through its streets. Her type won't.

– Where in the Bronx? she asked, yanking on his leash. Do you know the Mambo Room?... It's off Boston Road... I go there most weekends. My boyfriend plays in a band that plays there. Have you been there?

He shook his head. He'd heard about the Mambo Room. His father had been there. His father when he came in from California sometimes took his mother to a place off Boston Road which could have been the Mambo Room; drove her there in the long white Cadillac, all dressed up in shiny satin so tight round her bottom, he used to think, as he watched her from the window, that the dress would split if she bent over too far. Gave her a good time.

Camacho made a deep turn for the door. Mercedes at the Mambo Room? Her boyfriend playing with the house band? Crazy shit!

Still hugging her teddy bear Mercedes followed him outside, came up to the door of the tow truck, saying thanks for bringing her home, and maybe they'd meet again in the Bronx; Rico Rodriguez was playing in the Mambo Room this weekend.

His last glimpse of her was in the sideview mirror; she was staring after him, hugging the teddy bear which reminded him he had to get one for Cherokee's birthday, maybe the same size as the one Mercedes was hugging.

This white girl had a problem! Spoiled and pretty and weird, hugging a teddy bear; vanishing from his rearview mirror as he accelerated around a bend in the road. But, what the fuck, he'd got paid! Now he had to figure out how to get back onto the Eastbound.

He nearly shot past the entry ramp; he had to brake hard and the bag of mangoes rolled off the seat under the pedals at his feet.

Ah, yes, Manuel assured him, shuffling dominos under the *bodega* awning, there was a place off Boston Road, the Mambo Room, though it might be under new management; it was where the Puertoricannos came on Saturday nights, you got the best salsa there; Camacho's father sat in with the musicians a couple of times; they say even the great Tito Puente played there once.

He thought of asking Manuel if he'd noticed many white girls dancing there, but he didn't want to betray his curiosity. Besides Mercedes seemed the kind of girl who'd drive all the way to the New Jersey Meadowlands to see Bruce Springsteen. Not to the Bronx. Not the crime-infested, drug-plagued Bronx. Then again the music, once it got to your blood, no telling what you'd do, where you'd go, just to have all that brass and drums firing up your boilers.

Camacho wasn't much of a dancer; he asked Banuchi if she wanted to go to a nightclub; she didn't think he was serious. She wasn't happy these days with his habit of staying out late on Friday and Saturday nights; no, she wasn't interested.

He found the Mambo Room right where Manuel said it would be.

There were so many cars, shiny and new, he'd have to park a couple blocks away. No way would he leave his car parked out here. Then he spotted the Chevy Camaro, recognized the license plates. It was parked next to a fire hydrant. *The nerve, the fucking nerve of this bitch!*

No doubt about it, this was the place, this was where the weekend action started.

He stood at the door, taking everything in, the band revving it up on the platform. And Camacho thought he'd stumbled into something he had only vaguely imagined all these years. His father's world.

This was where the old man worked and played, with the tables packed tight, the exaggerated gestures of the men, the lascivious promise in every woman's smile, the scent of perfume and liquor, strobe-lit flashes, brass and heat, rump and cleavage, those horns like a flock of wailing birds, the *rakatakataka* of the drums.

His father came home from this place and slept all morning; when he awoke he coughed like death and searched for his first cigarette, all rumpled and stale-odoured, blue rings in his eyes. His mother heard the rasping cough, saw that sated glow on his creased face; and she sighed.

Camacho stood at the bar trying to ignore the quizzical stare of the bartender. He wasn't sure where to start looking for Mercedes. Was he really here to find Mercedes? He ordered a beer so that, holding the glass and sipping occasionally, he might seem more at ease with the scene.

Someone tapped him on the shoulder. Mercedes stood with her hands clasped in front of her, smiling as if she were his date, and this was the prom dance, and she had just returned from the lady's room. He feigned surprise; she wore a red dress this time; it made a neat tight wrap around her body; and her hair was down to her shoulders.

256

– I had this feeling we would meet again. Were you looking for me? she asked.

She stood close to him, looking up in his face; people kept jostling past, throwing her against him, her perfume, her friendliness, that neat trim body.

– I just love this music. I love this place. Do you want to dance? she said.

– I just came in… I'm not into dancing, Camacho said.

It sounded feeble and disappointing. She gave him a look of mock astonishment, then she casually threw her arms around his neck.

– I know why you're here. You've come to rescue me again, right…? Well, we can leave now if you like… But first, I have to tell this guy I'm with that I'm leaving. Wait for me…right here…don't move.

He'd imagined her to be somewhere in her mid-twenties, spoilt rich white girl, disdainful and generous in turn; he'd left his home, all smart clothes and cologne, not sure what he'd do if he found her; and now *what the fuck!* it seemed she was asking him to play his daytime tow truck role, take her home.

Still, he was intrigued by her schoolgirl friendliness, the popping up out of nowhere, then disappearing, swearing she'd be back; and all that stuff about knowing we would meet again, like the notion he had of some day seeing his father again.

He hadn't time to sort it out. She came back just as she'd promised. She stood before him, staring into his face with trust and a vague challenge. He wondered if perhaps she'd had too much to drink. Sensing the watchful eye of the bartender, the prurient eyes of others around him, he squared his shoulders and headed for the door.

Boston Road outside the Mambo Room was a scene of mild confusion: double-parked cars blocking the roadway, a group of not so young men and women arguing, you could almost taste the freshness of the late night air.

Camacho seemed to falter, fearing someone might recognize him; Mercedes hooked her hand in his arm as they walked away.

– Do you really need anyone to see you home? he asked.

– 'Course, I do. I always ask someone to see me home. Suppose my car breaks down or something, it's not safe for a girl like me…

257

I mean, I could take care of myself, but I'd feel a lot safer... *Look, you don't have to do this...*

He didn't have to do anything, but he'd look a fool if he walked away from her now. She stood near the Camaro, her legs slightly apart, lifting her arms to fix her hair.

A car drove by and two young heads leaned out the window, *Hey, babe, come with us, we won't hurt you.*

– What's the matter? she asked, not understanding why he looked so tentative.

– Nothing. I'll get my car.

As he started the engine a little confidence came back to him. It wasn't too late to drive away.

He came up behind her and for a moment the Trans Am and the Camaro stood idling on Boston Road, attracting envious stares from young people sitting on parked cars. He was so close to her rear he could see the teddy bear held by suction cups on the rear window looking back at him. The traffic lights changed; her hands signaled him to follow.

Only then did it occur to him he was in trouble. That little engine that purred supportively inside his body, rarely if ever breaking down, now threatened to stall; he was miles away from Cherokee and Banuchi; he lacked the will to pull himself together, take himself home. Under a clear midnight sky there was only the mystery and excitement of Mercedes.

The Camaro drove almost leisurely through the streets of the Bronx, not fearful of anything, its rear lights signaling its every intent. On the ramp to the highway it seemed to hesitate, slowing until the Trans Am was right up on its tail; then it shot away. Caught by surprise the Trans Am almost ran into a truck bearing down in the right lane. It was the first performance.

The Camaro was streaking away from its fast start; the Trans Am answered by switching to the left lane, its exhaust screaming, forced next to cut back to the center lane, pass a slower moving Mazda, then back again to the left lane, drawing on all the power it could call up from its twin carburettors.

It caught the Camaro at the tollbooths, inching forward on line, looking mightily pleased with itself.

Committed to paying the toll Camacho was reminded of how much the whole night had cost him so far. What if the Camaro bolted from the tollgates first, and disappeared before he could count his change? He'd have to turn around somewhere and pay a toll to recross the bridge. It wasn't too late to turn back, call a halt to this shit. *Swallow your pride, cut your losses, forget this bitch, man.*

The Camaro was waiting on the other side. He had to wind down his window to hear what she was saying.

– Sorry I almost lost you. Stay close to my rear lights, okay?

Who the fuck did she think she was? Who the fuck did she think he was?

He was ready now to show her his stuff. He grabbed the felt dice dangling from his rear-view mirror and massaged them for good luck; then he took off.

Stick to your ass? I'll stick to your ass. Before the night is over, I'll have your ass!

Now he was moving in unfamiliar territory. Were he in his tow truck he might have thrown more caution to the wind; he didn't want to put a scratch on his car. He switched off the car radio, the better to focus on her rear lights. Luckily for him traffic on the parkway was reduced to two lanes at 30mph so it was easy to stay close. Once they'd passed the obstruction she went back to her old tricks, switching lanes without warning, overtaking slower cars. He thought his tailgating might have made her at least a little cautious, force her to slow down.

On the Southern State highway the lanes opened to five, the bends were as sudden and sharp as the letter S; she streaked away again, the teddy bear waving goodbye; the Trans Am's tires screamed and he glided dangerously out of his lane to the right, then to the left, ignoring irate horns behind him, around him; pushing the pedal to the floor on the straightaways which brought him up close again.

But she was on her home turf and he was hitting the brakes more often. He had to fight his way recklessly forward, worried he might lose her if she took an exit, leaving him to barrel on, chasing after something that was always ahead of him.

Not once did she yield. Even after they'd come off the high-way, she raced through the streets of her town showing off her familiarity with the local roadway.

He pulled in behind her in the driveway and switched off his engine. He stepped outside his car and waited. She came up to him and hugged him with crushing affection.

– *Way to go!* You were terrific! All the way home! You made it all the way home, she said.

– What the hell did you think you were doing? What d'you take me for, some punk who likes to show off at night in a car? he said, stiff and serious.

– C'mon, lighten up. It was fun.

– You call that *fun*? I call that stupid reckless shit!

He looked around, not wanting to make a scene in her driveway.

– I'm sorry... really I am... listen, why don't you come inside? My father is away for the weekend...please...? I'm sorry about the whole thing.

She took his hand and led him up the concrete path to the door. He followed, still sulky, the tow truck operator not at all impressed with what he'd witnessed tonight. But he was in a mood to be mollified.

Inside the living room he released a huge sigh of relief as he sank into the leather sofa.

– You know, you're the first to see me all the way home, she said.

– What do you mean, the first?

– I mean, you... *are*... the first. Honest! All the way to my door! The others didn't stay the course.

– I'm not surprised. They probably all got killed or something.

– There was this black guy, he came close, I mean, real close! At one point he was far behind but he must have had eyes like a hawk... He saw when I came off the highway. I saw him in my mirror coming up real fast, then he ran a light – just by the gas station? – and out of nowhere this stupid cop shows up! Pulled him over... poor guy, can you imagine...?

Camacho looked at her in disbelief. *My God...what would have happened if the same stupid cop had pulled him over!* He could think of nothing to say to her right then, but sitting there, sulky and disapproving, wasn't going to cut it; and to get up and leave would give the impression he was truly ill at ease in this situation.

Relax. You're already in deep shit! Relax!

– How about something to drink, she said. Keep your spirits and your pecker up, as my father would say.

She left him in the big living room again; she was humming a leftover melody from the Mambo Room as she opened the refrigerator door and cracked ice cubes. He stretched his legs and looked around him.

Most of what he saw looked expensive; one or two things looked comfortably worn; everything hinted at her father's tastes and choice. Her father, he imagined, sat here, ate there, worked over there. Why did two people need so large a house? Why did they collect so much stuff, spreading it around so neatly, barely noticing it after a while.

– Life is all fun and games to you, right? he said, thawing out, wanting to show how relaxed he was.

– It's like crossing the road to the other side, she said, handing him his drink.

– The other side?

– The other side… you know… everybody's so stuck on *their* side, so scared of what's over there on the other side, the violence, the blacks, the shit that happens.

She sat on the sofa next to him, her feet tucked under her. Now and then she reached up and played with his ponytail.

– I'll tell you a little story. My father drove me into the city one day – I was six or maybe seven – and we were crossing this wide street. I mean, it was *the widest street I'd ever seen in my life*! Usually he'd take my hand but this time he crossed over alone, then he turned and told me to cross… I was fucking scared… I started to cry. He just stood there refusing to come and get me… *C'mon*, he waved, *cross over!* I thought I'd get killed, you know, a car or something would run me down.

– I'm amazed you're still alive today, he said.

– That's exactly the feeling I had. My father says it's like this… fear is the widest street you cross. Some of us never make it. If you cross to the other side you get this feeling… like *wow*… like you've conquered the world…now you can do anything you want, know what I mean?

Camacho thought he knew what she meant. The way he saw

261

it, she was a rich spoilt white girl, trying to justify her rich spoilt-child behavior.

He raised his glass to his lips more frequently, his body tense again; whatever he was drinking gave him a warm feeling inside, but it still couldn't steady his nerves.

She got up abruptly, excused herself and vanished inside. When she reappeared she was wearing a bathrobe; her breasts were bare; she didn't need to look at him suggestively to make the point. Still, she said in a matter of fact way:

– Aren't you coming inside?

Somewhere at the start of the night he knew it might come to this. What irritated him was the way she seemed always one step ahead, forcing him time and again to change lanes, throw himself into a lower gear, play catch up.

He had no story to tell about his father helping him cross wide streets. He knew what his *papi* would do in this situation.

She took him to this tiny room lit by a bedside lamp, the sort of place she might have lived in all her life, a secret cave, shut away from the world. In one corner a tennis racket; on a chair a wide-brimmed straw hat.

She stood with her back to him, removing her bathrobe, revealing the tight loveliness of her buttocks. His eye strayed toward the bed which was covered with a quilt, a patchwork of many colors. Mercedes turned and noticed he was not paying attention to her.

– My mother made that. She was good at this sort of thing.

She was standing with her hands to her side, already ahead of him, naked, awaiting his appraisal.

But his eye fell on a clan of teddy bears arranged on a shelf over the bed. He saw the one she'd hugged in his sideview mirror. He saw the poster of Bruce Springsteen on the wall. *Damn, he was right!* She was one of those Meadowland rock concert types, *Babe we were born to run!*

– *That*, she said, is a leftover college. Do you like it?

The half-jeering snap in her voice made him realize he was behaving inappropriately; he'd failed to take sufficient notice of her standing in front of him, her startling tuft, her small, upstanding breasts, neat beautiful things.

262

She was waiting for him to do something, say something, not stand gaping with his clothes on. He stepped forward and cupped her breasts in his hand. They were lovely to touch; he fondled them for a while, played with the nipples; they seemed made for the soft palms of his hands.

She lifted her head to be kissed but he didn't seem interested.

She unbuttoned his shirt and pulled back to admire his chest; then she put her arms around his waist and squeezed him like a giddy python. He was amused by her tiny upstart strength, her fine reckless intensity. His hands rubbed her back and then gripped her buttocks; they too were firm and lovely to hold.

For awhile they stood there exploring each other's bodies. This in itself intrigued him, this leisurely fondling, the stroking of each other's limbs, as if their bodies spoke a language that had nothing to do with desire.

– Are we going to stand here all night? she asked.

He removed his shoes and his trousers. But she had had enough of his preliminaries. She pulled him down and fell upon his chest, removing and tossing away his underwear; pausing to marvel at the mould of his thighs, then crouching over him, making him wince and twitch with her tongue. When he tried to move she told him to lay still; she wanted his submission.

And Camacho was delighted with her attention. Content to lie back – *Stay that way*, she hissed, *Exactly like that, don't move* – he closed his eyes and thought of his father, the old lion of the highways who belonged nowhere and to no one.

How he must have lived for these moments, this here and nowness, despite his greying temples, the flabbiness of his rib cage. How he must have relished these nights of not doing much, not over-exerting himself, his body nursed and loved into new vigours; lifting his arms to rub the woman's neck, fondling her breasts, massaging those tight buttocks, letting the whelps of their desire swarm over him.

Mercedes swarmed over him; she handled him; she arched and threw herself into him; her eyes expressed amazement; she asked only that he stay there wordless, his eyes closed, while she worked at her own pleasure.

263

When she thought she had had enough she lay on her side and waited for him to do as he wished.

But he wanted nothing more from her. His young lion's body seemed content to recover itself. He stared up at the ceiling, still in his father's world. Maybe later he would turn to her. He wanted to dream awhile.

She looked in his face. *What a strange man. Not asking for much. Fondling her breasts with his big soft mechanic's hand.*

Her fingers touched his lips. He opened his eyes just once, telling her she was strange woman, but good, really good. Then he drifted off, his chest damp with her drippings, until he was faraway and asleep.

In one night so much can happen, so little change. A news-paper van on its early morning run throws its bundle on the store's sidewalk. Walking by you glimpse a headline, the front page news of a mudslide in Venezuela burying hundreds of peasants; and right below that a photo of a smiling mother who gave birth to a baby in the New York subway.

Elsewhere you wake up, you scratch your withered genitals, discover your world is much the same; the locks on your door were not tampered with; the tethered goats are waiting; coffee and toast, box office tickets, the curlers in your hair, a national anthem, a cruel father's erection – everything unchanged, waiting to be made use of like tools in the crankcase of the world.

Camacho stirred when he heard the sound of insects and birds outside his window; light was skittering through the shades from an unaccustomed angle; he knew where he was but he was surprised he had slept over. Time like a fox had stolen a march on him.

He saw the bare buttocks of Mercedes on the bed and desire for her flared. But she was fast asleep and the morning light splashed on the bric-a-brac of her life, shoes, underwear, the hat, the tennis racket.

His car. Cherokee. Banuchi. Waiting for him on the other side.

As he stepped into his shorts she stirred in the sheets.

– You don't have to leave right now. We can do breakfast, she said, from under a tangled mass of hair.

264

He didn't want breakfast. He didn't want her getting up either. He wanted to leave and let her wake up later and find him gone. He wanted to get into his car, leave this room, these rump-strained bed sheets. He didn't know why this was suddenly important except that his father had done it this way, told his mother not to get up, no breakfast and messy farewells, taking off at the first light of dawn.

On an impulse he leaned over Mercedes and kissed her on both cheeks of her buttocks. She was drifting back to sleep *I'll let myself out*, he said. She stirred again but didn't answer.

His windshield was cloudy with dew mist; he set the wipers in motion and looked out on a hazardous morning sky.

It had rained so hard brown leaves littered the lawns. The battened-down neighborhood waited for the day's all clear. The Trans Am started quickly, backed gently down the driveway, and slipped away like an ocean bound ship.

He found the highway without much trouble and settled down to a leisurely drive.

The highway was taking him from the grotto of Mercedes to that other haven where Banuchi lay waiting. He pictured her lying there in her flimsy nightclothes; he pictured her buttocks which were broad and heavy. They were soft fleshy boulders on which Cherokee loved to romp, though once she lost her grip on the elastic of Banuchi's panties and rolled off the bed onto the floor, wailing as if badly hurt, but alright.

Would he make love to Banuchi? Would the road with its bends and tolls take him straight to the doorknob of their bedroom, to the moist cavern of her forgiveness?

He had no way of knowing. It might be possible to creep inside, slide under the sheets beside her, snuggle up behind her fleshy mound, and pretend he had come home hours before while she was fast asleep.

A white Lincoln Continental passed him fast in the left lane. It cut right in front of him. Ordinarily he would have made a counter statement, showing this little showoff in his fancy car what his Trans Am can do. But the morning air was crisp, the sky a placid grey, with an eternal stillness that called for nothing intemperate or rash from man or machine. He let it go.

And suddenly stretching before him, illumined by the shifting heavens, he saw a landscape that was free of cars, free of angular faces and tense jaws at the wheel; he rolled down his windows and, with his foot maintaining light pressure on the pedal, he gave himself over to the cruising trees, the infinitely pleasuring air; to that amazing freedom his father must have tasted as he drove back to the West coast, flicking ash from his cigarette through the window, the wind caressing his hair.

On grey mornings like this, at the end of any highway, waiting in a warm room, an event would uncoil from surprising deep sleep, show him a lane of flares, a route to his own private heaven.

That Sunday morning traffic was backed up for miles; a bottle-neck at Exit 6 off the expressway, causing confusion, delay and anger. There was a baseball game in the Bronx. You'd think that on a Sunday, drivers would be spared the commuter's daily agony of idling, moving at a walking pace, praying for release from those poisoning exhausts.

There are always accidents, though why today of all days? A ball game at the stadium, a flight to catch at the airport, "I came out to get a carton of milk", everyone feeling trapped, going nowhere.

Up ahead you glimpse a tractor-trailer in a twisted catastrophic state across the road. The usual problem. You glimpse too the car buried like a plow under the wheels of the tractor-trailer, ambulances flashing like the mobile homes of extra-terrestrials, police in dark glasses and ocean blue uniforms, weapons and hearts holstered. Tragedy on the road, arbitrary and stark.

A traffic cop is shouting: *Show's over. Keep it moving.*

Up ahead, there's a bend in the road, an exit ramp to forgetting. Release is at hand from the hopelessness that sometimes clogs our lives.

In the rearview mirror, if you walk back to the scene, forgetting for a while where you're going, you might find the driver. He's trying to reconstruct what happened; he's lit another cigarette; he's staring at his rig; he has his story, and a strange cold knot in his stomach that tells him he's still alive, but it's no use, *it all happened so fast.*

266

And there are always witnesses like skips of the heartbeat. Some who saw the whole thing. Some who saw nothing. If you ask anyone, *what happened here?* even as you get set to move on, he'd say, first, I *don't know*; then he'd recreate frame after frame an event that would rattle your heart's cage.

Take, for instance, the eyes of these two witnesses who were just about to cross the road when it happened:

See, the car came off the expressway back there and stopped at the lights. A young woman was standing over there at the intersection waiting for the bus.

– *Getouttahere!*

I'm telling you what I saw, muthafucker

– *At that hour in the morning, the only women out on the streets are whores. I know this area. Women work these streets, naked from the waist, from the crack of dawn.*

Well, this woman wasn't naked; she wore glasses; she wore a simple white dress; she had a Bible in her hand, and judging from the way she looked up the road she was waiting for the bus.

– *Tell me about it!*

The guy in the car had the green light, but he didn't move. Just sat there staring at her.

– *Muthafucker want to pick her up. At that hour any man in a car cruising these streets is looking for a quick morning boost.*

Hard to tell. He might have been struck by her pretty face, the way she held herself erect, the slim ankles under the dress, the bible clasped like a shield. He might have wondered, *what the fuck she doing here, all by herself?* In any event he pulled up beside her and asked where she was going.

– *Uh oh!*

To the House of my Redeemer, the woman said.

– *Uh oh! Stepping in deep shit!*

Seems like more words were exchanged, the guy's trying to persuade her to get into the car, craning forward to catch her eye, his arm extended on the passenger seat, foot on the brake pedal so that the car seems ablaze with the red lights of his desire. She tried to ignore him at first, looking up the road for the bus. Then her heart must have softened.

– *Or quickened!*

267

Suddenly she smiled, as if the guy had found the code to her vault; she said something to him, polite but firm, she was determined to wait for her bus; then she checked the watch on her tiny wrist and, throwing one last desperate look up the road, she stepped into the car.

— See, there you go! First mistake, right there! Never take a ride from a stranger. Unless you got business to take care of. You sure this wasn't no street woman with a new game?

At the bus stop? Carrying a bible?

— Hey, this is New York City! A priest unfrocks himself and, watch out, you got a pedophile in the vestry.

His heart must have pumped as the door slammed shut, their bodies locked in for the ride; helping her with the seat belt, noticing her smooth calves, the innocent eyes, a bit flatchested under the blue cardigan, but that's alright, her body ripening every minute under that dress. He thinks he hears something pounding on her walls, a sound like muffled passion just above the engine's whine, coming from where the bible rests in her lap.

— Oh yeah, like those girls from the Catholic high school, in their plaid uniforms and shit. When we was at PS 179, we'd call to them hot-thighed bitches as they walked by, cause we knew what they wanted.

Or thought we knew. Anyway, you won't believe what happened next. They're driving along, he's giving her the rap, "What you say your name was? Julietta? I have a cousin named Julietta. Where you from… the Dominican Republic? *Dominica?* You know, you looked so heavenly standing there at the bus stop, please forgive me, I couldn't help myself." And before you know it, they're crossing the bridge, they're on the Interstate.

— The Interstate? Getouttahere! Bitch waiting for a bus to take her to the House of Whatever on the Interstate? Is that what you're saying?

I'm saying, I don't know, anything could happen, a young woman in a fast car, getting away from the city, the wind in her hair, hot brass music, the red wine of freedom pouring through her veins.

— Yeah, right!

Miles and miles along the Interstate. Until he remembered he hadn't eaten. So they stopped for a bite. Now, the waitress recalls a gold chain on the hairy chest of the young man, and a young woman with curls of hanging hair, wasn't wearing no glasses, wasn't carrying no bible. Seemed all set for a hollering good time.

– *What did I tell you? Thick-fur bitch!*

All of a sudden it starts snowing, light dusty stuff at first; they paid it no mind; then swirls of snow coming thick and fast, blanketing the cars, which meant they couldn't get back to the city rightaway, the roadway's full of white stuff, high as a wedding cake. Ain't nothing they could do but check in at a Ramada Inn.

– *Oh yeah!*

Desk clerk recalls two people checking in, a young woman, modest and shy, on the arm of an older man, silvery-haired at the temples, neatly dressed, walked with a dignified air.

– *What did I tell you?*

But, dig this, nothing happened!

– *Whaddaya mean, nothing happened?*

One minute they're checking in, next minute they're checking out. Desk clerk recalls hearing a loud furious exchange in the lobby, the man shouting, "What did you get in the fucking car for?" and the woman answering, "I wanted to see how far we'd go before you turned back." The man staring as if there's been some mistake, he was crazy to get mixed up in this from the start; the woman saying, "But I asked you to take me to the *House of My Redeemer*, I told you your soul was at risk, you wouldn't listen." The man staggering back to the door, wanting to get away, plunging outside where it's still snowing hard, and all he can think of is finding his car.

"Are you going to leave me here?" she asks, rushing after him. He doesn't answer.

He sweeps off the snow piled like a curse on his windshield; the engine shudders, as if violently cranked, then responds; headlights, tires skidding, backing out; he doesn't give a fuck; he's heading back to the city; he has to get back to where it started, there isn't a roadway ice-slick enough to stop him; he throws one last lingering glance at the woman in his rearview mirror, she's standing in the thick-drizzling snow, hoping, praying his heart would turn; and that's when the truck he didn't see, or saw too late, ploughed into his darkening heaven.

– *Yes, Lord.*

ABOUT THE AUTHOR

N.D. Williams was born in Guyana in 1942. He went to Jamaica to study at Mona in the late 1960s and was very much involved in the student/youth uprising of the Rodney affair in 1968. He writes of being powerfully influenced by the radical, nativist currents in Jamaican culture – reggae and yard theatre – of this period. He lived for a time in Antigua before moving to the USA where he now lives in New York. In 1976 his novel *Ikael Torass* won the prestigious Casa de las Americas prize.

ALSO BY N.D. WILLIAMS
FROM PEEPAL TREE PRESS

Prash and Ras
ISBN 1-900715-00-7, 1997, £6.99
Disparate worlds collide in the two novellas that make up *Prash and Ras*. A young German woman joins a Rastafarian commune, and Indo-Guyanese Prash, escaping the socialist republic for New York, gets mixed up with drugs and discovers that freedom has its price.

The Silence of Islands
ISBN 0-948833-46-7, 1994, £6.95
Escaping the suffocations of her Caribbean island, Delia re-defines herself in America, whilst struggling with life as an illegal alien. Although no guide to her safety, it is in literature that Delia finds the greatest meaning and psychic protection.

The Crying of Rainbirds
ISBN 0-948833-40-8, 1991, £6.99
Passionate in their despair, the characters in these stories dream of wholeness and meaning in a postcolonial Caribbean they find it impossible to live in, yet impossible to live without.

Visit the Peepal Tree website and buy books online at:
www.peepaltreepress.com